The Mill

Cailyn Lloyd

The Mill

© 2022 Land of Oz LLC

All rights reserved. No part of this book may be reproduced or transmitted in any form or by any means, electronic or mechanical, including photocopying, recording, or by any information and retrieval system, without permission in writing from the copyright holder.

This is a work of fiction. Names, characters, places and incidents either are the product of the author's imagination or are used fictitiously, and any resemblance to any actual persons, living or dead, events, or locales is entirely coincidental.

Content guidance available under Acknowledgments.

ISBN: 978-0-578-37798-8

Cover design: Rose Miller

For Rosemary,
who got me thinking...

One

The mouse.

Someone had moved it.

The position and orientation were off slightly.

Chase Riddell invariably placed the mouse facing due north on the exact same spot: on a prominent knot just left of center on the oak desktop. His office was otherwise undisturbed. The desk and a brown leather swivel chair were the only furniture in the small, windowless room. The tawny brick walls were bare, as was the desk, except for a flatscreen monitor and the errant mouse.

The precise placement was a function of his OCD. He also hated odd numbers, unless they were multiples of five. The kitchen cabinets were studies in neatness and order, the bottles, cans, and cartons arranged by size and type. His clothing was similarly organized. He checked his locks twice whenever he went out, though crime wasn't an issue he expected to worry about.

The building had a keyed entrance, and his apartment had two commercial-grade locks on the door: a Schlage lever handle and a double cylinder dead-bolt. The windows were new, twelve feet above ground on the exterior, and equally secure. Management had no access to the unit without advance notice. The outside walls were brick and limestone block. The apartment was more impregnable than most bank buildings. He had chosen this place in Rock River Mills—an old paper mill converted to condos and upscale flats—partly for that reason.

He carefully examined the locks on the door, but there were no scratches or evidence of tampering. A quick survey of the apartment revealed that nothing else had been disturbed.

Nothing.

The computer seemed to be the target of the illicit entry.

Was that possible? And why? Was he being unduly paranoid?

He couldn't imagine how someone had broken in, but the wayward mouse was proof someone had. It was a serious problem.

Had they discovered the hidden files on his computer? Files filled with photos of deviant sexual acts. Images of domination. Rape. Murder. Just the thought of them brought a stiffening to his groin.

But if someone had, surely the police would be here, arresting him. Dragging him off to jail to face life in prison.

While it was unlikely a casual browser would find the incriminating files, he could assume nothing, since someone had breached his well-secured apartment, maybe hacked into the computer, and left zero evidence of his presence—other than the errant mouse.

What now?

He didn't know.

Chase only knew he had a problem on his hands.

Possibly a disaster.

Unless he found the asshole and killed him first.

Two

Lili stopped mid-step and closed her eyes.

Concentrated, trying to visualize the invisible.

Yes! Right there.

A vibration, a subtle shimmer. A sense of someone—or something—close by. On the other side of the wall maybe.

A moment later, the feeling was gone. But it had been tangible, her best connection yet.

Having lived in Rock River Mills for two months, she had sensed spirits in various parts of the building. Each had been subtle and ephemeral, unwilling to reveal themselves. Maybe they were just shy. She couldn't tell. Some ghosts were like that. But they were here, and she would draw them out eventually. The strongest presence felt female. Lili hoped it was Emma Kiekhafer, a girl who had died in an industrial accident in 1894.

Lili had spent the last three nights staking out the hallways around apartment 114 at the west end of the building. Over three thousand square feet in an open plan with twenty-five-foot ceilings, 114 was the largest unit in the Mills. High in one corner, a ten-ton industrial crane hung from a track. Sandblasted and painted, it was a striking element that graced the cover of the promotional brochure.

The entry door to 114 lay at the end of a softly lit corridor off the main hallway. A nearby exit door led to the courtyard, a lovely area shaded by oaks and maples with picnic areas and grills. A tiki bar served drinks during the summer months. Her apartment lay on the other side of the courtyard.

She walked back and forth in the hallway, sitting in various spots, meditating, trying to reconnect with the presence. When that failed, she lit two votive candles and placed them near the wall—an invitation to the spirits.

Still nothing.

Pacing slowly but relentlessly, she rolled her ankle and bumped into the wall. Mrs. Kaplan peeked out, and Lili felt herself blush as she sat and pretended to fiddle with her shoe.

She didn't know the Kaplans, but had seen their photos in the lobby on a flyer for a charity auction. Lili had heard rumors Mrs. Kaplan was unhappy with the unit, something about the bedroom feeling creepy. It sounded like an ironic metaphor, but the story had piqued her interest. She suspected spirits at work.

A moment later, Mr. Kaplan looked out, locked eyes with Lili, and walked down to where she was sitting. He was tall, at least six feet, with dark hair and a short beard. He was good looking, fit, and carried himself with a vaguely military air.

Accusingly, he said, "Do I know you?"

"Lili Paltrinieri, 124. You might've seen me around."

He shrugged. "Is there a reason you're lurking in our hallway?"

"Probably not a good one."

"Try me."

Lili contemplated several lies before settling on the truth. Technically, she could loiter here. It wasn't their hallway, but if they took an interest, her efforts might be more effective inside the apartment. "I'm psychic and I think there's a spirit in this hallway or your apartment."

"Oh, Jesus." He rolled his eyes. "Not you too—"

"Your wife?"

He nodded, then eyed Lili suspiciously. "How do I know you're not casing the place?"

"One, I live in the building. Two, do I look like a thief?"

"No. But maybe your boyfriend is."

"I don't have a boyfriend." Now she was sure he was a cop or ex-military from his questions and demeanor. Exasperated, she pulled a business card from her back pocket and handed it to him.

He eyed it, then pulled an iPhone from his pocket and tapped furiously for a moment.

"So you're the owner of Revelations, a metaphysical store," he said with a hint of derision. "Seems you're legit. You might as well come in and meet my wife."

Lili stepped in and scanned the room with an admiring eye.

It was stunning. The Kaplans had money. Real money.

A suit of medieval armor guarded the entrance to the large combined living room, dining area, and kitchen. The brick walls were decorated with an interesting selection of quality fine art from classic to modern, interspersed with sculptures on plinths, the atmosphere and lighting imparting the impression of a cozy art gallery. Two of the abstract canvases looked like Kandinsky originals. The furnishings were a careful mix of antique and contemporary. Expensive, modernist steel light fixtures hung from the high ceiling on long pendants. It looked like the hand of a professional decorator at work. The crane hanging in the far corner was an exquisite touch.

She now understood why they might worry about theft.

"I'm Raleigh Kaplan, and that's my wife, Olivia. Your name again?"

"Lili—Lili Paltrinieri."

Olivia Kaplan walked over from the kitchen area and extended a hand in greeting. A short, long-haired blonde, she was more cute than beautiful with an intelligent gaze. "So, Lili, why are you hanging out in our hallway?"

It wasn't their hallway, but pointing that out wouldn't be helpful. "I'm psychic and I think there's a spirit in the hallway or in your apartment."

"I knew it!" Olivia said, flashing a look of vindication at Raleigh. "Who is it?"

Lili briefly retold the story about Emma dying in the Mill in 1894, though she wasn't certain it was Emma she'd sensed.

Olivia's eyes widened with the telling of the story, and she looked at the apartment as if seeing it for the first time. Finally, she said, "That's awful. Why didn't they tell us? I don't know if I would have wanted this apartment if I'd known—"

"Babe, you love this place and had to have it." Raleigh gave Lili the stink eye, clearly regretting letting her in. "Knowing the story, I still would've bought it. Somebody died here over a hundred years ago. It means nothing now."

"But I didn't know the story when we bought it." She looked to Lili. "Is there anything else?"

Lili shook her head.

"It's getting late," Raleigh said. "You should probably leave."

It wasn't a friendly request.

Lili scurried out the door. She didn't much care for Raleigh Kaplan and felt a twinge of pity for Olivia. She seemed nice and exuded a pleasant aura. What was she doing with that guy?

She then spent a fruitless hour wandering the mill hallways.

Returning to her condo just after 1 a.m., she felt tired but not ready for sleep. There was more than one way to explore the building. Perhaps a little astral travel yet?

After a small glass of wine, she stripped and slipped into bed.

Relaxing every muscle and joint, she wiggled her fingers, enjoying the soft texture of the high thread count cotton sheets. She gazed at the white ceiling without focusing, receptive to the slightest disturbance in the ether, to the vaguest feeling or presence in her apartment, a space she had grown to love.

Her apartment, a warren of brick rooms, overlooked the Rock River. The kitchen was modest but modern, with an adjoining low-ceilinged dining area she had converted to a sitting room with a concealed flatscreen. The contractor had added a small second-floor office with a large skylight, accessible by a spiral staircase. Lili had turned it into a spare bedroom. Her bedroom sat in the left corner of the apartment. The window there, fifteen feet above the water's edge, let in the gentle sounds of the river, an ambient soundtrack more soothing than the apps people used to relax and sleep.

She had decorated the walls throughout with all manner of paraphernalia. Small antiques, clocks, old hand tools, gears, a camshaft, and other mechanical oddities. More esoteric items like runic symbols, crystals, zodiac signs, and framed Tarot cards—though she didn't read Tarot; she just loved the card designs. Interspersed were old black and white photos and enlarged images from the Hubble Telescope collection on canvas. There were bookshelves everywhere, stacked with books. It looked a bit like a museum.

While she loved the apartment itself, there was a deeper significance in choosing unit 124. In numerology, the numbers one, two, and four equaled seven, a number that imparted reflective and introspective qualities to the space. A *seven* home was an ideal environment for her spiritual nature.

Gradually, she reached a state of total relaxation, her inner eye a blank slate, the first step to embarking on astral travel, a spiritual discipline that allowed her consciousness to leave her body. To reach out and explore the world, a literal out-of-body experience.

Settling into the first stage of sleep or alpha phase, a semiconscious state, her mind drifted upward and floated near the ceiling, separate from her body but still connected by the astral cord.

She could travel anywhere, but she drifted back to 114 for another look, to see if she could connect with the spirit or spirits there, even though astral travel was only vaguely useful for ghost hunting. She wouldn't see Olivia or Raleigh. In the astral plane, she moved on a different level than the living. She couldn't snoop or spy on people even if she wanted to.

The Kaplan apartment was silent and dark when she arrived. Lili burrowed into the fabric of the room, seeking the hidden energies lurking there.

At first, it was still.

Tranquil.

A slight disturbance rustled the drapes framing the windows and then the room and all its trappings disappeared. Lili stared, agog at the cavernous space of a different era: the stark image of a factory filled with vapors and large machines. A pungent smell permeated the air. Bleach maybe?

She had slipped into a vivid, harsh world she could scarcely comprehend. How had people worked in such a place?

A restless shadow gave her a start.

Someone or something was watching. A vaporous presence more sinister than the female spirit she'd sensed earlier.

A ghost. A belligerent male spirit, like a dark cloud, eying her with a hostile gaze.

Lili felt trapped and vulnerable until she slipped out and drifted home.

The sensation of his glare stayed with her the longest.

Whoever it was, he seemed sinister and territorial.

As she returned to her body, the memory sent an icy shudder through her.

From the base of her skull to the tips of her toes.

Three

Emma Kiekhafer was dead.

Had been for years. After an industrial accident in 1894, she had crossed over and become a permanent resident of the mill.

Late last night, she had stumbled upon an ugly situation and now struggled with the implications of it. The man in apartment 139 was some sort of deviant or monster, possibly both. His computer contained horrid pictures of rape and murder, and they obviously aroused him. He had pleasured himself at the computer in a disgusting and horrifying ritual.

How had he gotten the pictures? Had he taken them himself? Was he a sick, perverted killer? She feared he was. The man was cautious, his proclivities a closely guarded secret, his doors secured with heavy locks. Given the furtive way he looked through the images, he knew his behavior was immoral, illegal.

Honestly, who constantly looks over their shoulder in an empty room?

Emma dwelt on the issue for hours before deciding to do something about it.

Perhaps she could direct someone like the police to the computer.

Then she paused, confused by her runaway thoughts.

Why did she care?

Really, as awful as the man was, why did she feel compelled to do something? Interfering with the living seemed unwise—though she had done so once before without suffering harm.

She wasn't certain. Ema only knew the dreadful images upset her deeply. It wasn't an emotional reaction. She didn't experience emotions the way she had in life. Oddly, she felt upbeat most of the time.

It was something else.

Emma paced through the hallways a few inches above the plush carpeting, thinking, digging down to the root of her angst.

It was a quality-of-life issue, she decided—ironic with her being dead and all.

A moral issue certainly, but also a matter of keeping the peace. That guy threatened the atmosphere in the mill. He would upset the balance. The worst-case scenario could be as bad as the chaos that followed Frank's murder. Or maybe she was just being a goody two-shoes. She tended that way. Still, her ambivalence regarding her personal comfort versus the moral issues caused her to question her supposed good intentions.

Adding to her discomfort, Emma sensed someone watching her, trying to summon her. While she enjoyed having living souls in the building after so many years of emptiness, the sense of prying was annoying, intrusive, and needed to stop. She was familiar with the sensation. When the mill was abandoned, someone had hosted several ghost tours. Between the odd devices they brought and the incessant probing, it drove her crazy. They upended the atmospheric flux in the building for days.

Things were simpler in the old days. Back then, Emma amused herself by reading the magazines and newspapers lying around the cafeteria and staff rooms. Then the mill closed and she lost all contact with the world. It sat vacant for over twenty years, empty beyond the occasional adventurous teens and those annoying ghost tours. Emma grew listless and bored.

She rested for long periods of time. It wasn't sleep because she didn't dream. It felt more like hibernation. She shut down and went away mentally. To where? She didn't know, but it felt necessary. Maybe that was how ghosts slept. Or maybe she needed to recharge, like a battery. Emma didn't really understand her state of being. Was she a blob of ether? A cloud of electrons? A figment of some perverse dream world? It was a mystery and not a subject covered in books.

When the Mill renovations began, she was horrified, certain she would hate it. The noise was no issue, but the construction and change in floor plans caused disruptions in the energy fields passing through the mill. The ripples squeezed and distorted her personal space, making her feel uncomfortable and out of sorts.

When the construction stopped and the living moved in, the disturbances ceased.

The renovations made life interesting again. With the living came positive energy flows and auras that made the place brighter, warmer. Emma liked it. No gloomy, eerie ambiance for her. It was a silly stereotype of the living that ghosts were mournful creatures who came out only at night. She liked the light, found it rejuvenating. If she wandered mostly at night, it was only because the building was quieter in the wee hours.

When people returned, they brought fewer magazines and newspapers. Something in the world had changed. But they brought books.

Lots and lots of books. Emma loved to read and did so voraciously. Emma didn't need to open a book to read it. She literally dove into the book, reading page by page as she floated through the text. As a spirit, her hands weren't very useful, so that technique was the easiest. It was a comfortable way to read, even if comfort wasn't really an issue.

Overall, the renovations had been a good thing.

Emma remained young at heart and curious, so after the conversions took place, she snooped in the apartments for books. Observing, reading, she learned the world had become a very different place. Technology, machines, cars, computers. Fascinating stuff—though little of it affected her life in the mill. The newspapers she missed were apparently hidden inside computers only now, she couldn't find them. She had swooped into a computer once, but it wasn't like reading a book. Inside the box, she found nothing but a confusing jumble of wires and metal parts.

Observing people using tablets, phones, and laptops, she wanted to learn and understand how they worked. They represented a way to venture out into the world, even if she was a prisoner in the mill. So far, she had made little progress toward that goal.

Emma also liked to lurk in various apartments and watch TV. She could keep up on the news without newspapers, and she *loved* watching movies.

In the past few weeks, she had noticed an increasingly negative energy flux on the east end of the building. Emma went snooping and discovered the sick, creepy pervert looking at nasty, violent pictures on his computer. She was convinced he was involved in criminal behavior.

After the man went to bed, she tried to find the images, hoping to answer that question, but couldn't figure out how the computer worked. She had watched him use a handheld device to look inside the computer. Emma had fiddled with it and moved it slightly, but couldn't make it do anything useful. Evidently, moving it wasn't enough. Some other action was involved.

Emma needed to learn how to use computers and now, she had a reason to delve into tech—though wasn't sure she could actually utilize such skills. Books had provided everything she needed and she wasn't adept at manipulating physical objects. Haunting rooms, rustling curtains, and slamming the occasional door was the extent of her ghostly repertoire.

The guy in 202 had a wonderful library, including many books on computers. With an entire shelf devoted to the subject, she was drawn to *Computers for Dummies.* It sounded ideal.

Emma dove in and read about memory, hard drives, keyboards, and the handheld device, the mouse. Now she understood why passing through a computer revealed nothing. The knowledge was all written in code on hard drives and memory chips. The computer turned that code into words. Reading about the mouse, she realized she had been doing it wrong.

A fresh problem arose. Computers needed a password.

She could watch the man enter his but would it matter? Emma doubted she had the dexterity to handle the mouse or enter a password. Maybe it was wishful thinking that she could actually do something about the guy. Still, she had once written a message on a dirty mirror. Anything was possible with determination.

Emma spent most of the night reading until she felt she understood computers.

When dawn broke through the windows, she headed to her lair high in the building, the skylight outside apartment 222, directly above the walkway where she'd lost her life. The sunlight was glorious.

She could feel neither warmth nor cold, but the light bolstered her spirits and made her feel alive. It was counter-intuitive. The sun and memories of life should make her blue, she felt, but the effect was quite the opposite. Just as well. She was dead. No point in dwelling gloomily on things that couldn't be changed.

Emma sighed. It had been a busy and exhausting night.

She needed to recharge.

When she woke, she would formulate a plan to deal with the problem in 139.

She might be a ghost, but Emma knew how to make things happen.

Four

Three in the morning.

Lili walked the hallways of the mill like a wraith. Along every passage, north to south, east to west, she absorbed the energies of the structure, particularly well preserved in the thick stone and brick construction of the walls. She avoided the Kaplan apartment for a few days after Raleigh had chased her away.

Built in 1880, the Rock River Paper Mill was a remnant of the golden age of paper making in Wisconsin, once one of the largest mills in the state. Lili had toured most of the apartments in the complex when they first went on the market and knew what lay beyond the hallway walls, even if she couldn't see the decor. Her memory was impeccable and photographic.

As she wandered, she caught occasional glimpses of the past. Strange machinery, vats, huge rollers. Vague smells of the paper-making process.

Walking past 106, she felt a little tickle. A spirit lived in that apartment, though tonight, she had little sense of who or what they were.

She was searching for an impression of the accident back in 1894.

The newspaper articles from the era had no useful information beyond the basic details. Lili easily recalled the article because of its prim, surreal wording.

> **Shocking Accident at a Paper Mill. Girl Torn to Pieces**
>
> Saturday morning, between 9 and 10 o'clock, the Rock River Paper Mill was the scene of a terrible accident, in which a young and interesting girl was hurried into eternity without a moment's warning. Emma Kiekhafer, an employee in the mill, was engaged in carrying rags on the third floor when she fell through a trapdoor onto the whirling machinery below and was instantly severed in twain. The spectacle of the mangled body, it was said, was a most horrid one. The body was almost cut in two just below the shoulders, and there were numerous other bruises and lacerations. The face, however, was not touched and presented an appearance of peaceful repose, as though she had fallen asleep.

Given the horrible manner of her death, Lili doubted the poor girl's face looked anything like peaceful repose.

Despite her constant wandering, she still had no idea where the accident occurred and couldn't picture the machinery. Maybe it was just as well. Some things were too terrible to visualize and best left unseen.

She wondered if any of the residents were aware of her nighttime strolls. They would surely consider her odd, which was fine. She had been different, even as a child, a loner with an uncanny sense of the thoughts and feelings of the people around her. She passed through high school in a cloud of smoke, mostly weed. Her brother went to college and medical school and had been their parents' pride and joy. That was fine. Lili didn't resent him and loved him dearly. She took a year-long apprenticeship with a spiritual medium in Madison near the University of Wisconsin, the closest she ever came to college.

With an SBA loan, she opened her shop on Franklin Street but struggled at first. Lili was good with her kind of people—those who embraced the paranormal. She delivered prescient reads on the lives of her clients. Her advice was useful more often than not. She wrote a quirky and humorous blog. Made enough money to bank some. Her parents never really approved of her path in life, but Mom gradually accepted it. Her father developed a grudging respect for her financial acumen, even if he thought she was crazy.

Lili preferred to think of herself as eccentric and happily embraced her inner weirdo. She was obsessed with the paranormal in every form. A practicing Wiccan, she rejected the Catholicism she grew up with and embraced aspects of Taoism and shamanism. She sold metaphysical items and saw customers for palmistry, numerology, and séances from her shop downtown.

Walking past 202, she sensed something inside, a presence. She stopped and leaned against the wall, clearing her mind, probing the slight disturbance.

A female spirit.

The strongest connection she had felt yet, but with an odd presentation. The presence seemed fixated on computers, passwords, and learning to handle a mouse. Prosaic and decidedly not ghostly.

Still, Lili felt certain it was Emma.

Or was that wishful thinking?

Was she trying to force a connection? Invent something that might not exist? The very nature of ghost hunting and spirit seeking encouraged false positives. In the quiet darkness, it was easy to imagine things. Lili lingered, but the presence slowly faded to black.

If it was Emma, she seemed shy, a quirk at odds with her earlier history in the mill. Newspaper accounts in the years after her accident recounted frequent sightings of the ghostly girl of the night shift, stories that had drawn Lili to Rock River Mills.

No matter. Lili would eventually draw her out of her shell.

Maybe she should concentrate on 114 for now.

It was late, but she continued wandering. As a rule, she needed only four or five hours of rest and could sleep in tomorrow. She never opened the store before noon.

Lili walked to the stairs at the west end of the building and down to the main corridor. Sitting, she leaned back against the north wall of 114 and closed her eyes. The Kaplans couldn't see her here. Their doorway was farther up, down a side hallway—though she was visible to the other tenants coming and going. She didn't care.

Clearing her mind, Lili opened herself to the auras emanating through the wall.

At first, she detected little more than static. The space was dark, no hint of the presence from the night before. Lili relaxed and grew drowsy. It wouldn't be the first time she dozed off in a hallway.

As she fell into an alpha sleep state, she smelled bleach, then glimpsed a shock of blond hair and a man falling from above against the backdrop of vats and machinery.

Lili startled awake.

Holy shit!

The Kaplans had an otherworldly occupant. An unexpected guest. A dude. She had been right last night in sensing a male spirit there. While she hadn't found the machinery room where Emma died, she had stumbled on to something equally interesting. Lili wondered who the man was.

While they had moved some walls during the conversion of the building into apartments and condominiums, Lili knew the original floor plan. This apartment lay over the footprint of a room that once held vats of pulp. She had walked the hallways adjoining the unit many times and sensed little, vague flashes.

Last night, she caught a stronger jolt.

Now she understood. Something bad had happened in that space unrelated to Emma's death and she had just caught a vivid glimpse of it: a man falling, a flash of someone lying dead in one of the vats. It didn't feel like a mishap.

Was there a story she'd missed?

Lili intended to find out. Researching the event moved to the top of her list.

Back in her apartment, Lili spent hours searching through local news stories on a newspaper archive, searching for an accident or some death she could connect to that apartment. When she found it, she wanted to kick herself and congratulate herself in equal measure. She had overlooked the story for two reasons. It fell outside of her sweet spot of research from 1880 to 1920, and the headlines referenced the name of the victim but not the mill.

She was right about one thing. It wasn't bad luck nor an accident. It was murder.

In 1936, they found Frank Zivkovic dead in a vat with a heavy weight tied around his neck. Suicide was the initial determination. But suspicion fell on four of his co-workers after an anonymous tip. During the installation of a new machine, some items had gone missing: two reels of copper wire and a toolbox.

Frank had evidently overheard four men talking about the stolen goods and reported them to a supervisor. He leaked the information back to the thieves.

The district attorney presented a simple case. The men confronted Frank, beat him, and tossed him into the vat. Lili shuddered, reading the story as she visualized the encounter in technicolor. Sometimes, her imagination was a curse.

The accused maintained their innocence but were convicted and sentenced to life in prison. Two of them died there. The other two were paroled in the late '70s. The supervisor received five years on a conspiracy charge.

Lili wondered why the story hadn't resurfaced when the plans were floated for the condo project. It seemed odd since the trial had generated a great deal of publicity. Maybe the owners had found a way to bury the story, though lesser stories had surfaced during the renovations. Like the stories about Emma that had first piqued her interest in the building.

Of one thing she felt certain: the murder must have made a deep impression on the fabric of the mill. She would be more receptive to it now that she knew where to look. Frank's death certainly explained the weird vibe in the Kaplans' bedroom.

The only problem was Raleigh. He wasn't receptive to her ideas. Maybe she could strike up a friendship with Olivia.

One way or another, she was going to connect with Frank.

She wondered, though, recalling the male figure glaring at her last night.

Just how angry was Frank after all these years?

Five

Emma was a celebrity once, years ago.

As the ghostly girl who haunted the night shift, she became a star of local folklore.

But she wasn't the only spirit in the mill.

A creepy guy lurked under the floors. Already there when she crossed over, he had never shown himself. Emma didn't know his name but sensed a dark, repellent vibe from the cellar. Oddly, there were no doors or stairs leading down there, but if there were, she wouldn't go looking. If he was content to skulk about in the dark, she saw no need to snoop and upset whatever balance existed between them.

Still, his presence gave her the heebie-jeebies. It seemed ironic to be a ghost afraid of a ghost.

Frank in 114 had been murdered in 1936. Tommy died in what was now 106. That sad soul got his head crushed between paper rollers in 1963. She hadn't met them either, but they were harmless, their presence mere blips in the building aura. Emma only knew their names, having witnessed their deaths. Oddly, she couldn't enter either of those rooms, some aspect of the mill she didn't understand. It was a strange state of affairs. In the time the four of them had lived there, their paths had never crossed.

Maybe only she had the ability to wander. Others had died here over the years, but their spirits hadn't lingered. She didn't understand that either. Perhaps they had lived better lives and gone straight to heaven—if there was such a place. She wasn't particularly bad in her last life though maybe God didn't agree. She guessed this was purgatory or limbo and that she would have to suffer through her sentence, though really, it didn't feel like suffering. It didn't feel like anything at all.

The stories—her celebrity—were the catalyst for the later ghost hunts and tours. Of the four ghosts, she seemed to be the most visible to the living.

It was always *Emma this* and *Emma that* in the articles. They never saw Frank or Tommy and she didn't know why, but enjoyed seeing her name in the papers. In a way, she lived on.

Maybe she was just that talented. She had the impression Frank and Tommy weren't very smart. She had quickly learned how to make herself visible to the living, mostly in her quest to haunt Mr. Bodman, the original mill owner. Though she once enjoyed playing the starring role, she grew tired of the attention and disruptions it brought. She no longer cared to be seen or sought after. The girl of the night shift had retired. She intended to live in peaceful anonymity ever after.

Except for a new wrinkle. The man in 139 was probably a dangerous rapist and a murderer and she had decided to do something about it.

Emma drifted within a book, reading in unit 202, trying to wrap her mind around modern technology.

While learning about computers, she discovered they were connected to a thing called the internet. At first, it was almost beyond her comprehension. She had to read about electricity and surprised herself when she understood the subject after sufficient study.

Emma hadn't done well in school. She wasn't stupid, but girls had no reason to study. They were expected to marry, raise a family, and manage a household. It was understood that boys were smarter and would handle the serious thinking. Later, as she read more and more, Emma realized that wasn't true. Women had written some of the books she read. Women were scientists. Women could vote.

No longer tethered to traditional ideas about girls and women, she saw herself in a different light. That she could read and understand so many subjects was mind-boggling. It gave her a thrill as well. She almost wished she could go back to school and earn a degree.

But that was dumb. She was dead.

While it was easy to read books, she couldn't easily handle things in the physical world. Manipulating something like a keyboard or a mouse required dexterity that her current skill set didn't allow. She was working on it.

Quite by accident, she had discovered that a flat screen thingy called an iPad was easier to influence. By sliding herself across the glass screen, the device somehow tracked her motion. Problem was, she didn't fully understand the device, and her fingers alone seemed ineffective. She could manipulate the screen, but to what end? And the skill was of no use in handling a mouse.

She spent a few more hours honing her knowledge of computers and wandered over to 139, hoping to find the man at his computer. Usually, she lurked at the edges to avoid being near him. He gave her the creeps. But she needed his password.

Alas, he was gone.

She peeked through the door to the office; maybe the computer had been left on.

Emma startled, taken aback.

The computer was gone! He had either moved it or gotten rid of it.

Did he suspect someone was on to him? How? Had he seen her?

She fretted. There were other explanations, but Emma sensed it to be true. He knew someone was watching him.

Now what?

She had to think. She wanted to direct people to the computer, to find the awful pictures inside. Now, the evidence was gone, and she was at a loss for a cogent plan.

Emma wandered aimlessly for a while before returning to her roost in the skylight, hoping to rest on it.

But it was futile. She couldn't rest.

Besides the creepy man in 139, the snooping person was still prying, further disrupting the tranquility of the mill. She had sensed them pause earlier, outside 202, while she was reading. Now they were somewhere lower in the building, the probing more intense, more concentrated. Emma floated through the building, searching for the source of the disturbance.

To Emma, the building looked just as it did a hundred years ago, except the renovations now overlaid the older structures, superimposed in three dimensions. Every alteration to the Mill was preserved here in this dimension. Or perhaps merely in her memory. She didn't know.

In some areas, the old and new aligned well. In others, they lay at odd angles, welded together like op art. The structures and changes weren't ephemeral—she liked that word and prided herself on her vocabulary. No, the changes appeared rock solid but provided no impediment to her wanderings. She passed through any material: brick, stone, or steel. They might look solid, but she floated through them like a breeze across a meadow. Except the outside walls. She could enter them but not pass beyond them. Another aspect of her life she failed to understand.

Her life?

Though technically dead, she had consciousness, awareness, but lacked substance. This was a life after death, she assumed. She had been raised to believe in God, but the mill was a mystery. It wasn't heaven. It wasn't hell either.

She finally found the source of the disturbance: a woman lurking in the hallway outside 114.

Emma recognized her. She lived in 124. Tall with red hair, brown eyes, thin and waifish, not unlike Emma when she was alive, except that her hair had been blonde, her eyes blue. Good Anglo-Saxon stock, her father had declared frequently. She had come to realize her father was a racist. So much so, he had hated anyone born south of the Alps, even Italians. His dinner table talk was often a litany of rants against coloreds and foreigners. She and her mother never said a word. In her father's house, women were to be seen but never heard. He drank too much and often batted her mother around for transgressions, real or imagined. Once a month, he gave Emma an examination to confirm that she remained a good girl. It was a mortifying and humiliating experience. Emma couldn't wait to move out of that house and away from that awful man. She just hadn't imagined it happening the way it did.

Careful what you wish for.

Wasn't that what they said?

The woman seemed determined to stir up trouble. Emma drifted over to 124 and snooped around. She quickly learned her name was Lili Paltrinieri and she owned a metaphysical shop called Revelations.

Great, just what she needed. Some woman who fancied herself a psychic.

She was obviously trying to connect with Frank. Emma fumed for a moment. Why couldn't the living just leave well enough alone and stop bothering them? She was quite content here and didn't need some phony psychic stirring up trouble. Emma considered appearing and scaring her, but decided it wasn't worth the effort. Besides, it would only confirm the spirit presence the woman sought and might draw ghost tours back into the building.

A low profile was best, she decided. Better that Lili pestered Frank than came looking for her.

Apartment 114 had been the pulp room long ago and the story of Frank's death had been a big event. She had watched it all play out. Heard the whispers. The accusations. The confrontation and a man's death.

Four men murdered Frank. Beat the poor guy and tossed him into a pulp vat.

A crime that might have gone unpunished.

If not for her.

Six

Danielle Hamlin ran flat out.

Following her favorite trail at the edge of the river, she tried to burn through her melancholy mood to achieve a positive mindset for work. She had a crucial meeting this morning with a new client.

A meeting with the DA followed to discuss a plea agreement on a current case, a charge of embezzlement of $130,000 against the office manager of a local building contractor. Such cases were often mind-boggling examples of greed, broken trust, laziness, and stupidity. A trusted employee grew greedy or larcenous, pilfering small amounts of money at first, becoming more and more brazen as they escaped detection. The business owner was often too busy or clueless about the day-to-day expenses, or too lazy to monitor the employee or put checks and balances in place. Eventually, the theft became obvious after the business suffered substantial financial loss. Her client was an amoral, greedy bitch masquerading as a suburban mom. Nevertheless, she was entitled to a good defense and Danielle would give her the best.

Sweating and huffing from the workout, she keyed herself through the side entrance and jogged up the stairs to her condo.

On the east end of Rock River Mills, unit 241 was almost two thousand square feet, an open plan space with fifteen-foot ceilings. It was sparsely but tastefully decorated with steel, light woods, and fabrics. The walls were greys and whites. The living room overlooked the river through large windows, the kitchen on the west wall featured white cabinets, grey quartz countertops, and a Wolf range. A granite-topped island divided the kitchen from the living room. It was a polar opposite to her parents' house with its heavy brown furniture and cabinetry.

She grabbed a glass of ice water from the fridge, striding through her bedroom and bathroom to start the shower. The run hadn't relieved all of her anxiety. Segerman, her boss, was about to retire, and Dani worried her chances at a partnership rested on today's client meeting. Segerman's son would become partner, but a second partnership was up for grabs and would go to either her or Ryan Cassell. She felt confident she was the better attorney. Did her boss agree?

After a three-minute shower, she dried her hair. Danielle had laid out clothing for the day: a white blouse and a stylish tailored black suit with a fitted jacket. She wore only light makeup for a subdued natural look, but no jewelry beyond diamond stud earrings. Her appearance was tasteful and serious. Feminine, but not sexy.

Normally she would jog down the stairs outside her condo, but her car was closer to the lobby, so she took the elevator. No jogging today. She didn't want to break a sweat before the meeting. She sweat far too easily and it was a constant curse.

A courteous man held the door for her as she stepped out into the sunshine.

She thanked him but felt his eyes follow her as she walked to the car. It gave her a little chill.

Danielle had no idea why.

* * *

Chase saw her out of the corner of his eye.

As he opened the lobby door, she stepped out of the elevator. Her hair was long and dark, her profile flawless. She was dressed professionally in a business suit: a white blouse beneath a fitted jacket that lightly accented her feminine qualities, the gentle curve of her breasts. The slightly flared pants revealed a slender profile. Her walk was fluid and seductive. He stopped and held the door until she walked past with a "Thank you" and hopped into a BMW in an assigned spot. The spell was broken when someone stepped around him to exit the building with a not-so-subtle glare.

But he was hooked. He felt compelled to follow her.

A bad idea. Still, Chase turned on his heel and walked back to his car, forcing himself to maintain a nonchalant air. He watched the BMW leave and pulled out seconds later, following at a discreet distance.

The woman drove across town to a freestanding building next to the Walmart, the offices of Segerman and Bosch, Attorneys at Law. She might be a paralegal, but he thought not. She drove a Beamer, so she was probably a junior partner. If so, her name would be listed on the company website. She could be a client, but she entered through a locked side door.

Okay, not a client.

He drove back to the mill, telling himself any interest in the woman was dangerous. Against the rules—though they were his rules. He could bend them to suit.

Locked in his apartment, Chase grabbed his laptop and found her on the company website. Danielle Hamlin, a criminal defense attorney.

Walking out to the front lobby, he grabbed his mail and saw the name Hamlin over the doorbell for 241. So, she lived there. How had he missed her before now?

His interest in Danielle was reckless and could lead to trouble. He knew it but was already hooked. She was precisely his type, and once he fixated on a woman, he couldn't stop obsessing over her.

His OCD was like that. If an idea took hold, it was difficult, if not impossible to shake.

Just by thinking about this woman, he was breaking several of his rules. Never pursue a woman who could be traced back to him, and therefore, no neighbors, especially in the same building. Never take more than one woman a year. Only six months had passed since he'd taken Megan. Never—

He realized Danielle looked a little like Megan. Dark-haired, slender, with a narrow facial profile and a slight overbite. Prettier even.

Chase walked to the stairs at the end of the hall and up to the second floor. He didn't know the rest of the building well and was surprised to learn that 241 was almost directly above his apartment. How had he failed to notice this stunning woman? He shook his head at the egregious error.

Time for bed. He walked back to his apartment.

Chase worked nights this week and slept during the day. As he slid into bed, he continued to dwell, unable to erase that face from his mind. Thinking about her might be stupid, but such rationales seldom dissuaded him from doing so. He realized he was already plotting how to take her. Maybe his rules were overly strict. Living in the building wouldn't make him a suspect. Of all the residents, he would be the last to fall under suspicion.

Why take the chance?

There were plenty of beautiful women out there to choose from. Taking Megan had been carefully planned and executed. Six months later, the police still had no clues.

He could devise an equally careful grab for Danielle.

Chase knew he shouldn't even consider it.

But her face was all he could see.

Seven

Lili poured a glass of chardonnay.

A moment later, someone knocked on the door.

Olivia Kaplan. Dressed in tight jeans and a green *Salt Life* tee, she had pulled her hair into a ponytail. "I hope you don't mind me stopping by."

"No. Come in. Glass of wine?"

"Sure." Olivia's eyes swept the apartment with a look that suggested she was seeing exactly what she expected to see. "I love your decor. Some people might find it busy, but I think it's very creative—perfect."

"Thank you," Lili said, pleased. The busy look was intentional.

She grabbed another glass from the kitchen, tipped a generous pour, and handed it to Olivia. She motioned to the sitting area. With a seven-foot ceiling, the space had a cozy feel. Lili had furnished it with a loveseat and two oversized chairs, thickly stuffed and wonderfully comfortable. The center coffee table held an assortment of flameless candles for ambiance. She preferred the real thing, but candles would darken the ceiling with soot.

Lili was curious about Olivia's motives for stopping by. "What can I do for you?"

Looking pensive, Olivia delayed making eye contact, then said, "I checked you out. You have excellent reviews. People seem to feel you're the real deal."

"Ah, thanks."

Olivia fiddled with a loop of her hair. "I'm convinced there's something wrong with our apartment. I think you understand it."

"I wouldn't say 'wrong.' Unsettling maybe," Lili said, though after the other night, she knew better. "What are you experiencing?"

Olivia sipped her wine and struggled still to make eye contact. "I feel a little stupid talking about this and Raleigh is hostile to any mention of ghosts."

"Many people are," Lili said. "I'm not. You can talk openly here."

"It's a bunch of little things. Sometimes, I feel like I'm being watched." She looked at Lili, an eyebrow raised. "Paranoid, right?"

"Maybe, maybe not. What else?"

"Sometimes there's a smell." She wrinkled her nose at the memory. "Like bleach."

"I've smelled it too. In the hallway."

"Really? So I'm not crazy?" Olivia's shoulders relaxed.

"No. But more than a few people think I'm crazy, so my opinion might not be worth much," Lili said with a self-deprecating laugh.

Olivia tittered, then gave Lili a pensive glance. "Would you consider coming down and doing a reading or whatever it is you do?"

"What about your husband?"

"Raleigh's gone to Paris on business."

"I would love to." Given that Frank was murdered in that apartment, it was perfect, but she withheld that information. She sensed Olivia was tightly wound. Better she didn't know, for now.

"I'll pay your normal fee—"

Lili waved her off, thrilled to be invited into their apartment. "Don't worry about that. You're a neighbor. A bottle of wine will suffice."

"Awesome." Olivia smiled, a genuine look of gratitude.

After a stilted pause, Lili said, "So, what do you and Raleigh do?"

"We're art dealers. I handle the research and sales. Raleigh handles acquisitions."

That explained the decor and professional look. "Your place is gorgeous."

"Thank you."

"Your husband looks and sounds like he's military."

"Ex-military. He was in the Army. Special Forces."

"Whoa. So he's dangerous."

"Not really," Olivia said with a dismissive shrug.

Lili wasn't convinced. Steering clear of Raleigh seemed prudent. They chatted a bit more—small talk—until Olivia finished her wine. She said, "What time?"

"How about nine?"

"Sounds good."

⋆ ⋆ ⋆

Lili packed a small satchel with her gear: a crystal ball, incense, a purple candle, and a small wooden wind chime. She wasn't a fan of Ouija boards or standard séances as an avenue to talk to spirits. They were too easy to manipulate in group settings. As the medium, only her participation and perceptions mattered. Her clients weren't always happy to simply observe but it was her show.

Instead, she used a crystal ball, not as a fortune-telling device, but a spirit medium. She didn't offer fortune telling, interested only in the here and now. It wasn't possible to foresee the future, to see events that hadn't yet happened. Suggesting the future was knowable also implied that free will was an illusion, and she didn't believe that.

Lili scooted across the courtyard and rapped twice with her knuckles.

Olivia opened the door holding two bottles of wine. She set them on the table next to the door.

"I picked up two. I hope you don't mind. Thanks for doing this."

"No problem," Lili said casually, tried to hide her excitement. She performed a quick read of the room and decided the dining area would be an ideal spot to work. The ceiling was highest just above and she had a nice direct line of sight from the door to the exterior windows. The energy flow would be ideal there.

Lili set her bag next to the Queen Anne-style table. It looked like antique cherrywood. "This okay?"

"Set up wherever you like."

Lili hung the chime set from the light hanging over the table. Turning around, she placed the candle on the sideboard behind her and lit it. Then she lit a sandalwood incense stick and set it on a ceramic tray.

"Can you dim the lights, please?"

Olivia grabbed her phone and fiddled with it until the room was almost dark. "How's that?"

"Perfect."

Lili set the dark wooden box that held her crystal ball on the table and tipped the lid back. The clear quartz ball was about three inches in diameter, quite small compared with the stereotypical crystal ball. It had cost her over fifteen hundred dollars on eBay and was a far superior instrument to the larger, cheaper glass balls. She set the crystal on a felt-lined wooden stand.

"Okay. For the reading, I am going to use the crystal ball to contact any spirits present in the room. I did some research. It seems a man named Frank Zivkovic died somewhere near your apartment in 1936, so I'll be looking for him in particular."

Olivia gave the room a wide-eyed gaze. Yep, definitely tightly wound.

"You are an observer, not a participant, so you need to remain quiet while I'm working."

"Understood." Olivia touched the chimes. "What's with these?"

"Placed over the crystal ball, they'll pick up any disturbances in the energy fields."

"Oh."

Lili left her hanging to add atmosphere to the reading. "If you're ready, we'll start."

Olivia nodded, looking apprehensive.

Lili took the crystal ball and held it in her hands. Eyes closed, she cleared her mind of extraneous thoughts as the quartz warmed slowly in her grip. She reached a relaxed state and felt a familiar sensation as her mind bonded with the crystal. Setting the ball on the stand in the near-dark room, the indirect light of the candle on the sideboard cast a wan light on the crystal, allowing Lili to gaze into it. She relaxed further and locked her eyes on the interior of the ball where a mist had formed. Her concentration became absolute as the apartment faded from view.

As she completed the psychic connection with the crystal, the mist cleared. At first, the ball was dark. Then the grimmer aspects of the room came into focus. Grey, industrial, raw. There were large vats in the room, an iron catwalk overhead. It was a surreal vision.

The wind chime rattled slightly, and she caught movement at the corner of her eye.

Somebody was here!

Lili spoke quietly. "Frank? Is that you?"

The chime rattled a bit more.

"Frank. You can talk through me."

The smell and harsh light of the factory was a bleak, forbidding vision. Hard to believe people ever worked in these conditions—

"What do you see?" Olivia said.

Shit.

The question broke the connection and snapped her back to the present. Lili shook her head and tried to remain calm. "Olivia, you can't talk while I'm attempting to make contact. I was almost there."

"I'm sorry. I'll shut up." Olivia sat, eyes down, face reddening, and pursed her lips tight.

It took another ten minutes to return to the old factory. The chime rattled slightly.

Lili whispered, "Frank?"

She sensed a presence over in the area of the bedroom. Someone stared at her, but refused to show himself.

Lili again whispered his name.

The chime rattled and a deep male voice boomed inside her head.

Leave me alone!

Those three words catapulted her back to the present like a slamming door.

Lili jumped back in shock and almost fell off her chair. Overt, angry reactions from spirits were uncommon.

Olivia stood up and took a step back. Her voiced pitched up several tones. "What happened?"

Shaking her head, Lili said, "That was strange. He's here—Frank's here, but he told me to get lost."

"Was he mad?"

"I think maybe he was."

Eight

Danielle loved police procedurals.

Books, movies, television—they were all good, especially with a hint of romance. With her legal background, she fancied herself an expert on the subject. She also considered herself situationally aware at all times. Perhaps she spent more time monitoring her surroundings than necessary. Her father had taught her the requisite skills and insisted she take a self-defense class as a teen. He had seen the worst the world could offer serving in Afghanistan and wanted his daughter trained sufficiently to handle herself in any situation. Danielle also carried a Sig P365 in her purse and practiced at a local range once a month.

His background and views influenced her decision to live in Ash Grove, where crime was rare beyond domestic violence, drugs, and petty theft. She had led a sheltered life. Never had a difficult or possessive boyfriend. Had never been stalked or harassed, though she had friends who had dealt with both. She just had an ex-husband who liked to play the field.

Maybe she was being unduly paranoid, but she noted a car following her in the rearview mirror. She was reasonably certain the same car had followed her yesterday and the day before. Dark—black, maybe. It hung back behind several other cars. It might just be someone who drove the same route every day. If so, they would continue on if she deviated from her normal path.

Dani took a right on Taft instead of going straight on Main.

The car turned as well.

Crap!

She turned three blocks up and steered back toward Main. The car followed. She turned into the Kwik Trip and pulled up to the store. The dark car slowed but continued forward. She didn't get a good look at the driver and he didn't turn to look at her. Maybe she was being paranoid, but couldn't shake her unease.

Danielle slammed the steering wheel with her hands.

She had screwed up. Despite the training, the situation had rattled her. She should have snapped a photo of the car or the license plate. Still, by pulling into a busy location, she had done one thing right.

When she arrived at the office and mentioned her experience to Don Segerman, he insisted she report it.

"There's nothing to report. It was just a feeling."

Segerman, grey-haired and casually handsome, had a resonant baritone voice. "Nonsense. If you think someone followed you, I'd trust your gut. I'm calling Tom."

Picking up the phone, he called Tom Isaacs, the police chief and one of his golfing buddies. Segerman briefly explained the situation. Looking up, he said, "Any idea who it might be?"

"No. No one I can think of. This has never happened to me before."

Segerman passed the information along, then said, "Make and model of your car?"

"BMW 330i sedan."

"License number?"

Dani rattled off the details.

"What time do you leave for work?"

"Seven-forty, give or take a few minutes."

They talked for another minute and Segerman signed off with, "Thanks, Tom. Appreciate it."

He turned to Danielle. "They'll have an officer tail you to work for a few days, starting Monday, just to play it safe. Okay?"

Danielle walked to her office to check her messages. She should have felt better, but a small anxiety remained. Another worry on top of the others. The client meeting had gone well enough, but the woman hadn't yet retained her for representation. She and the DA had arrived at a reasonable plea deal for the embezzler, but the woman balked, trying to avoid jail time. That wasn't an option. And Segerman had delayed the partnership decision for another week without explanation, shaking her confidence that she would win it.

All that anxiety on top of her normal state of melancholy, a consequence of a year alone after the divorce. The split had been agreeable enough. Dean was a loving philanderer who simply failed to understand the principal precepts of monogamy. She didn't mind living alone but missed having someone to talk to about her day, to give her a hug when she needed one. A best friend. She had friends who were supportive at first, but they were married and had drifted back to their normal, domestic lives.

Dating was a nightmare. She was attractive and knew it, but tried to not treat it as a weapon or her only asset. At times, it was a curse. Too many men hit on her, as did a few brazen women. Yes, relationships always started with physical attraction, but she needed companionship more than she needed a sex buddy right now. She didn't date people through work, and dating sites were impossible. She was mostly bombarded with messages from men who had little in common with her. Danielle wasn't a sports fan, didn't care to fish, and as much as she loved the outdoors, hated camping. Holiday Inn Express was the closest she ever ventured into the wilds. This was all spelled out on her profile and yet, almost all of the messages she received came from guys holding a dead fish in front of a tent. She wasn't an elitist but wanted to date someone with equal intelligence and education, not some dude content with a GED.

The creepy experience of being followed had unsettled her, and the situation felt much more real now that they contacted the police.

It was real, she decided. Someone had followed her.

She just couldn't imagine who.

Or why.

⋆ ⋆ ⋆

Chase shook his head and drove home.

He was done tailing Danielle Hamlin. It was dumb, reckless, and he worried she suspected the tail. She had made several unexpected turns today. If he wasn't careful, he would get caught. As a cop, he prided himself on his knowledge of crime scene science and the mistakes people made that resulted in arrest.

So why was he being so careless?

Sadly, he knew why and couldn't control it; felt the slippery tentacles worming into his brain.

Danielle.

A full-blown obsession. He had to have her.

The woman had become the only thing he could think about. Friends called her Dani, but he found the nickname trite. He had followed her on foot as well, learning her routines. Like the morning run. In those efforts, he'd been much more discreet.

From here, he would practice a more subtle mode of observation. He had placed an inconspicuous mini camera near her apartment in the hallway, connected by Wi-Fi to his computer. From the recordings, he was learning her schedule and those of her neighbors to prepare for the big event.

She ran every morning, the same route like clockwork at 6 a.m. No one else came or went. No boyfriends. No girlfriends. She looked more and more perfect. There was only one other apartment along that hallway, an older woman who seldom ventured out and never appeared before noon.

Really, Danielle was ideal. Something of a loner whose absence would likely go unnoticed for days. The early morning looked like the best time to grab her. Suspicion would fall on her run through Rock River Park.

And yet, the idea seemed incredibly foolhardy.

Regardless of the risks, his infatuation with the woman grew and festered.

Crowded out almost every other thought.

An obsession that felt indestructible.

Nine

Emma felt increasingly uneasy in the mill.

A relatively stable energy field passed through the building and she was sensitive to any fluctuations within it. The renovations had changed the field modestly, an irritating sensation, but not unbearable. Now, this Lili woman was stirring things up and the deviant in 139 was creating stronger distortions. With turmoil on each end of the building, she felt squeezed. Caught in the grip of an invisible vise.

A death led to serious upheavals. Frank's murder had caused disruptions that took months to settle down. Emma had witnessed his murder years ago and felt compelled to bring him a measure of justice.

She remembered it vividly as an ugly, violent event. Four men beat Frank and threw him from the third-floor catwalk into a pulp vat after tying a weight around his neck.

The authorities suspected suicide, but Emma knew the truth. She saw the men steal some tools and materials during the installation of a new machine. They killed Frank after he reported the theft. It angered her because they might've literally gotten away with murder.

Emma felt pity for Frank, too. She had sensed his last moments, the terror—which felt so much like her own death—and had been profoundly affected by it.

She tried to write notes, but her physical skills were almost non-existent. Finally, she found a way. The mill manager had his own washroom. Manager or not, he was blue-collar, and his dingy bathroom reflected his status relative to the stuffed shirts in the front office. The mirror was dingy, too. No one had washed it in years. After hours and hours of effort, slowly wearing through the grime with her fingers, Emma scrawled a simple message:

Ed killed Frank

The manager was a good guy. He liked Frank and, after reading the message, connected the theft to the murder and called the cops.

The police came and took the mirror. Then they questioned Ed. A day later, they returned and arrested three of Ed's co-workers. A trial followed. Emma followed it religiously by reading the newspapers in the break room. All four were convicted and sentenced to life in prison. The author of the note that broke the case remained a mystery.

Emma hoped her efforts brought Frank some measure of peace, but she would never know. They couldn't communicate. Some strange facet of her life in the mill.

Oh well.

Over the years, other people had died in the mill—it was a dangerous place to work. In most cases, they transitioned to the next life in a process she didn't understand. They went to heaven? A different dimension? She had given up trying to make sense of it. The answers weren't in any of the books she read. The Bible said that people went to heaven or hell, but Emma had growing doubts about that book. And where did the mill lay in the grand scheme of things?

Stuck in this place, she relived her death often. Emma felt anchored to the spot, returning every day to the skylight to rest at the scene of the crime. Why, she didn't know. She could rest only there; nowhere else. Another strange quirk of her existence.

The machine was long gone but she could still picture it vividly as a mess of shiny whirling metal. She had no clue what the machine did, but her fall took place in slow-motion. It felt like an eternity as she floated down and the blades, like fangs, tore her asunder. There was no pain, just the horror of watching her beautiful, youthful body cleaved into pieces that would never be made whole again. A terrifying Humpty Dumpty dismemberment, her consciousness and vision remaining acute for what seemed like hours as her life slipped away. She knew it was mere seconds, but the memory played like a wretched horror movie.

Worse, she never felt Jacob's embrace again. Beautiful Jacob, the man of her dreams. A tall, dark-haired gentleman with brown eyes. Her memory of their last day together was vivid and cherished, an antidote for the darker memory of the whirring blades.

A Sunday, she had packed a picnic lunch and met Jacob in the woods just past Braverman's farm. There was a clearing by a brook in the middle of the oak grove. She had worn a beige, ankle-length linen dress. He was still dressed in the somber suit he'd worn to church that day. They sat in the sun and ate sandwiches, drinking cider from a jug he brought.

They talked, discussing their plans for the future: a house, a baby, maybe a move away from there. Joking and laughing, they imagined a day, a year ahead, when they would be husband and wife. She couldn't stop looking at him, and he seemed equally fascinated with her, even after two years of courtship.

They kissed. He fondled her breast—as far as they had ever gone. But the sun and cider made her bold and a little reckless. She touched him, then drew his hand to her. After arousing each other to breathlessness, he loved her in that clearing, the most exhilarating fifteen minutes of her brief life.

Three days later, she was dead. Gone. A life unlived. Her dreams erased.

In a way, she felt an affinity for the mill. Jacob had worked there the rest of his life and a small amount of his energy remained even now. Little more than a hazy photograph on the wall, really. She wondered how he could work there, knowing how she had died, then imagined he did so to remain close to her. She had attempted to appear to him, but he never saw her. Not everybody did. She didn't understand that either.

She had also tried to leave many times over the years but the outer walls of the mill were an impenetrable barrier. Emma was resigned to her life there. She suspected the sex by the stream had nixed her chances at heaven. Thus, she remained the girl she had been in 1894, a love-struck teen pining for a man she could never have. Jacob worked his whole life in the mill. Emma had watched him marry, grow old, and retire. She didn't know when he died. Now that she was learning about computers, perhaps she could look it up.

She held exactly one grudge in her life: an ire directed at the original mill owner, Mr. Bodman.

The accident was his fault. His carelessness led directly to her death. Really, in her mind, it had been murder.

He had installed a flimsy trapdoor with a flimsy latch over a dangerous piece of machinery. She had walked over it every day until the morning the latch failed and she plunged to her death.

Emma never let him forget it.

She learned the trick of making herself visible to the living early on and quite by accident. It was a matter of entering a certain energy state—like finding a secret path through the woods. Once she found it, she quickly learned to find the hidden opening until she could appear at will. Just pop right up and make scary faces. She haunted Mr. Bodman and made his life a living hell. She didn't want him to forget her death for one second. One day, he stopped showing up. A new owner took over soon after. Chasing him away had given her some solace over her untimely death.

The mill was her home and she didn't want the meddling woman from 124 messing with it. But she had more pressing matters right now. She had to expose the dangerous man in 139 and she needed something more sophisticated than a message scrawled on a mirror.

Ten

A loud rap on the door startled Lili.

"Lili!"

Raleigh. And he sounded angry. She opened the door cautiously.

"What did you tell Olivia?"

"Why?"

"She won't sleep in the bedroom. Something about Frank."

Lili crossed her arms and murmured, "Nothing—other than his name."

"Why would you do that?"

"She asked me to come over and do a read on the apartment."

"And you told her there's a dead guy living in our bedroom?"

"That's not exactly what I said—"

"That's what she heard." Raleigh pointed a finger at her and said, "You keep your fruitcake ideas away from my wife and stay away from the apartment or I'll file a complaint with the manager."

"For what?"

He stomped off and bellowed, "Stay away, Lili!"

Lili stood for a moment, stunned by his outburst.

Wow! What an ass!

She had been dead right about him—definitely someone to avoid. How did Olivia live with such an intolerant jerk? Even if he didn't believe in ghosts, he could at least be sensitive to his wife's feelings and concerns. Lili felt she and Olivia had bonded last night and opened a friendship. It was nice. She had many casual acquaintances but few friends she could call for a spur-of-the-moment lunch or dinner out.

It was in the nature of her life as a psychic and a metaphysicist that her life was often a solitary affair. One punctuated by odd hours and odder investigations. She wasn't always understood and was occasionally the object of derision. Most of the time, she didn't mind, sometimes too engrossed to even notice. Still, a friend in the building? That would be nice.

Hopefully Raleigh would chill out or go away on business again. For now, she would wait until Olivia contacted her.

She was more interested in Frank. Hostile spirits were a rare occurrence for her and they were usually lost, confused souls that ultimately warmed to her efforts. She got a darker vibe from Frank. The dude had been murdered. Maybe she needed to try an approach gentler than barging into his space with a crystal ball. Maybe she could help Olivia as well.

Her phone rang. Olivia. Lili hesitated before tapping the green icon.

"I'm sorry," Olivia blurted. "I didn't know he was going to do that."

"It's okay. Raleigh's not my first angry husband."

"Really?"

"Like Raleigh, the husbands or boyfriends of my clients aren't always receptive to my ideas."

"So you're not mad?"

"No. Not at all." Lili was a little mad, but it wasn't Olivia's fault.

"Good. Can we get together again soon?"

"Yeah. I'd like that."

After their conversation, Lili had a glass of wine, took a nap to recharge, and made a stealthy return to the hallway outside Olivia's condo just after 1 a.m.

Sitting against the wall, Lili allowed her consciousness to drift, emptying her mind of all thoughts. She preferred to astral travel from her apartment, but felt the proximity to 114 would improve the chances of connecting with Frank even if it was riskier.

There were plenty of doubters who believed astral projection was merely a figment of the traveler's imagination. That could be true, she supposed. How would she know? It felt real, though. And she saw details of places she had never visited in person. Later, when she went to those places, they looked exactly as they had during her astral journey.

Lili reached a state of complete relaxation and slipped into the first shallow, semiconscious stage of sleep. This wasn't something she could do with another person. It was a solo venture and only somewhat useful for ghost hunting. In the apartment or any similar space, there were multiple energy levels. A ghost could inhabit any one of them. She could easily glide past a spirit and never see them. Still, hit or miss, it was the gentlest approach she could take with Frank.

Ten minutes passed before her mind and spirit reached the desired astral state.

Her consciousness rose up and away from her body, drifting through the wall. Like sweeping through the frequencies on a radio looking for a station, she changed her energy state constantly as she moved. The apartment was quiet. For an hour she worked, probing and sweeping the apartment, finding no evidence that Frank was present. But she was in his world, the old pulp room clearly visible with a faint sketch of the Kaplans' apartment superimposed like a hologram on the space.

She spoke gently in an ethereal astral voice. "Frank?"

⋆ ⋆ ⋆

Frank stirred.

Most of the time, he rested—a vague condition like sleep. Time was a fuzzy concept. Maybe he rested for weeks or years. He had no point of reference, no perception of time passing. No day or night. The mill looked the same as it did the day he died. The pulp room was a grim space without windows, garishly lit from above. A landscape of grey concrete, bricks, and iron vats.

But not exactly the same. Superimposed on his world was a faint overlay: walls, doors, windows, furniture that fit neatly in his space. The overlay was completely weightless. He could walk or wave a hand through any part of it. He also had an impression of movement within the overlay. They almost looked like ghosts. But that was absurd. Frank wasn't a bright man but knew he was the ghost here.

The pulp room where he died was a closed space that he couldn't leave. He couldn't see outside, couldn't open any door, was aware of nothing beyond the walls. And though the overlay had openings that looked like windows, no light passed through them. He might as well be in jail.

It was a horrible irony. He had lived life as a good Christian and, after hearing the conspirators discuss the theft of materials, had reported it to his foreman. It wasn't an act of loyalty to the company. He liked his job, but he didn't owe Rock River Paper a thing. No, the theft violated a commandment, one of the big ones. He just hadn't considered the danger in telling.

For his efforts, God rewarded him with a beating, death by murder, and exile in this purgatory—or hell. He had no idea which, but he didn't deserve this fate. He had been a good kid. Always listened to his parents. Never sassed. Died a virgin. Other than a few white lies, what could he have possibly done wrong?

Whatever his sentence, he prayed in his waking hours for it to end. He walked the perimeter of his prison in the meantime until he grew tired and rested again. Oddly, he never felt lonely here, just cheated.

Tonight, something odd was happening—again. Someone or something was poking around in his space. It was annoying, like being jabbed with a finger.

Why couldn't they just leave him alone? Being trapped here was bad enough.

He ambled around the room, squinting, trying to better visualize the overlay, suspecting the problem arose there.

Frank spotted an opening. A small hole that looked like a tear. Through it, two eyes peered at him, and someone called his name. A soft voice from the other side.

Whoa! That was creepy.

Now the probing felt like a poke in the eye.

It needed to stop.

A diaphanous figure, a wraith, materialized in his space.

In frustration, he stared into the eyes of the figure as he conjured up something to scare her away. He puffed himself up into a hideous thing—all teeth and eyeballs—like a luminous piranha and yelled in a big voice:

Leave me alone!

* * *

Lili screamed inaudibly and fled from that horrendous sight.

What the fuck was that?

In her astral state, she got confused and disoriented. Suddenly, she was beneath the building.

Oh shit.

Was there a basement? Based on the sensation, there had to be, yet she had seen no doors in the building that suggested one. No stairs. The elevator stopped at the ground floor.

It was the second time she'd felt something underground. But it was inscrutable, hidden by darkness. Something to investigate? Or better left alone?

Finally, she reoriented her astral projection, drifted back to her body, and gently reconnected.

When she stood and walked toward her apartment, the basement sensation lingered and grew stronger. Why had she never noticed it before? It was like something had switched on in the building. A new ghost? The excursion may have been risky but felt enlightening regardless.

In the last few days, the building had come to life. There seemed to be ghosts everywhere, but she was exhausted.

Right now, it was time for sleep.

Lili brushed her teeth, stripped down to her panties, and slid into bed.

As she drifted off, a name came to her. The thing in the basement.

Eamon O'Keene.

Who the hell was Eamon O'Keene?

Eleven

Chase secured the apartment with his phone.

The deadbolt on the door snapped to the locked position. The alarm panel lit up, ran a security check, and a green light flashed on. The system was armed and ready. The day after the apparent break-in, he installed interior cameras. Today, he put the finishing touches on a high-end alarm system. He hadn't felt it necessary before; considered the apartment to be impregnable. Now it truly was, the door and the windows protected by sensors. Satisfied, he shut it down.

The errant mouse had reminded him, despite all his knowledge, that he had blind spots and had to worry about being overconfident. No matter how careful he was, there were situations he couldn't plan for and certain unknowns he couldn't anticipate.

In the end, he concluded there had been no illicit entry, that a passing truck must have shaken the building sufficiently to move the mouse. Heavy truck traffic did roll by occasionally. Nothing else made sense. The apartment *was* impregnable. But he felt safer with the recent changes in security, especially since he anticipated taking Danielle soon.

So safe, he decided to move the computer back to the office. The computer was hidden in his man cave, which was literally a cave of sorts.

The entrance was under the floor in the bathroom and skillfully concealed. Chase lifted the carpet strip at the doorway, held in place with powerful neodymium magnets. Then he removed the baseboard on each side wall, also held in place with magnets. The floating vinyl flooring rolled back easily, revealing the trapdoor that led into the underground passages of the building.

Learning about the existence of the basement had been serendipitous.

Chase had become friends with the lead contractor on the Rock River Mills project, Dominic Garcia. They frequently hung out at O'Malley's Sports Bar. One night, Dom, loaded and chatty after winning a large fantasy baseball pool, had confided in Chase and told him about the access to the basement spaces they'd discovered under the building. The spaces hadn't been marked on any blueprints and weren't structurally significant. Knowing no one would be the wiser, they closed them up to avoid an inspection and incurring any regulatory delays. The story came up because inspectors had recently shut down work on a Green Bay project after an excavator discovered Native American remains and artifacts in a basement crawl space.

Later that night, Dom Ubered home in a drunken state and Chase hoped he would forget he had spilled the secret. The subject never came up again.

Chase didn't forget. He had been looking for a small farm, considering a house in the country ideal for his particular needs. Instead, he took the money his sweet Aunt Karen willed to him and dropped it on 139 in Rock River Mills. Somewhat isolated on the east end of the building, the apartment and concealed basement hallways beneath were a dream come true for a guy with his particular interests.

He cut into the bathroom floor for access. With no apartments above or to either side, the construction noise wasn't an issue. He built a solid, hinged door that sat flush with the floor and looked identical to the surrounding underlay. No one would suspect a door, even if they pulled up the flooring. A remote activated spring popped it open for access the basement. With the vinyl flooring in place, stepping on the hidden panel sounded indistinguishable from the adjoining floor. He tapped the apartment electricity for lighting and plumbed hot and cold water into the basement—all hidden inside the bathroom wall.

That was almost a year ago.

Chase waited six months before snatching Megan Rice, his first planned abduction. The experience had been everything he imagined and then some.

He'd stalked Megan for weeks. Followed her from the bar and, convinced the road was otherwise clear, pulled her over with a small police flasher on his dash. He walked up, tased her before she suspected anything was amiss, yanked her out of the car, and applied a neck hold that rendered her unconscious. After binding her with duct tape, he tossed her into a sportsman's trunk in his truck.

He grabbed her phone and purse, dropping the phone into a Faraday case to block the cell signal, and drove away. Just under forty seconds had elapsed.

Wearing gloves and a nylon stocking, he left no prints, hair, or DNA.

There were no houses on that stretch of road. No cars passed the location. He had taken every precaution.

Committed the perfect crime.

Returning to the mill, he casually wheeled the trunk into the apartment. Megan was gone, never to be found again. The memories still thrilled him to the bone. He chuckled at his little pun. He was so damned clever. But he'd locked those memories away on a hard drive in the basement, and he wanted to revisit them.

Chase clicked the remote and the trapdoor popped up an inch.

Reaching into his lair beneath the apartment, he flicked the lights on. Metal rungs descended to the concrete floor.

The computer sat on a bench in a somewhat cozy room with brick walls. A pair of comfortable deck chairs and a camping table sat where he and his friend, Eamon, hung out and gabbed, often for hours. In an adjoining room, two long hallways led west beneath the rest of the building.

He had mounted a flatscreen on the opposite wall and usually left it on for Eamon. A small refrigerator filled with beer sat beneath it. On the left, he had filled a cork board with pictures of Megan that were gradually being supplanted by pictures of Danielle. In the top right corner, a few stray photos of Stacy—his first conquest—peeked through.

Eamon lived in the basement. He wasn't visible, but he was certainly real. They started talking soon after Chase opened up the basement passages. Chase had spent a lot of time down there cleaning, organizing, and making improvements. Adding lights and wiring. A basic bathroom with a shower. The plumbing drained into the Rock River. Part of the river ran through a tunnel under the building, a truly fortuitous discovery.

Eamon had spoken first, a simple, "Hey, friend."

The voice hadn't surprised him. He had sensed a presence in the basement, and the voice was proof of it.

Chase replied with a casual, “Hey, bro.”

Eamon claimed to be Irish and had a convincing accent. Their conversations ran the gamut from sports to women. Eamon had been fascinated by the business with Megan and an eager watcher. It was almost like having a cheering section and only reinforced his feelings of prowess and superiority.

Chase grabbed two bottles of beer and set them on the table, sitting down and taking a long pull from his. Eamon never drank his beer but said he liked the smell of it. He usually showed up a few minutes after Chase sat down.

A moment later, Eamon spoke. “The new colleen is lovely. When are you going to take her?”

Colleen was Eamon’s quirky Irish word for girl.

“Don’t know yet. I want to be fully prepared. This one feels riskier.”

“Nonsense. What are you fecking waiting for? You’re as ready as I’ve seen you.”

“You think so?”

“I know so. What I don’t understand is why you don’t.”

“Just being careful—”

“Sounds like you’re being a wanker.”

“Hey, you know me better than that.”

“I’m beginning to wonder.”

“What’s gotten into you, you cranky fucker?”

Eamon laughed. “Just taking the piss, mate.”

But Chase wondered: was he being too cautious? Losing his edge? Really, he was ready. What more would he accomplish in waiting, other than possibly missing out on a virtually perfect girl?

Chase clicked over to the Milwaukee Brewers game and they argued about strategy. Eamon was still trying to master the finer points of American baseball.

An hour later, Chase grabbed the computer tower and returned to his office.

* * *

Chase walked into work just before 11 p.m. and checked the late shift mailbox. It was empty, but he saw a note for a squad from an earlier shift. As of yesterday, they were running a loose tail on a Beemer 330i. So she *had* suspected. But they listed the vehicle of interest as a dark sedan with no further details. So really, they had nothing.

Again, his perceptions and instincts had been spot-on and he had avoided detection. He trusted those instincts to see him through the next adventure. It was dangerous. It would always be dangerous, but he would take her anyway.

He assumed he had the danger gene. Nothing scared him. Becoming a cop made him feel even more invincible.

His interest in the law?

It came from his need to skirt it, not obey it.

Chase had to work the next two nights, but he was off Thursday, Friday, and Saturday. Maybe Eamon was right. He was being too careful.

Saturday morning would be perfect.

Twelve

Martin Kettridge doodled at his desk.

A senior detective with the Ash Grove Police Department, he was bored.

He had closed two cases in the past week and only two remained on his plate. Normally, he worked five to seven cases at once.

The office wall to his left was adorned with photos of his children, Alissa and Brendan, from baby pics to their high school photos. Both were in college now. Behind him, a small wall of fame bore a degree in Criminal Science from UW-Madison and other sundry awards. The third wall contained a photo collage of his fishing catches, including a six-foot sturgeon snagged on Lake Winnebago. A relaxing Terry Redlin print, a sunset with a cabin and a flock of geese, hung next to the door.

The first remaining case, a series of random, opportunistic thefts, would probably solve itself. Eventually, the offender or offenders would screw up and they would make an arrest. Case closed.

The other, a missing persons case, was more perplexing. He spent a lot of time mulling it over.

Six months before, the department received a report of an abandoned vehicle on the shoulder of Estabrook Road, a secluded area just inside the city limits. They traced the car to thirty-two-year-old Megan Rice, a dental hygienist. When an officer was unable to contact Megan by phone or at her listed address, he contacted her parents. They hadn't heard from her in the past few days. That wasn't unusual.

They then received a call from her ex, Ryan Rice. Ryan and Megan had a ten-year-old who had been with Dad all weekend. When he took the boy home on Monday morning, Megan wasn't there and couldn't be reached by phone. That was unusual. Megan never missed a pick-up or a drop-off.

Later that day, she failed to show for work.

By Monday night, the chief had deemed Megan a critical missing person and threw the full weight of the department into the search. Street cops performed a widening search in neighborhoods and fields around the car. They brought in dogs and a helicopter. A crime scene crew pored over the car but found nothing suspicious.

Martin and fellow detectives interviewed the parents, family, friends, and co-workers. He interviewed the ex in depth, but he was home with the son, and they had watched movies Friday night. She had no known boyfriends. Over the next few days, he assembled a reasonable picture of her movements the last day anyone saw her, the previous Friday. After work, she dropped her son off with the husband. She was later seen at Clancy's Tavern, a bar just outside town with a band and a dance floor. She apparently went there every Friday and hung with a group of friends. Megan was an attractive, outgoing woman and drew the interest of several men who jockeyed for her attention.

Looking at her photo, Martin decided she had a face that might attract the wrong kind of interest.

Megan left the bar just before midnight. She might have been tipsy, but she wasn't drunk. The bartender thought she had a Cosmo and a couple of beers. No one recalled anyone paying undue attention to Megan or leaving around the time she did. The bar had a camera but sadly, it was broken. Her purse and phone were gone, and the phone went dark that night. Nothing else was missing.

To Martin, it felt like an abduction.

There were alternative possibilities. Now and then, people simply walked away from their lives. Tired of the grind. A secret lover. A medical condition even. Suicide was a darker possibility. Sometimes they popped up elsewhere, years later, with a new name and a new life. Once, a woman had walked in to report her brother missing. Turned out he was sitting in a jail cell thirty feet away.

He dug into her past, asking her family the hard questions: history of mental illness? Drugs or alcohol? Gambling? Nothing in her profile suggested any instability. Megan was a devoted mother, a loyal employee, and had a clean record.

They plastered her picture everywhere, but nothing developed, not a single sighting. Her credit cards and bank accounts remained untouched. The phone stayed dark.

Martin had a bad feeling. He suspected Megan Rice was dead and had been disposed of somewhere nearby.

He glanced at his phone. Lunch time.

Walking to his car in the station lot, he grabbed his rod and reel and a crawler crib that kept his nightcrawlers alive and happy. He strolled the short distance to the walkway along the Rock River. The sun was warm. The air smelled vaguely fishy and a couple of crows cackled noisily up-river. Sitting on a bench, he baited the hook, set a bobber, and cast the line twenty feet out.

While he enjoyed the warmth and fresh air, the details of the case churned along in a lazy stream of consciousness as he looked for a missed detail or the insignificant clue that would break the case.

He had visited the site on Estabrook Road multiple times. A crime scene team returned to scour the area with a cadaver dog. There was not one errant object, tire track, or fingerprint. No evidence of a struggle. No houses or traffic cams nearby. Just the car, abandoned on the side of the road like a discarded shoe.

He interviewed every neighbor within a mile of the location. Re-interviewed friends and family. Every person at the bar that night, especially the bartender. Occasionally, Martin went to the bar just to hang out. To watch the patrons, the regulars. Some of it he did on his own time.

Six months later, they still had nothing.

Martin burned through his break without a hit on the bobber or the case. He performed this ritual at least once a week just to keep it fresh in his mind. What could he do? There were no edges to pick at. The woman had simply vanished. It was possible she had been the victim of an alien abduction given the complete lack of evidence.

He shuffled back to his car and put his gear away.

Megan might still be alive.

But his gut said she was dead.

Thirteen

Emma felt conflicted and angry.

With the computer gone from 139, she questioned her initial reaction; second-guessed the threat the man posed. Perhaps he was simply a sick voyeur and not a dangerous rapist, though really, was there much difference? Just having that dreadful stuff on his computer was a crime.

With no proof, with nothing to direct people to, what could she do? Could she haunt him like she had Mr. Bodman? Scare him out of the building? That sounded desperate. Besides, not everyone was afraid of ghosts. Perhaps she just needed to take it easy and relax. If she did, he might bring the computer back. It was a little early to embark on a scorched earth campaign.

Meanwhile, Lili had focused her efforts on Frank, causing disruptions that reverberated throughout the building. She wondered how he was handling the attention but would never know. They were forever segregated from each other. Maybe they repelled each other like two similar magnetic poles. Or maybe, it was just one of the rules.

A mystery she had no hope of fathoming.

Sooner or later, Emma knew Lili would come after her, and she worried about the prospect. Lili had a strange ability, like magic or witchcraft. Somehow, her consciousness could float through the building like a ghost, though it remained tethered to her physical body by a luminous cord. Emma had never seen or heard of anything like it. She watched the woman drift right through the wall of 114! It was frightening. Maybe the woman was powerful in ways she didn't understand. They didn't explain the trick in any books she had read—though the answer might lie in Lili's library. Regardless, it seemed wise to steer clear of her.

Contemplating what she could do to keep her at bay, she wondered: could she intercept Lili during her travels? Swoop in and scare her like the ghostly angels in *Raiders of the Lost Ark?*

That movie seemed to play every other week somewhere in the mill and she loved it, partly because as Jacob grew older, he'd looked like the Indy character, only more handsome. When Jacob worked in the mill, it had been wonderful to linger in his presence, but also torture. She would never touch him again. He looked different, too, more like a sketch than a real person.

Three years after her death, a wedding ring appeared on his finger. She understood and was happy for him—and heartbroken. Jacob had been so nervous when he proposed to her. His hand shook; he was unsteady going down on one knee. Thrilled that a dream had come true, she had cried at the depth of the moment. It almost brought a tear to her eye now, but that wasn't happening.

Dead girls didn't cry.

While swooping in and scaring Lili sounded compelling, it probably wouldn't work and could be dangerous. Beside, the woman wanted to see ghosts, so it would only encourage her. And if she was truly powerful? What were the risks? Emma shook her head. These weren't nice thoughts anyway. Just last week, she had wanted to be left alone. Now she was contemplating going full demonic.

She needed to do something counterintuitive but nothing came to mind.

Instead, she felt paralyzed by indecision.

Just lie low? Use the time to learn the poltergeist trick? Over the years, she had learned how to nudge larger objects like doors to perform what she considered ghostly deeds. Her skills were imperfect and didn't always work. In her understanding of classic hauntings, people expected ghosts to slam doors, rattle chains, and rustle things. Until now, she had been content to appear at will and scare people. Through reading, she'd learned the most noteworthy ghosts were poltergeists who tossed things about. Someday, she aspired to be a poltergeist. To have some real fun.

Reading about it was one thing. Actually throwing stuff around? How would she learn a skill like that?

Drifting over to 208, Emma surveyed the apartment. The previous tenants were two women who lived together like husband and wife. It took some getting used to, but the arrangement wasn't as disturbing as she imagined. Furnished and currently vacant, someone had staged the apartment for prospective tenants or buyers and it was chock full of objects she could experiment with.

If she could only figure out how.

The kitchen was tucked in a corner, set off from the living room by a forest green L-shaped granite counter. Two place settings had been laid out: wine glasses, napkins, plates, silverware. Emma spied the forks. As good a place to start as any.

Emma spent the next hour trying to shove a fork onto the floor.

She managed to move it slightly. Nothing impressive. The act certainly wouldn't scare anyone. They might even laugh. But Emma wasn't a quitter.

She had to be doing it wrong.

Then she thought about the iPad.

Her fingers did nothing when she poked the screen, but if she slid across the surface of it, the device reacted to her presence.

Initially, she regarded the interaction as a mere curiosity. Then she wondered how it worked, read up on the subject and understood. The screen was sensitive to touch. When someone placed a finger on the glass, it drew a small electrical charge to the point of contact and the device sensed the location of the finger.

Somehow, the device sensed her presence, too. It had to be electrical.

Still, what could she do with the skill? People did little but play games on them. She didn't understand the games and had little interest in learning them. But the iPad could also be used to navigate to the internet and write notes. That would be useful. Better than a dirty mirror.

Would the skill work with other inanimate objects? It seemed doubtful, given that she could readily pass through anything, including stone and metal. And the iPad only worked because it was powered by a battery.

Having learned about electromagnetism, she had a thought. If she could interact with an iPad screen, then she must carry a small electric charge, too. Could she interact with objects electrostatically? She had studied the subject but did she truly understand the concept?

No harm in trying.

She spun in a loop and swept across a butter knife.

Nothing happened.

She tried it faster, then slower with the same result. Nada.

Then came a flash of insight. If the interaction was electrostatic, maybe she needed to sweep ultra close to the metal.

Emma eyed the knife, then swept over it at a microscopic distance above the surface.

It flew off the table and landed halfway across the room!

Holy shit!

She did it! Emma swept along the hallway and knocked a framed print off the wall before stopping to consider the concept further. Would the same effect work with just a hand?

After a couple of practice swipes with her hand, she knocked a fork to the floor, though with less force.

Emma was thrilled. She felt like a genius, though she was uncertain how the skill would be of any use. Lili already annoyed her. Any demonstration of the skill would only draw Lili's attention when all she really wanted was to expose the man in 139.

And what if Lili was dangerous? Avoiding her seemed wiser.

Still, Emma was excited about her new skill.

But she also felt tension growing in the mill, like a storm about to break.

Fourteen

Lili dropped her purse on the island.

Feeling frazzled, she thought about turning in early. The shop had been crazy. She'd hosted an unusual number of readings over the past two days, leaving little time to attempt another connection with Frank. She wanted to better understand his situation, but also felt anxious about the prospect. Frank seemed quite hostile. She'd had a few similar confrontations in the past. Surly, ornery spirits who were angry at their circumstances, or aggravated by the intrusion. Frank seemed a little of both.

She wondered how Olivia was doing. Was he still bothering her?

Maybe she should stick to looking for Emma, though she was also curious about this Eamon O'Keene dude. She had run extensive searches in the newspaper sites, looking for him—wasted hours on it—but found no reference to the man. None. It was inexplicable.

Her phone rang.

Olivia.

Oh, good. They hadn't talked since the night Raleigh yelled at her. She still hoped the two of them could become better friends.

Without preamble, Olivia said, "Glass of wine?"

"Sure. Where?"

"Your place?"

Lili looked around. Her apartment looked tidy with a bonus: no Raleigh.

"Sure."

Olivia arrived fifteen minutes later, comfortably dressed in designer sweats, a bottle of wine in hand. A girl after her own heart.

Lili took the bottle and motioned to the cozy sitting area with the low ceiling. Olivia curled up on the loveseat. Lili handed her a glass of wine and sat in her oversized armchair.

"How have things been by you?" Lili asked.

"Quieter in the last few days. After he came back from your apartment, Raleigh made a big deal of yelling at Frank and telling him to get lost."

"I thought he didn't believe."

"He doesn't. It was all for my benefit." Olivia shook her head. "I know he comes off as gruff, but he's really sweet to me."

Unconvinced, Lili opted to change the subject. "Where are you guys from?"

Olivia swirled the wine in her glass. "Chicago. We got tired of the rat race and the traffic. We took the gallery online a year ago, and now we're no longer paying a fortune in rent for a tiny space on Michigan Ave."

Lili nodded in understanding. "Business good?"

"Never better. Best move we ever made."

"So, how'd you guys meet?"

"Typical Raleigh style." Olivia did a little eye roll. "I was at a bar one night and some guy was hassling me. You know how it is."

"I do." And did she. Lili rarely went out alone for that very reason.

"He came over and asked if the guy was bothering me. I nodded with a look of desperation. Raleigh squeezed the dude's shoulder, kind of like that Spock move, and walked him out. Then he bought me a drink, no strings attached, and walked back to his table. I finally went looking for him."

"Sounds vaguely romantic." And not surprising, having met the man.

"I thought so." Olivia stood and wandered, looking more closely at the decor. "I'm curious. Why did you take this particular apartment?"

Lili explained her belief in numerology and the power of the number seven, then added, "But that wasn't the only reason I took the flat. Essentially, I came here hoping to interact with the ghosts."

"You knew?" Olivia said, mouth agape.

"I was reasonably certain. I'd sensed something when I toured the building. I knew in time, some of those who had passed here would reveal themselves. They always do in old buildings, especially when they have a history like this place. You know about Frank already."

"I'm not sure I believed before this. I do now."

"Cool, isn't it?"

Olivia pursed her lips with an uncertain nod. "The jury's out on that."

After a sip of wine, Olivia said, "Where do you hail from?"

"Appleton."

"Husband? Boyfriend?"

"Never married. No boyfriend."

"Are you...?" Olivia trailed off with a shrug.

Puzzled for a moment, Lili said, "No, not gay."

"Parents?"

"Both my parents are dead." Lili paused, surprised by the question and the depth of the sadness she still felt. "My father missed a turn on a foggy night two years back and skidded into a lake. They both drowned."

"Oh God. I'm so sorry."

"Thank you. I miss my mother deeply."

"Your father?"

"Not so much."

Olivia looked shocked. "Why?"

"My father thought I was crazy. And he would have hated this place, the expensive appliances and high end furniture, the busy decor, the fancy location. He was a simple man who made a fortune in the market by buying and holding Amazon and Apple years ago. He was good at making money, but he hated spending it. He was all business and only seemed interested in how financially savvy I was."

"That's too bad."

They sat silent for a minute, and Olivia then said, "Have you connected with Emma yet?"

"No. I've sensed her presence, but I haven't made contact."

"Can we try it now? In here?"

Lili frowned, caught off-guard by the strange request. Having already tried, she didn't think it would work. Maybe just as well with Olivia present. "Sure. We can try."

"Let's do it."

"You're not scared?"

"No." She hesitated. "Maybe a little. Mostly, I don't like Frank in my bedroom."

"I get that." Lili laughed but knew there might be little they could do about it.

Reluctantly, Lili got up and grabbed her things, setting the crystal ball on the coffee table. Maybe this wasn't a good idea. She didn't need another angry visit from Raleigh. Turning the lights and her flameless candles off, she lit incense and a wax candle that she placed behind her on the half-wall dividing the kitchen from the sitting area.

She whispered, "Remember, you need to be quiet."

Olivia zipped her lips like a child. It was cute.

Lili then focused on the crystal, her mind connecting. The quartz grew warm, and the mist formed.

The room seemed to cool by several degrees.

When the fog cleared, she had trouble visualizing her surroundings. Grey, dank, cold, it looked like a long hallway, completely foreign to any place she knew. It wasn't her apartment or the space that preceded it.

She felt a tingle at the nape of her neck. This was creepy.

A dark figure appeared down the passage, receding—not walking, but drifting away like a furtive shadow.

It wasn't Emma. Or Frank.

Then she knew.

It was the basement even though she had been assured there wasn't one. She'd asked the manager in the front office. Talked to the maintenance guys. They told her the same story. No basement in the building. Never had been.

So where was she? And what was this thing?

It stopped and turned slowly.

She saw a man staring her down with a malevolent gaze, the dead-eyed look of a ghost. Lili tried to pull away, but she felt stuck. Trapped.

Frozen.

He leered at her, somehow threatening and lecherous all at once, like a sexual predator.

As he drifted toward her, he puffed up his cheeks and spat out one word:

Boo!

He disappeared with a laugh.

Lili jumped back and knocked the crystal off its stand. "Holy shit!"

"What?"

Lili held a hand over her heart. She couldn't tell Olivia the truth. She was already nervous about sleeping in her apartment. Finally, she said, "I got lost for a moment. It spooked me."

Olivia eyed her doubtfully. "That can happen?"

Lili nodded.

Truth was, Lili suspected she had just met Eamon O'Keene.

And he was way scarier than Frank.

Fifteen

Danielle tapped her phone to silence the alarm.

5:30 a.m.

Same time every morning, even on weekends. Just like clockwork.

It felt like a grind some days, but the routine kept her grounded. The regular hours, the vigorous daily exercise, kept her melancholy mostly at bay. She had grown accustomed to sleeping alone, but waking by herself was a work in progress. She could get a dog, but with her hours, it would be cruel for the dog, and she had no interest in a cat. Dani was glad to have a quiet weekend ahead. Having the police tail her to work all week made her feel foolish. Now she felt certain she had overreacted. At least she was alone on her runs.

For a moment, she considered falling back to sleep and taking an extra hour.

Nope. Couldn't do it.

The coffee had just finished brewing, timed to coincide with the alarm.

Dani drank a half cup and slipped into her gear, a black lululemon short-sleeve top and running shorts. After eating some yogurt and a keto bite, she laced up her Nikes, dropped her phone into her waist pack, and checked the time.

Six o'clock sharp. Maybe her life was a little too regimented?

She shook her head, flipped the deadbolt, and opened the door—

Something—someone—moved at her. Large, dark, like a shadow. Something slammed into the center of her chest.

A fist?

It was a paralyzing blow. She couldn't breathe, couldn't call out, felt so stunned she couldn't resist when a man pushed her into the apartment, twirled her around, and pulled her into a neck lock.

As she struggled to breathe, to fight back, the world went black.

* * *

Chase strolled along the corridor, a sportsman's trunk in tow, trying to avoid dwelling on the myriad of things that could go wrong.

At this early hour, the building was silent, the hallways empty, not a creature astir—none he could hear, anyway. It was Saturday morning and people were sleeping in. The trunk was a mundane item that no one would question in the halls. Many people used them to store their overflow in the storage lockers. He had one added feature, a narrow bar behind the wheels to erase any impression of the wheels and his footsteps in the pile of the hallway carpets. He knew the only camera in the building covered the lobby. The owners' association had nixed cameras elsewhere in the mill as overly intrusive. Some apartments had door cameras but none did in this hallway.

The plan was simple—in theory. Danielle ran the same route at exactly the same time every morning. A serious creature of habit. He would take her as she opened the door on her way out. His risk of exposure would last only a few seconds.

Still, so many ways it might come unraveled. What if she left early? Or late?

What if some moron wandered along the hall? Though until the last moment, he could easily abort. Pretend he was lost or something.

What if the punch failed to work and she screamed?

Naw. He had experienced a well-placed punch to the solar plexus personally. It was almost like being hit with a Taser, only much quieter. It stunned him. He couldn't breathe, couldn't make a sound for several seconds. The perfect technique to neutralize her. The second step was trickier—

Chase pushed all doubts aside.

His senses were heightened, alert to every nuance of the building, any footsteps or sounds that would turn him around.

As he approached the door, he slipped driving gloves on and pulled a nylon stocking over his head. He wasn't worried about being recognized, only concerned that he leave no hair or DNA behind.

The building silent, he heard light steps inside 241 as he set the trunk down.

Almost like a dream—the moment felt surreal—he heard the latch disengage as he leaned against the wall by the jamb.

The door opened and she stepped over the threshold. Chase pivoted and punched her hard in the solar plexus.

His aim was perfect.

Her body crumpled as her face evolved from task-focused to stunned shock. He pushed her back, grabbed her right arm, and spun her around, pulling her into a rear chokehold. The pressure on her carotid arteries would quickly render her unconscious. As she recovered from the punch and struggled against him, the hold worked like magic and she fell limp. He gently shut the door with his foot and laid her on the floor.

Less than twenty seconds had elapsed, and the attack had been virtually silent. He had forty to fifty seconds to complete the next and most critical step before she stirred.

Duct tape. Every handyman's friend.

A piece went around her head to cover her mouth. Then the wrists and ankles. He ripped her fanny pack off, folded her limp body in half, taped her at the knees, trapping her arms, then taped her ankles to her head. When she came to, it would be impossible for her to move.

He laid her body in the felt-lined trunk. Tossed her purse in as well. Grabbing it would obfuscate the investigation—the detectives would wonder if she ran off. Chase found her phone in the fanny pack and checked for a calendar or upcoming appointments, but it was locked.

No matter. He would destroy it once they reached the basement. He tossed the phone into the trunk and snapped it shut.

Checking the hallway through the peephole, he opened the door and set the lock, closing it silently behind him. He removed the nylon and gloves and shoved them into a pocket. Little could go wrong now.

He felt calm and in control.

With a casual gait, he wheeled the trunk to his apartment, going through the stairwell to avoid the elevators and lobby.

A moment later, he closed his door and set the locks and alarm with his phone.

Perfect!

He had executed the plan flawlessly. Danielle was in his apartment and he had left no evidence behind. Once someone realized she was missing and reported it, the detective on the case—most likely Martin Kettridge—would pursue two avenues. One, that she had been abducted.

With her car in the parking lot, they would almost certainly focus on her daily run. Most of the attention would fall on the trails in Rock River Park. The missing purse would be a question mark. They would have to consider that she might have simply run off.

Nothing would point to him.

Danielle Hamlin was gone. Vanished.

Just like Megan.

He congratulated himself. A silent pat on the back. He was a fucking genius. Even grumpy old Eamon would be impressed.

The bathroom floor was open and waiting. She remained unconscious and easy to handle—she couldn't weigh over one-twenty. Tossing her over his shoulder, he climbed down the rungs and carried her to a small room with a cot, laid her down, removed the tape, and locked the door. The walls were brick and the ceiling concrete. All had been treated with soundproofing foam. She could scream for hours and no one would hear. He had tested that room with a boom box at peak volume. Only a little of the bass penetrated his apartment. He heard nothing outside his door in the hallway.

With luck, no one would miss her before Monday or Tuesday.

Sixteen

Lili awoke with a start.

Her eyes snapped open and alit on the ceiling.

Something was wrong. Confused and disoriented, she couldn't identify the source of the unease beyond some change in the aura of the building. She had no memory of a nightmare, no lingering impression of a dream. Just raw anxiety that would prevent further sleep.

Lili couldn't recall ever having a foreboding this intense.

She rolled and glanced at her phone. 6:02 a.m.

Ugh.

Far too early to be awake. The sun had just risen.

Lili slid out of bed, grabbed her robe, and brewed coffee.

Sitting at the island, she felt dizzy, shaky. Maybe she was getting sick. No, she didn't have time for that—she had to work today. Lili choked down a piece of toast and took a shower. The hot water helped, but her angst remained. Lili sat in Lotus position and tried to meditate it away. When she left for work, she felt better, and the walk in warm sunshine further lifted her mood. A vague feeling that the change was because of leaving the mill lingered. She couldn't imagine why.

Two women waited at the door of the shop. The Larsen sisters, Marilyn and Peggy. Middle-aged, matronly, they had spent most of their adult lives caring for a father ailing with Parkinson's. Neither had married and they now struggled with a lack of purpose after his death. They couldn't let go of their father, even though Lili had suggested it would be healthy to do so. They scheduled a session twice a month, hoping to contact him, but the crystal had been cold every time, and Lili never faked spiritual connections. Even Dad seemed to know it was time to end the relationship, but the sisters came back diligently, ever hopeful the next session would be different.

Today, Lili struggled with the ritual. The store was unusually busy with a steady stream of customers for crystals, amulets, art, and tarot cards. She really needed to hire somebody to manage the counter.

At one o'clock, she announced, "Sorry, ladies. We can try again in two weeks if you like."

Peggy said, "Two weeks. Same time, please."

Lili decided next time was their last. Taking their money was beginning to feel like larceny.

At three, Diana Paresky arrived. Twenty-six, short, with shoulder length mousy hair, her aura was dark, and she wanted Lili to help her improve it. She suffered from depression and hypochondria but refused to see a doctor, wanted no medication, and believed only a spiritual cure would make her feel better. Sometimes Lili felt more like a therapist and less a medium.

By the time she closed the shop at seven, the unease of the morning was mostly forgotten. As she walked home, she received a text from Olivia.

Are you stopping by tonight?

Sure. 9?

Yep!

When Lili stepped through her apartment door, she felt a tinge of the morning's jitters, but they quickly evaporated with a little meditation and mindfulness. She tossed a spinach-romaine salad with a raspberry vinaigrette, poured a glass of wine, and sat, answering shop and blog emails while she ate and relaxed.

Lili felt a mixture of curiosity and anxiety as she prepared for the second reading with Olivia. Usually, the ghosts or spirits she contacted were passive, offering vague information, as if they resided in a fog, that nothing was clear to them. Only rarely had she been admonished by ghosts and while Frank had made no threats, his voice had been chilling.

Then there was this Eamon dude. She didn't want to end up in the basement with him again. Frank might be surly, but Eamon felt darker, evil maybe. And she worried about Raleigh. That man was scarier than any ghost.

What's the worst that can happen?

Lili shrugged. She wasn't easily put off and felt mostly thrilled by the events of the past week. A little fear and adrenaline never killed anyone. People often paid for similar hair-raising experiences.

At nine, she grabbed her satchel and walked across the courtyard to the Kaplan apartment. Olivia was waiting with two glasses of wine.

Lili spoke with a conspiratorial whisper as she walked in. "Raleigh mustn't hear about this, sweetie."

"Not a peep." Olivia zipped her lips.

Lili set up at the dining room table and again reminded Olivia to remain quiet. Besides the crystal ball, candle, and incense, Lili set out a food offering to let Frank know she planned a casual, friendly encounter.

Olivia dimmed the lights, and Lili eased into a meditative state as she connected with the crystal. She gently probed the space of the apartment, sending relaxing waves to soothe Frank and make him more receptive to contact.

The room was quiet at first. So much so, Lili worried Frank had left.

Had she driven him away?

Then she noticed a disturbance at the edge of her vision. Turning her head did not bring it further into focus. It remained at the edges, a darker shadow lurking in the umbral light, fluttering like wings.

Big wings.

A faint whooshing sound followed.

An impinging sense of danger sent a cold shard of anxiety through her. The atmosphere was creepy and unnerving.

While most of her séances were quiet, placid events, she had also tangled with unruly spirits. Ghosts who were angry at their circumstances, who might yell like Frank or toss things around like a petulant child. This was neither, but she had no time to ponder further.

A vibration shook the room, centered on the table where they sat, spreading outward, rattling frames on the wall and glasses in the kitchen.

Lili spoke forcefully. "Settle down, Frank!"

The table shuddered violently. Olivia looked horrified.

Lili tried to hold the table still, trying to conjure a move that would stop the ghostly tantrum, afraid he would upend it and knock her crystal onto the ceramic flooring.

She grabbed an amulet and held it up in her fist. "Frank! Stop it!"

The room fell silent.

Oh good, it worked!

Then the lights flickered and the candle blew out. A moment later, the crystal ball cracked in two with an ugly popping sound.

Olivia jumped up and backed away, wide-eyed. "What the hell was that?"

Lili held the table in a death grip and shook her head, feeling disoriented and stunned.

Shit!

What just happened?

She closed her eyes. When she opened them, her prized crystal still lay broken on the table.

"I don't know." Lili handled the broken pieces of quartz, shocked, feeling a sense of loss. That crystal was like a dear friend to her. "Clearly, Frank doesn't want to talk to us."

Silence hung over the table.

"What do we do now?" Olivia said.

Shaken, Lili pondered that very question. She had just lost a very expensive crystal. She had a backup, but this was her favorite. A couple of bottles of wine wouldn't cover the cost of a new one, but now wasn't the time to discuss it.

"We may have to consider an exorcism if you want to get rid of Frank permanently," Lili said.

"For real? They do that?"

"I know someone who can perform the ritual."

"What should I tell Raleigh?"

"That's your problem," Lili said, harsher than she intended. She had no interest in dealing with Raleigh. He had been spooky angry the night he came to her apartment. She packed her things, including the broken ball. "That was my favorite crystal."

"Yeah." Olivia eyed the apartment warily, then looked at Lili with a look of desperation. "I'm not staying here by myself."

Lili should have realized that might happen. "Grab some pajamas. You can stay with me."

She waited while Olivia packed a small overnight bag. They walked across the dark courtyard. It was a warm night and the stars glittered overhead like ancient gems.

As they stepped through the doorway, Lili pointed to the loft. "There's a bed and bathroom up there. Make yourself at home."

"Thanks. Are you going to bed?"

"God no. It's way too early." Though she felt tired—she had woken at six this morning—Lili didn't think she could sleep just yet.

"What do I tell Raleigh?" Olivia said, wide-eyed.

Lili, still unnerved by the experience, said, "I don't know. Just don't blame me."

They stayed up for hours, talking about ghosts and hauntings before turning to other topics.

Something was happening in the Mill. With Frank. With Eamon, the mystery soul she was unable to connect to the building. And she'd had no luck finding Emma.

Lili was a skilled medium. Always in control. But not here. She was missing something.

Lili had no clue what it was.

Seventeen

Emma drifted through the mill, brooding.

A powerful new wave had roiled the energy fields. While Lili and Frank remained a problem on the west end, a stronger disturbance had erupted on the east side, a disruption almost as unsettling as the mess that followed Frank's murder. She knew who was responsible, even if she didn't know why. Emma could discern no substantial changes in the building. She had witnessed no acts of violence. The police hadn't visited. No one had died. Everything appeared normal but clearly wasn't.

Given the strong negativity emanating from the apartment, Emma feared the worst: that the man *was* a violent criminal and had committed another vile act.

She had also uncovered an unsettling detail while drifting through his paperwork. The guy was a cop. Cops were supposed to be good people, agents of law and order, but this man was anything but. He seemed patently evil. Perhaps only she could see it. She didn't understand the contradiction. Another subject she needed to study further.

Emma remembered a similar disturbance about six months before. Emma hadn't been able to pin it down. It emanated from beneath the floors, but she couldn't venture down there to investigate because the cellar was off-limits. Unable to determine the source of it, she resolved to ignore the problem by throwing herself into a study of ancient history, particularly the Roman Empire. It was fascinating stuff and a pleasant distraction. The problem slowly dissipated and calm returned to the mill.

Then she ran into the deviant in 139 and Lili started poking around. Now she wondered if that guy had been responsible for the earlier disturbance—if his horrid pictures were evidence of a crime from that period.

She had to know, worried his behavior would lead to greater trouble in the future.

Emma stopped. Again, why did she care?

Perhaps she was better off reverting to a detached existence and ignoring the events in the mill. It seemed wise to avoid the man and the turmoil he created. She felt happier that way. Really, the business of the living wasn't her concern—unless they made her life miserable.

Clearly, that was the risk here.

No, that was wrong. Why was she thinking that way? Where was the Emma who had done the right thing and avenged Frank's death? Fought the good fight and sent four murderers to prison? Instead, she was trying to trivialize things while the situation escalated. If that man was hurting women, she had an obligation to do something. That was the crux of the matter.

But with the computer gone, what could she do? She had no evidence to make a case.

A dilemma to be solved. She would find a way.

Emma slipped into the apartment and wandered about, trying to gain a better sense of the problem. It felt inscrutable, lying somewhere beneath the floor in the cellar. How did he get down there? There were no stairs leading below ground level in the building. Had there been once? She couldn't remember.

The turmoil down there was palpable and unnerving. A mix of emotions.

Fear, despair, pain. Was he holding a hostage?

Drifting into the office, Emma stopped.

The computer was back! Exactly what she needed. Actual proof.

She would access the computer, confirm her suspicions, and find the pictures to expose him.

Would her new tricks work? Emma slid across the mouse and moved it. The monitor lit up and a prompt for a password appeared. She had read that *password* was the most common password, which seemed logical. She slipped over the keys and typed the letters in. The process seemed to be working.

The screen flashed a reply: *Password is incorrect. Please enter your password.*

She tried again. This time, nothing happened. The keys refused to respond.

What the hell?

Her new technique had arbitrarily stopped working. Crap. If she lived to be a thousand, she would never understand this place.

Then she heard a clatter in the next room.

He was here.

Even better.

Emma slipped through the wall and hovered in the bathroom, watching. The negative aura was especially potent here, but remained beneath the floor.

Watching him, she finally understood how that was possible.

The guy removed a metal carpet strip and two pieces of baseboard. Rolling the flooring back, he exposed heavy wooden planks beneath. He clicked something in his hand and a section of the floor popped up. A trapdoor. He pulled it open, revealing a dark space beneath.

He flicked a switch under the floor and the space lit up. Emma craned her neck to look through the opening, but she could see nothing but an amorphous white square. She knew a room lay below; it simply wasn't visible to her.

So frustrating. So illogical.

As the man climbed down, his body disappeared at floor level, much like she did passing through a wall. She tried to follow, but couldn't. The opening was a solid barrier. Impassable. Just like the outside walls.

An arm reached up and closed the door.

With no idea what was down there, without access, what could she do?

The man was doing something awful down there. Emma just knew it, sensing pain and suffering. She needed to stop him. Expose him and the let authorities arrest him just as she had with Frank's killers.

But how?

Then she imagined a way. She could make contact with Lili. Cooperate with her to end this nightmare. Lili seemed to have some telepathic capabilities. If she truly was psychic, she must feel the energy disturbances flowing through the building, too.

With the ability to leave her body, could she venture into the cellar to see what this awful man was doing?

Lili could then point the police at Chase Riddell and have them grab the computer.

It might work.

Emma hadn't tried to contact the living since Frank's murder, had no reason to, so she wasn't sure how to proceed. What were the risks? If Lili was psychic, they should be able to talk to each other, but Emma feared she could place herself at risk, too. If the woman was indeed powerful, could Lili get inside her head? Control her and steal her autonomy? Hijack her soul? She'd read about such things.

Emma found the prospect frightening. She was her own person and couldn't risk it. She would communicate in writing like she had with Frank. Find a way to send a note.

Lili spent a lot of time on her iPad. That might be the best way to get her attention. Send a message but maintain some distance between them.

She was wasting her time here. Hurrying up to 202, she dove back into the book on iPads, convinced she could use it to talk to Lili.

One thing was certain. It was only a matter of time.

Chase Riddell was going to jail.

Eighteen

A muscle spasm jolted Danielle awake.

For a few seconds, she felt a surreal unease, like emerging from a nightmare. Then reality set in.

The room was nearly dark, a faint wash of light creeping in beneath the door. Her chest hurt. She vaguely remembered being punched. Her wrists were sore from fighting bondage, her body aching from assault and rape. The room smelled of disinfectant.

She couldn't wrap her head around it. It felt unreal and terrifying. With no idea where she was, the disorientation was awful. Panic rose and fell in nauseating waves.

Trying to get her bearings, she put her hands out to explore her surroundings.

A thin mattress and a metal frame. She was on a cot.

The floor was cold, damp. Concrete.

A door without a handle.

No way out.

A prison cell.

* * *

Lili tossed and turned.

Deep in REM sleep, she was trapped in a dark place. It felt damp and smelled faintly pungent.

Bleach?

She explored the space with her hands. Brick walls and a concrete floor.

A cell.

She was locked inside. Fear and panic rose to a near unbearable level.

Then Lili would try to rationalize the dream and return to her apartment. Moments later, she was back in the box. Over and over, the nightmare played in an endless, unstoppable loop.

She hated these types of dreams and the absolute sense of dread and desperation that accompanied them. In the past, they had preceded periods of anxiety and depression. There was no reason she should be sliding down that slippery slope again. She was happy with her life. The store was doing well and she had great clients. She had a new friend in Olivia. Other than her run-ins with Frank and Raleigh, life was good.

Finally, she broke out of the recurring sequence and reached consciousness, hyperventilating, soaked with cold sweat.

She glanced at her phone.

Six a.m. Way too early, again.

But she couldn't go back to sleep and risk returning to that awful nightmare. No, she had to get out of bed and make coffee to break the cycle.

She rinsed her face with cold water while the coffee brewed, an action that did little to alleviate the anxiety and dread she felt. Maybe an apartment in this building hadn't been a such a great idea. First, she angered a ghost who wrecked her favorite crystal, and now this dreadful nightmare. Had Frank come to torment her, hoping to scare her away?

Maybe an exorcism was exactly what this building needed.

Then she remembered Olivia sleeping upstairs. Oh Jesus, the last thing she wanted this morning was a house guest. As she poured a cup of coffee, Olivia padded up behind her. "Morning."

"Morning. Coffee?"

When Lili turned, Olivia stared and said, "You okay?"

"Why?"

"You look—frazzled."

"I didn't sleep well."

"I did. That bed is awesome. And yes, coffee, please."

They sat at the island with their mugs, silent in their thoughts. Lili was still trying to shake off her nightmare. Olivia sat, sipping coffee and nibbling on a fingernail. It was clear her anxiety was off the charts. Who could blame her?

Finally, Olivia said, "I think I'm moving out until this Frank business is settled."

"What about Raleigh?" Lili also wondered where Olivia planned to stay. She had settled in here a bit quickly. As much as she liked the woman, she wasn't ready for a roomie.

"I don't know. I hope we didn't make a mistake buying that place."

Lili shrugged. "We'll figure it out."

Finishing her coffee, Olivia stood and said, "I'd better get back to the apartment. Raleigh's due home soon."

She popped out the door with a worried frown on her face. Probably trying to decide what to tell Raleigh. Despite their clear understanding to leave her out of it, Lili suspected Olivia would throw her under the bus.

How long before Raleigh came over to bitch at her?

Oh well. She had bigger concerns.

It was Sunday and she was off. It seemed like a bad thing. Too much idle time to fret and dwell on the nightmares. Trying to be proactive, she emailed her therapist, asking for a quick internet session. She loved online therapy. So much easier to talk when the therapist wasn't in the same room, staring at you. Her therapist was a sweetheart and very responsive when Lili needed to talk.

The day was sunny and warm. After breakfast, she took a long walk along the river. The sun and fresh air soon dispelled the dark feelings, and Lili decided she had overreacted. It was one bad night. At the apartment, her therapist had responded and, after a brief conversation, agreed that Lili had read too much into the dream.

Lili spent two hours online tracking down a new crystal and ordered a three-inch sphere.

Ugh. Seventeen hundred dollars—

A knock at the door. She jumped up and looked through the peephole.

Raleigh.

Shit. She didn't need another chewing out, but Raleigh didn't look angry; he looked concerned.

She let out a sigh and opened the door, ready for anything.

"What can I do for you, Raleigh?"

"Mind if I come in?"

"Going to yell at me?"

"No, and sorry about that." He looked genuinely contrite. "No yelling. I need a favor."

She directed him to a seat at the kitchen island. "Coffee?"

"Sure."

Lili poured them both a cup and sat. "What's the favor?"

He eyed her for a moment with an indeterminate gaze, then said, "I don't believe in the paranormal—ghosts and all that—but Olivia does, and that's what matters. I want her to feel at ease again. She loves our place, but now she's talking about moving out. I wanted to blame that on you, but being honest, she was already uncomfortable in the bedroom."

Lili stifled the urge to make the obvious joke and decided she may have misjudged Raleigh. He was acknowledging Olivia's anxieties and discomfort and seemed genuinely concerned for her happiness. But what did he want?

"I'd like you to do something to help her feel at ease. Feel comfortable again in the apartment."

"What did you have in mind?"

"Olivia said you mentioned an exorcism."

"I did."

He gave her a wary side-glance. "I think the idea is crazy myself, but she thinks it'll work because you said it would. That's all that matters, that she believes it'll work."

"You want me to fake something?" Lili said, taken aback. "I don't do that."

"No. Perform the actual ceremony."

"Will you be there?"

"No—"

"You should be there. Your wife will appreciate the support."

"Okay. I'll be there," he said with vague resignation.

"Give me a few days."

He nodded and drained his cup. “Sounds good. Thanks for the coffee.”

Raleigh waved as he walked out. Lili stood, questioning her decision to get involved. The memory of the nightmare returned in full force for a moment, and she feared Frank wouldn’t take the interference lightly.

She hoped an exorcism was the answer.

Nineteen

Chase stood in the shower.

Washing the scent of sex and the woman off his body, he was quite pleased with himself. Feeling strong and confident, it was hard not to gloat. He had plotted and carried his plan out flawlessly. Left no evidence. Saw no one. The perfect execution of a perfect plan. He had worried about taking too many risks, but everything had worked out. His prize was magnificent.

He felt more relaxed than he had after taking Megan. It made sense. He was getting better at this and would continue to do so. The first woman, Stacy, had been an impulse, and luckily, he hadn't been caught. Hence the rules—though he noted ruefully that he was already bending them.

This time, he wouldn't get nervous and kill the woman so quickly like he had with Megan. He would keep this one longer and planned to savor this experience to the fullest. He wanted to go downstairs and take her again, but he had a shift scheduled. It would be hard to leave, but he needed to resist temptation and maintain a normal routine at all costs.

Chase toweled off, shaved, and dressed in street clothes. He kept a low profile in the building. Never wore a uniform or showed a badge. Never left a squad car in the parking lot. Kept his occupation discreet.

Finished early, he walked to his office to check email and the news.

Fuck!

The mouse!

Someone had moved it again!

What the hell was going on? Prepared for this eventuality, he grabbed his laptop and brought up the security software.

The app showed no incursions into the apartment. He didn't expect otherwise. The system was the best on the market.

So what the hell was going on?

He brought up the office cam focused on the desk and played the feed in reverse until he noticed the mouse jerk.

Huh?

He played the feed forward in slow-motion. The office was empty and yet the mouse moved—*all by itself!*

Did some keys on the keyboard move as well?

What the fuck?

Chase checked the time stamp. Yesterday afternoon. He puzzled for a moment, then realized who the culprit was.

Eamon. Had to be. Was that dirty old bastard peeking at his pictures?

Chase checked his watch. He had time for a little vodka.

He reopened the basement door and dropped into the room below, forever marveling at his good fortune in discovering this place.

The warren of rooms and hallways beneath the mill were fascinating, beyond his wildest dreams for a secret lair. Long passages ran the length of the building. A centrally placed room between them led to a well or drain that emptied directly into the river. He suspected they had used it to illegally dump toxic waste back in the day.

A simple hole in the floor, two feet in diameter, the edges had been crusted with grunge. He had cleaned it meticulously because it turned out to be perfect. Megan, dissolved in lye, went down that hole and into the river along with random fragments of bone. That would be Danielle's fate, too.

He pulled a bottle of Stoli from the freezer. Poured a finger for Eamon and two for himself.

Chase took a sip of the ice-cold liquor, enjoying the freezing burn on his palate.

Perfect!

He often enjoyed a little boost before work. The job was dead boring 99 percent of the time. Chase would keep vodka in the squad if he could finagle it, but no, even a flask was too risky.

Chase waited patiently for his buddy. They felt like kindred spirits. Eamon liked the idea of taking Megan. Encouraged it. Seemed to understand his needs, though Eamon had gotten nervous once he'd actually nabbed Megan. Or maybe he was just being cautious. He sounded like he felt concerned about Chase.

His friend hadn't been around for the last few days, which was surprising.

A moment later, Eamon arrived. "Nice catch! She's lovely."

"Thank you. Hey, have you been in my office lately?"

"Nope. I stay down here. Why?"

"Someone's been snooping around my office."

Eamon was silent for a bit. Then he said, "There's a colleen who lives up above. Might be her."

"How? I've got locks and an alarm system—"

"She's like me."

Chase took this strange exchange as a sign of his phenomenal abilities. He could commune with the dead, clearly a unique gift bestowed upon only the most extraordinary of people—as if he needed any further proof of his superiority. He forever imagined people watching him, marveling at his genius and talent.

"Who is she?"

"Some dead bitch—to borrow your word. Watch out for her. She's crafty, and a goody two-shoes to boot."

Chase also understood his *friend* might be a figment of his imagination, but he saw it as a benign thing. He had always been a little different, but he never questioned his sanity. He felt perfectly lucid and focused. He was simply taking care of his needs. Men had been doing it since the beginning of time. He had no time for quaint dating rituals. Sadly, modern society frowned on men taking women, but no law could trump biology.

Her disappearance had raised no flags thus far. He couldn't get into her phone so he didn't know if she had weekend plans. Being Sunday, she wasn't working, so he figured he had another day or two before her absence was discovered. Regardless, nothing pointed to him. He was home free despite the risks he had taken grabbing the woman *right inside his building!*

Ha!

Now, she would remain missing until the end of time.

He hated to think of this as the perfect crime. It was a risky mentality.

Still, it felt perfect.

Twenty

Martin gazed out his office window.

The day was sunny, the sky dotted with fair weather cumulus. A couple of kids fished along the river walkway. He longed to be out there, too. On a call with his son, he swiveled when the desk officer dropped a memo on his blotter.

Danielle Hamlin, age 32, possible missing. Lt Farber wants you on it.

Martin gave it a quick glance and frowned. "Brendan, something's come up. I'll call you back."

He followed Abby Eriksen to the front desk. She had been with the department for a year. Attractive with short blonde hair and green eyes, she was married, much to the chagrin of the younger officers. A no-nonsense twenty-something, she was an outstanding officer and well liked.

"What do we know?" Martin asked.

"The mother reported her missing. Her employer, Don Segerman, called her this morning after Danielle failed to show for a second day without calling in."

"Last time anyone saw her?"

"Friday."

"Four days already. What have we done so far?"

"Mom tried her phone and email. I asked her the standard battery of questions. No urgent or chronic medical conditions. No odd behavior. I sent a squad to her address at Rock River Mills. No answer at the apartment. Her car is sitting in the lot. I checked with the hospitals, the sheriff, the state patrol, and the morgue. The mother and father came over and opened the apartment. No sign of her. Phone and purse are gone, too. Her carrier says the phone is off the grid." Abby gave him a wary glance. Martin knew what she was thinking. He didn't want another disappearance to be the cure for his ennui.

"Husband? Boyfriend?"

"An ex. He hasn't seen or heard from her. No boyfriend."

"Where's the ex?"

"Milwaukee. Also an attorney. No apparent issues there. An amicable divorce according to the parents. Thing is, Don Segerman called the chief last week. Danielle thought she was being followed. A squad tailed her to work last week but noted nothing out of the ordinary."

Martin felt an uneasy twist in his midsection. At best, a creepy coincidence. At worst...?

"Okay. Open a missing persons file and enter everything we have plus the contact info. I'll get started right away. Where do the parents live?"

"Appleton."

"See if they can come in now and talk to me. If it's been four days, we're getting a late start on this."

Abby nodded and began typing furiously.

Martin returned to his office, thinking about Megan Rice. The parallels were eerie. Two professional women who disappeared with just their purses and phones.

A serial killer?

One type of case he never imagined handling. His case load was mundane. Robbery. Some drug-related violence. Occasional domestics involving aggravated assault. Homicides and sex crimes were rare, and he liked it that way.

Nope. Too early to make that leap.

He sat and opened an internet search on Danielle as he checked her vitals in the newly opened file.

Friends and family called her Dani. Age: 32. Height 5'6". Dark-brown hair, green eyes, one-hundred-twenty-five pounds. No criminal record beyond a speeding ticket. She had never been the victim of a crime. Criminal defense attorney at Segerman and Bosch. College UW Madison followed by UW law school. She was strikingly attractive based on the photo in her professional profile. She had a profile on LinkedIn, a Facebook page, and an Instagram page. Her social media had been quiet lately. There was nothing negative in her online profiles.

He then searched the ex, Dean Hamlin. He had a Facebook page. It looked like he was dating and doing well for himself. No criminal record.

Martin assembled a list of people to interview after he met with the parents.

* * *

Jeff and Sarah Sikorsky arrived an hour later.

The father looked anxious. Tall with a strong face, prominent chin, and brow ridge, he didn't look like he rattled easily. The mother, an older version of her daughter with a little grey creeping in, appeared close to tears. They drew a picture of Danielle indistinguishable from that of a hallowed saint. Honest. Reliable. The heart of an angel. He understood, though he was more pragmatic in assessing his children. They were great kids but hardly perfect.

The ex was a philanderer, but the divorce had been amicable, and they had both gotten on with their lives. The four of them still met for dinner occasionally.

"Have you talked to any of her friends?"

"Yes. None of them have talked to Danielle lately. She's been incredibly busy at work."

And avoiding the loneliness of divorce, Martin thought. He knew the feeling well.

"Was she seeing anyone?"

"No," Mom said confidently.

Hmm. Martin wondered if Danielle told her mother everything. "When did you last talk to her?"

"Friday night; we usually talk once or twice a week."

"How did she seem? Everything okay?"

"Perfectly normal. A little stressed by work, but she was handling it."

"Hobbies?"

"Running, hiking, kayaking, reading. She ran along the river every day at six a.m."

"Every day?"

"Yes. Like clockwork, she'd say."

The father added, perhaps to reassure himself more than anything, "She's trained in self-defense and carries a gun."

"Good to know."

He then asked the tough questions. Did Danielle drink? Gamble? Any history of mental illness or suicide attempts? The answers were an emphatic no.

After a little more conversation, Martin assured them locating their daughter was a department priority. Perhaps she had just taken off for a few days. A breather from her busy schedule. They didn't believe him; he could feel their pain. He couldn't imagine having his daughter go missing.

Next, he called and spoke to Don Segerman, asking many of the same questions he'd peppered the parents with.

Closing, Martin asked, "How seriously did you take Danielle's sense of being followed?"

"Very. Danielle is very perceptive, very sharp," he said. "That's why I insisted she report it."

He trusted Don Segerman's assessment and felt more certain something bad had happened to Danielle.

Still, the situation didn't technically rise to the level of a critical missing. There was no evidence of foul play. Regardless, Martin decided to go loud and wide with the media. They needed all the eyes they could muster to find Danielle Hamlin. An attractive young woman would likely generate a lot of media interest.

* * *

Martin stood in Danielle Hamlin's living room. The parents had earlier granted permission for a search of the apartment. They had noted nothing missing beyond her phone and purse.

On the east end of the mill, 241 was a large open plan apartment, sparsely but tastefully decorated with steel, light woods, and fabrics. The walls were painted in whites and greys. The living room overlooked the river through large windows. On the west wall, an island separated the kitchen from the living area.

The apartment showed no signs of a struggle.

After a first superficial pass, he discovered nothing. No notes, no calendar, no doodles. He suspected everything was inside the missing phone. Nobody wrote anything down anymore. It all went into their phones.

In a small office, he found a laptop, an iPad, and a printer.

They had permission to search the iPad but not the computer, which contained privileged legal information. He grabbed the iPad to hand over to their computer forensics guy.

Officers had interviewed the neighbors. No one remembered seeing her over the weekend. None had door cameras. The only security camera in the building covered the locked lobby and the mail slots. Danielle did not appear anywhere in the footage going back forty-eight hours, but she could have used the locked side entrance.

Her parents said she ran along the river every morning. Martin sent officers to walk the trails, particularly in the wooded areas of Rock River Park, looking for signs of a struggle, drag marks, or discarded clothing.

The sum of all this effort? Nothing.

The ex had a solid alibi. A crime scene crew would soon arrive to check for any forensic evidence. Martin suspected they would find nothing.

With no evidence of a struggle, no evidence a crime had been committed, it was possible Danielle Hamlin had just walked away. It happened occasionally. Often, mental illness played a role. There was no evidence for it, but she worked long hours and had been vying for a partnership. A lot of stress right there.

Regardless, she was gone, had left no clues behind, and no evidence of when she went missing.

On a second pass, Martin noted personal touches seemed quite sparse. A few family photos: mom, dad, and a sister? Strangely, one of her and the ex in a happier time. Some kids, maybe nieces and nephews. That was it. Danielle kept her feelings close at hand, he suspected. No hidden caches he could find. No prescription drugs in the medicine cabinet. Nothing untoward in the refrigerator or freezer. The garbage was nearly empty. No sign of a gun.

Only one possible clue. Danielle's report that she felt a car had been following her. A vague report, a dark or black vehicle. Sadly, the town had never felt the need for traffic cams. Either she'd been followed or had been setting the scene to disappear.

Martin desperately hoped Danielle had just run off for a few days.

Met a new guy. Took a break from the pressure of work.

In his gut, he feared she was dead.

Or would be soon.

Twenty-One

Lili was trapped in the dark box again.

Part of her knew it was a dream—a nightmare—but the cycle was relentless and unbreakable. She pulled herself out of it, tried to dream of something else, only to find herself back in the box.

Several iterations later, a door opened and someone walked in.

A man, though she could discern no details. He looked like a three-dimensional shadow in grey. He yanked her from the box and dragged her to another, brighter space. She saw a mattress. He threw her down and quickly restrained her—ropes or straps, she couldn't tell which—it didn't matter given her overwhelming terror. She lay spread-eagle. Then the shadow attacked her, climbing on top and forcing himself on her.

It was beyond awful.

The ordeal was horribly vivid and visceral. She couldn't escape it. Couldn't scream. Couldn't even open her mouth—it had been taped shut.

She had never experienced a sexual assault in real life, but she imagined it would be just as horrifying. She couldn't decide whether the inability to see her attacker's face was a blessing or a curse. Her imagination filled in the details in the worst way possible.

The nightmare ran for hours and multiple violations before he led her back to the box. At no point could she wake herself and break away from the vision, no matter how hard she tried.

Sometime later, she finally woke up.

Lili rolled out of bed, ran for the bathroom, and threw up. Not much came up, but her stomach kept spasming for several minutes. She leaned her head against the cool, hard porcelain, crying and shaking uncontrollably. As the horror slowly subsided, she was left with a terrible anxiety. What did this mean? What had pushed her dreams into that hellscape? Was she suffering from some mental issue? A sign of a physical disorder? Were the nightmares related to Frank and the problem in Olivia's apartment? While she didn't believe in an ability to see into the future, the dreams felt like an omen. She felt exhausted, physically and emotionally. And she had to work.

Lili brushed her teeth, made coffee, and tried to put her fears in order, her mind at rest. As she drank the coffee, she lay back and performed several relaxation techniques. The nightmarish images receded. She texted her therapist, who responded immediately and expressed grave concern at the violent nature of the nightmares.

Had she been truthful in saying she had never been assaulted?

Yes.

Any history of night terrors or PTSD?

No.

Did she feel threatened now?

No, not really.

She left out the exorcism. She felt anxious about it, but she would only be an observer.

The therapist approved her plan of meditation and relaxation techniques and scheduled a video session in two days to follow up. Lili worked the routine until she felt ready to face the day. Then she took a twenty-minute catnap that was refreshing and dreamless.

Dressing for work, Lili grabbed the can of pepper spray and her Taser from a drawer in the closet. Into her purse they went. If anyone came after her, they would rue the day.

A minute later, she grabbed for the Taser in a practice draw.

She brought it out and up fluidly, her finger at the ready. Her reflexes were good.

Feeling the weight of the nightmares bearing down, Lili called her friend to arrange for the exorcism.

Mateo Martinez was a former Catholic priest with a small, nondenominational church in Milwaukee. Given his background, he was familiar with the classic ritual—though he seldom resorted to it. He preferred the far gentler Taoist rituals. Mateo had been born in Puerto Rico and had married an Asian-American woman after he left the church. She taught him the Way of Tao. He was just the person to handle Raleigh and his skepticism.

He was free tonight and happy to help.

Lili sighed with relief.

* * *

Mateo arrived at eight.

An inch shorter than Lili, he was a slight man with a clipped beard, longish dark hair, and intense green eyes. After Lili briefed him on the situation, they walked across the courtyard to the Kaplans' apartment.

Raleigh greeted them graciously.

Lili suggested the dining room table to Mateo, pointing out the high ceiling above and the direct line of sight from the door to the exterior windows. "This okay?"

"Perfect."

Mateo lit incense and candles to set the atmosphere, placing amulets at what Lili knew to be favored points of Qi in the apartment.

Sitting down, he addressed Olivia and Raleigh. "This ritual is helpful when someone has disturbed a ghost or spirit intentionally or unintentionally. It sounds like the initial event was unintentional, but then you started probing, which aggravated the situation."

"That's what I felt," Lili said.

"I won't be performing the conventional rite," Mateo said, eyeing Raleigh. "The problem with the Christian ritual is that it assumes all ghosts are demons and are therefore bad. In Taoism, not all ghosts are evil. They have the right to occupy their own spaces in the world."

"I don't want it in the apartment," Olivia said. "This is my space."

"I'm going to persuade Frank to stay in his realm. If he does, you won't see or sense his presence again."

"That would be good."

Lili hoped he'd stay out of her head, too.

They sat at the dining room table. Lili sat across from Mateo, as an observer and not a participant. He directed Raleigh and Olivia to sit in the living room on the sofa. Olivia seemed immersed in the experience, while Raleigh looked suitably skeptical as he held her hand.

Mateo laid out a food offering, a fresh piece of homemade bread. He then laid out papers that looked like fake Chinese money.

"These are Joss Papers. We'll burn one while I talk to Frank."

"Where did you get those?" Lili asked.

"Amazon."

"You're kidding, right?"

He shook his head nonchalantly. "No. I'll leave some and have Olivia burn one every week for a month to reinforce our efforts here."

At first, it was a quiet affair. Mateo sat with eyes closed, connecting with the room. He murmured, a low chant, gently summoning Frank to the table. Five minutes later, Mateo began a one-sided conversation.

"Why are you here, Frank?"

Mateo cocked his head like a dog listening to his owner. A minute passed. Lili wished she were part of the conversation but resisted the urge to speak.

"I understand, Frank, but you need to stay in your space."

The table shuddered slightly—Frank announcing his displeasure.

"Settle down, Frank. We're asking you to stay in your space and leave these nice people alone."

The table bumped sharply.

Mateo continued, "Yes, they'll leave you alone, too."

The table jolted again.

Lili was fascinated. She hoped it impressed Raleigh. There was no faking this—though for an exorcism, it still felt a *little* tame.

Mateo maintained a calm manner and tone. "Come on, Frank. You don't belong in their space; you have—"

The table jerked sideways, and the bread fell to the floor.

The room grew cooler, the atmosphere taut as Frank resisted.

A standoff.

Mateo spoke sharply, with a little menace. "Settle down, Frank. Don't make me send you away."

The table shuddered violently. Both Lili and Mateo pressed down on it to keep Frank from tossing it aside. She saw a note of alarm in Mateo's normally placid expression.

"I'm warning you, Frank!" The table strained under their hands and glassware in the kitchen rattled.

Mateo, eminently serious, raised a small wooden cross in his right hand but kept his head tipped down, eyes closed. Then he spoke quickly, a harsh sounding invocation or prayer in Latin.

Fascinated, Lili felt her hackles rise. She had so many questions but knew better than to interrupt. She wondered what Raleigh thought. If he didn't believe, he didn't believe, but this was the real deal.

Until now, Frank had remained hidden from view but appeared briefly over the table with a frightened expression before evaporating into the tabletop. Olivia yelped, and Lili thought she heard Raleigh snicker.

The table and glasses fell still.

Seconds later, Mateo looked up and opened his eyes. "He isn't happy about it, but Frank is going to stay where he belongs."

Olivia said, "It worked?"

"I believe so, yes." He handed the remaining Joss Papers to Olivia and suggested she burn one at least once a week.

Lili felt a sense of calm. The building felt quieter than it had in days.

Mateo looked at Lili with a look of gentle admonishment. "And you'll leave Frank alone, too. Yes?"

Lili nodded.

As Mateo collected his things, Raleigh managed to rein in his skepticism and said, "That was interesting. Thank you."

"For your wife's sake, I hope Frank behaves. Your disbelief is evident."

Raleigh smiled sheepishly. "Busted, huh?"

Mateo nodded with a tight smile. "Good night, friends."

Lili walked Mateo to the lobby, hoping this exorcism would end her nightmares as well.

She hadn't mentioned Eamon.

Why, she didn't know.

Twenty-Two

Emma shook in fear and anger.

Something frightening had just occurred. Busy reading in 202, she felt a sudden, sharp shock wave pass through the room.

Emanating from the west end of the mill, it exerted a powerful, disturbing effect on the energy fields. It wasn't Frank. She sensed his disorientation too, though she wasn't sure how.

Emma wandered toward the source of the disturbance. A second surge struck her fifty feet from apartment 114. Emma had never experienced anything like it, some kind of pressure wave flowing through the building. It scrambled her brain. She felt weak and diffuse, like she was evaporating. It took considerable concentration to restore her coherence.

Soon after, Lili and a strange man walked out of the Kaplan apartment.

Of course. That woman was to blame—again.

Were they trying to push Frank out? What kind of trouble had he been up to? Would she be next? Who did Lili think she was, moving here and making trouble? Emma felt like retaliating, blowing over to her apartment and tossing the place, but no. Bad idea. She didn't want that kind of negative energy directed at her, and petty vandalism was a poor way to deal with the problem. In reading about karma, Emma understood good behavior was a virtue and that better karma might be her way out of the mill.

Besides, the best way to protect herself was to befriend Lili. Better to be on her good side than to incur her wrath. While Emma couldn't peer into the cellar, she felt certain Lili could.

Could they collaborate? Could Emma maintain a safe detachment from her? Would Lili be receptive?

Of course she would. It was probably her wildest dream to actually connect with a spirit. Together, they could be quite a team.

Emma briefly imagined herself as a force for good, a girl warrior. Kids these days believed in superheroes, and she liked the idea of it, going out, fixing stuff, saving people—

Nonsense. It was a silly dream. Especially for a dead girl stuck in limbo.

And it was risky.

But there was plenty to do. The police had visited the mill yesterday. A woman was missing. Emma felt certain the criminal deviant in 139 had taken her and was holding her in the cellar. Lili might be her only way to warn someone and save the woman, but Emma feared the weird, scary power that Lili possessed.

The solution lay in the iPad.

Confused, Emma returned to 202 to continue studying something called apps. An app sounded like the secret to writing messages.

But Emma was having second thoughts. Worried about making direct contact with the living. Was it even allowed? Leaving a message was one thing.

Then she imagined that poor woman, trapped in the cellar.

Did she have a choice?

Sigh.

Sometimes, she longed for the days before the renovation and the quiet of the empty old mill.

⋆ ⋆ ⋆

Frank was pissed.

Exorcism. That's what they called it, and it enraged him. Scared him, too.

Sheesh! He was a simple, dimwitted ghost, not a demon.

The experience had been brutal. It started innocently enough. A calm voice speaking to him, trying to befriend him. Then the voice started giving him orders.

That intruder had no right to boss him around.

And what was with the food?

Criminy, he was dead!

But when Frank resisted, the preacher cast a powerful spell that created an intense pressure, forcing him against the walls and into the very crevices in the brickwork. Dead or not, it was painful, and he felt powerless against it. The discomfort was bad enough, but the implied threat was worse. Being sent away? Dispelled?

It sounded like termination. Death for the dead. Something very bad.

It had started with that woman sitting in the hallway, poking at him. There was little he could do to retaliate. He tried bothering the people living within his space, but his efforts had been mostly useless. He had rustled the curtains and blown on the nape of the woman's neck, giving her a start. Made some scary faces. Laughable efforts, really.

He wasn't much of a ghost. And now, they had wielded some magic power against him. Clearly a warning.

Angry or not, Frank decided to lay low to avoid bothering these people. He didn't want to invite another exorcism and had no desire to discover what being sent away entailed. It wasn't fair. They were invading his space, not the other way around. At least when this was still a paper mill, people left him alone and seemed to accept his occasional appearances, even if he startled someone now and then. They didn't call an exorcist.

He wondered if they were bothering that stupid girl as well. Little Miss Goody Two Shoes lording over the mill like a princess. Frank had never seen her; he just knew she was around, free to go wherever she wanted. Totally unfair.

Of course, nothing in his brief life had been fair. Why should this be different?

That annoying ceremony wasn't the only thing that had set him on edge.

He had felt uneasy lately. There was something wrong in the building. Something new, an unfamiliar presence, stirring in the cellar hallways.

Could they talk? Cooperate in some manner?

Probably not. He wasn't very smart but concluded that if he was unable to leave the room, the other ghost probably couldn't get in. Yet somehow, a woman had done it the other night. Wafted right through the wall of the pulp room, just like a ghost, even though she was one of the living. She was also making his life miserable.

Frank understood none of it.

How did someone get into the cellar, anyway? Those passages had always been a closely guarded secret. Twice, he'd been sent down there to dump barrels of sludge. He didn't know what it was, but his supervisor had sworn him to secrecy. No one was to know what he was doing. Each time, the guy slipped him a twenty, an amount equal to a week's pay. Had he done something wrong in dumping the barrels and accepting the money? Was that why he was stuck here?

Who knew?

He just knew his punishment wasn't much of a lesson if he didn't understand what he'd done wrong.

Right now, Frank just wanted that woman and these people gone.

By any means possible.

Twenty-Three

Lili tossed and turned.

Deep in REM sleep, she was in the grip of a nightmare that felt as tangible as the walls around her. A shadowy figure had assaulted her for hours, an assault on her body, mind, and soul. Her terror and despair were intense, and she couldn't dispel them.

Mercifully, the assault ended, and the man dragged her back to the box in near darkness.

Her cell.

He tossed her onto a cot. The door slammed and a bolt slid closed. There was a thin blanket. Lili covered herself and lay shocked and despondent. She couldn't stand much more of this.

Locked in a nightmare in a room of horrors, she groped around. The cot was cold cast iron. Her hand bumped into something on the floor.

A bucket padlocked to the wall. She knew exactly what that was for.

Ugh.

Not the slightest thing to use as a weapon. All she had was an abundance of time. Time to remember the horrors of the previous few hours. Too much time. An endless amount of time to anticipate the next assault, to wonder how long before she died, to pray for deliverance or death. She contemplated suicide, but all she had was the blanket and nothing to hang herself from.

The room smelled dank with a faint undercurrent of bleach. She knew bleach was used to clean up crime scenes, to cover up murder and assault. And that's what this was, a crime scene in progress. She knew how it would end.

How her life would end.

The hours passed with slow, exquisite horror, time stretching before her like an endless desert. She shook with fear, from a constant wash of adrenaline through her veins. Sometimes she dozed but never reached deep sleep. Ironically, the horrors of the past few days awaited in vivid nightmares—as if it wasn't enough to have lived them firsthand. Nightmares within a nightmare, like an endless set of mirrors reflecting the horrible reality of her existence.

She drifted through memories of her parents. Her father was tall with a prominent chin and brow ridge, a strong but kind face. Her mother—

What?

The nightmare had taken an odd twist. Those people weren't her parents. Yet they lived in a house that felt like her childhood home, her childhood bedroom—only that wasn't hers either.

It was disorienting and yet her mind kept reverting to those false memories, searching for sanctuary within them.

She heard the bolt slide back on the door.

Lili startled awake in a cold sweat, overwhelmed by terror, her eyes darting around the room—

Her bedroom, her bed, her life.

She rolled from bed and ran for the bathroom, vomiting a thin stream of bile as her insides railed against the horrid images and feelings that had assailed her sleep.

Then she cried. She couldn't go on like this. These nightmares seemed to represent some kind of psychological breakdown.

Lili laid her head on the cool porcelain and closed her eyes.

She took a breath. Then another. Collecting herself before contacting her therapist, certain she'd need hospitalization.

She had lost the plot.

A minute passed. Then two. An odd clarity slowly cleared the fog in her brain. This was no mental issue.

It was a spiritual one.

The dreams? The nightmares? They weren't hers. That explained the false memories. Instead, Lili felt certain they represented reality for someone else. Someone nearby. And she was convinced that someone was Danielle Hamlin, the woman who had been reported missing Tuesday evening. She lived in this building, and somehow Lili had forged a psychic connection to her.

The memories were Danielle's memories. She was being held against her will and assaulted.

She had to report it.

Now.

⋆ ⋆ ⋆

Martin stared at the Terry Redlin print on the wall, a placid scene he normally found relaxing. Today he felt like ripping it off the wall. Megan Rice was probably dead. Danielle Hamlin might be dead or suffering horrors worse than death. Perhaps they had been abducted and trafficked in the sex trade. He imagined no good outcome right now.

One disappearance had been easier to rationalize. He remained hopeful Megan had run off for whatever reason—some outcome besides abduction and murder. Then she would be alive. Still, why would a doting mother just leave? It didn't feel right. And two unrelated women absconding from Ash Grove in six months? A coincidence? Not likely. Improbable. Especially these two women.

Danielle had no hint of instability in her profile. She had loving parents and an idyllic childhood. An amicable divorce. Well educated and responsible, dedicated to her work. No known history of mental illness. But she faced undue stress at work. Perhaps it was more than she could handle?

Neither woman was the type who just took off, leaving their families, clothes, and cars behind. Only their purses and phones were missing and the phones had been dark since.

No, two women disappearing without a trace looked like a pattern, and yet, he still had zero proof any crime had been committed. A third woman vanishing would clinch it, but they couldn't wait for a third disappearance to confirm a pattern.

The extension to the front desk pinged. Abby Eriksen.

"I have a woman on the line who says she has information about Danielle Hamlin."

He perked up. A break?

"Put her through." After a click and a pause, a female voice said, "Hello?"

"Yes, ma'am. Detective Kettridge speaking. How can I help you?"

"My name is Lili Paltrinieri." She paused, then said, "This is going to sound strange..."

He felt the first quiver of doubt. Any information presaged by the words *this is going to sound strange* was probably very strange. When she didn't continue, he said, "Go on."

"I live in Rock River Mills, and I think Danielle is here somewhere."

Martin had a bad feeling about the direction the call was taking. Something in her tone. Maybe he was wrong. "Have you seen her?"

"Not exactly."

"If you haven't seen her, why do you think she's there? We've been through her apartment. Is she staying with someone?"

"I said it would sound strange." There was a long pause. She then spoke in a rush. "I'm psychic and I've had dreams about her."

Shit!

He wasn't going to entertain this nut no matter how well-intentioned she was. He wasn't in the mood. "That's nice. Thanks for the tip."

Martin set the receiver down, ending the call.

I'm psychic and I've had dreams.

Jesus. He had no time for such lunacy.

Twenty-Four

A moment later, Martin shook his head.

He wasn't rude as a rule. The woman might be a nutcase, but he could have listened politely, ended the call more professionally. A measure of his frustration; a poor excuse for rudeness nonetheless. He hadn't even bothered to jot down her information. Martin buzzed Abby's extension and asked for the woman's name and number.

He tapped the numbers in. A moment later, she answered.

"Sorry, we were cut off, Lili. Your last name is Paltrinieri?"

"Yes." She spelled it out for him, followed by her address and apartment number.

"Okay, Lili, tell me what you know about the disappearance of Danielle Hamlin."

"I sense your skepticism, Detective, but I'm not crazy. People believe in this stuff or they don't. I sense you don't."

Perceptive—or a lucky guess, he decided.

"I have my doubts. I also believe it won't hurt to hear you out."

"Very open-minded of you," she said with an edge. "Anyway, believe it or not, I'm psychic and I moved into the Mill partly to explore the place—I'd call it the most interesting building in town. There are ghosts here if you believe in such things."

He was wrong. It might hurt to hear this woman out. "And Danielle is one of the ghosts?"

"No. I'm convinced she's still alive."

"How could you possibly know that if you haven't seen her?"

"Dreams. I've had dreams, horrible nightmares. That woman is going through something awful, and I think it's happening somewhere in the building."

He might regret it, but asked, "Any idea where?"

"Listen, I know you're skeptical, but I believe these dreams are real. I don't know where in the building, only that it's dark and the walls are brick. I understand that's not very helpful."

"Have you looked for her?"

"No. I'm a psychic, not a detective," she said with a sigh. "The guy holding her is crazy."

"This guy. You know what he looks like then?"

"I only have a fuzzy impression. I don't think I could draw a sketch. Not yet anyway."

How convenient.

Martin bit his lip. This woman with her dreams and theories was probably a waste of time. On the other hand, he wasn't busy, and given the complete lack of evidence in the case, he had nothing to lose. There had been well-publicized cases where the police were assisted by a psychic. Had it been luck? Or some genuine ability? Who knew? His lieutenant probably wouldn't be amused, though.

"Okay. Can you come down and make a statement?"

"Now?"

"Now would be good."

* * *

Martin's extension buzzed ten minutes later.

Abby Eriksen spoke. "Ms. Paltrinieri is here."

"I'll be right there."

Martin steeled himself and walked up front, prepared to meet a crazy cat lady wearing an ugly knit sweater despite the warm weather.

He couldn't have been more wrong. Lili Paltrinieri was in her thirties, perhaps five foot eight, with dark red hair and brown eyes. She was thin, waifish even, and quite attractive, dressed in a blue knee-length summer dress. She might be crazy, but she was no cat lady.

He extended a hand. "Ms. Paltrinieri. Nice to meet you. You can follow me."

She shook his hand firmly with solid eye contact. She wasn't wearing a ring.

Reaching the office, he put a hand out. "Have a seat."

She sat gracefully in a feminine way he found attractive.

* * *

Lili eyed Detective Martin coolly.

He was trying to be sincere, but not succeeding very well. An attractive man in his early forties, he was tall, with mousy brown hair and blue eyes. He had a scar on his right temple. It looked like something had glanced off his skull, and she immediately thought: *bullet.* He was in fair shape—but not great—nicely outfitted in dress slacks, a tie, and a fashionable tweed jacket.

He settled into his chair and said, "Do you know Danielle Hamlin personally?"

"I've never met Danielle. I didn't know what she looked like until her picture appeared online."

"Okay. Some basics. Where do you work?"

"I own a small shop on Elm Street—Revelations—a metaphysical store. I sell New-Agey stuff. Crystals, amulets, incense. Tarot cards. I do some palmistry, numerology, and act as a medium for people hoping to connect with loved ones who've passed."

"So, you're a shopkeeper, a fortune teller—?"

"A soothsayer."

He gave her a look of surprise. "That's a thing?"

"No. But it's pretty obvious you're a skeptic and that you're just going through the motions here," she said, slightly perturbed. She could read his dismissive stance perfectly. "You have no leads, so you're trying to convince yourself you're doing everything you can."

"You can read my mind?" He gave her an exaggerated, wide-eyed look.

Good, she had pierced his smug attitude. "No. It's just the aura you're giving off."

"What you say is true...but I am trying to keep an open mind." He regrouped and looked her in the eye with a more sincere expression. "So, tell me what you—um, suspect."

Lili wasn't sure how to start. She had dreamt about violent sexual assault. It was a profoundly personal narrative. She opted to leave the explicit details out.

"I occasionally have dreams that reveal things about people. Sometimes I know them, sometimes I don't. In this case, I realized I was sharing an experience with someone else. She was tied down and a man was raping her. She was terrified and knew, eventually, that she was going to die. The man was a shadow. I only know he was tall with fairly short hair. He talked, but I couldn't understand him."

"That sounds perfectly awful." Martin gave her a genuine look of concern.

"It has been. Beyond that, I can tell you she's being held in a small dark room. A basement, I think. She has a cot with a crappy mattress and a thin blanket. There's a bucket padlocked to the wall for—you know."

He nodded, closing his eyes. He seemed truly affected. Retelling the story was sending Lili into an anxious tailspin. Her palms felt sweaty. She fought to maintain her composure. It was vital that he believe her.

"So why do you think this is happening in the Mill?"

"I think it's a proximity thing. I'm dreaming it because it's happening nearby. And the walls I could see were brick, like the walls of the mill."

He nodded. "Makes sense."

"The rest is a hunch. I accept I could be wrong, but I don't think so."

"Anything else?"

"Not really."

"So why do you think you're, um—channeling Danielle?"

"Another hunch." Spoken aloud, it sounded ridiculous. Why would he believe such a crazy story? She hoped she was wrong, that this poor woman wasn't being held hostage and suffering through rape after rape. But the dreams felt real, and the alternative was madness—that she had simply lost her mind. Lili didn't think she was crazy. "You either accept that I'm psychic or you don't. It can't hurt to look."

He nodded, then shook his head.

"Okay. Your story sounds—unbelievable. But as you said, we have nothing to lose in performing a search of the common areas, the basement, the utility rooms. We won't be able to search individual apartments and condos. No judge will grant us warrants without more substantial evidence."

"It's not in an apartment. I'm sure of that."

"Anything else?"

"Not really. Do you believe me? Even a little?"

"A little. I am a skeptic. My lieutenant will be much more so. While you sound sincere, you've given us precious little to act on. If you see anything else, an idea of her location, the face of her attacker, let me know. I'll listen."

"Thank you."

She couldn't tell if he was sincere or simply humoring her. She sensed he liked her, found her attractive, despite her sketchy story. No matter. She had no interest in a man who made her feel like a member of the lunatic fringe. That was often the story with men. They were drawn to her until they fully understood her interests and hobbies.

As he saw her out, she worried mostly about going to sleep later and being plunged back into Danielle's nightmares.

But she had a fix for that.

Tonight she was sleeping with the prince of darkness.

Doctor Xanax.

Twenty-Five

King of the World.

Looking out his windows overlooking the river, Chase felt just like Jack Dawson in *Titanic.*

Everything had unfolded according to plan. He didn't understand why he had been so nervous with Megan. He was intelligent and resourceful. Planning, execution—he excelled at all of it. His prize lay beneath his feet. And what a prize it was. She was a beauty of the caliber he deserved. The sex was awesome. In time, she would come to realize what a catch he was.

He paused.

She would come to realize?

Was that a justification? Was he equivocating? Trying to find a reason not to kill her? Why?

A growing worry about getting caught like the anxieties he had with Megan?

Fear drove him to kill her prematurely. Really, it was a lapse in confidence, and it had surprised him. This entire business was a tightrope act of risk versus reward, as in most endeavors. The risks were huge.

The rewards astronomical. He recognized himself as a work in progress. The learning curve was steep and came without guides or manuals.

The voice of his friend, Eamon, the voice that had helped spur him on, had suggested it was time to get rid of the woman already.

Ridiculous.

Why was he listening to him, anyway? This was his moment of glory.

But he viewed Eamon as a compatriot, a friend.

His friend? He might be evidence of a disordered mind. He'd had imaginary friends as a child—his parents encouraged it—but nothing this real, this vivid. Or was it? Could his friend be a manifestation of his special brand of genius? No way to know and no one to ask.

If he was going to create an imaginary friend, this dude with his quirky Irish accent and dry humor seemed perfect. Too bad they couldn't go to O'Malley's and hang out—though he did enjoy their chats in the basement.

Eamon seemed much more real, more independent than his childhood buddies. Chase didn't direct his thoughts. Eamon wasn't a parrot like his earlier friends. He was a ghost, a spirit, and he chose to commune with Chase. Surely, that alone was proof of his superiority.

Occasionally, he would view himself with a saner eye and realize—or fear—that he was losing it. Were these the thoughts of a sane man? But who had defined sanity in the first place? Was it a legitimate definition? Chase thought it doubtful that many of the great men of history would pass a standard definition of sanity.

Maybe he was a little crazy.

But not in taking Danielle. Illegal or not, he was only grabbing what was rightfully his. Feminists had run amok, giving women inordinate and undeserved power. He and his online peers truly believed these radical bitches meant to kill and erase every last man from the planet. The original sin had been giving them the right to vote.

Now they were overrunning every male domain, including the legal profession and law enforcement, so it was doubly delicious that Danielle was an attorney. Really, he was fighting back, striking a blow for men everywhere.

Even if he was a tad crazy, he functioned at a very high level. Did his job well. Never missed a shift. Maintained civil relationships with everyone on the force, even the female officers, while hiding his disdain for them, knowing they had no place on the force beyond secretarial roles.

It was irrelevant in the end. He was who he was and had a valuable role in society as a warrior, an alpha male. His little quirks weren't really an issue. Everyone had quirks. He was happy with who he was.

Chase had begun to understand his particular idiosyncrasies on his sixteenth birthday.

He had been dating Paige for almost eight months. They had messed around but hadn't done the deed. He was in imminent danger of becoming a sixteen-year-old virgin, a fate almost worse than death among his fellow sophomores. While he didn't have any real friends, he listened to the locker room talk and realized he was falling behind. In danger of being tagged as a loser. But he wasn't. He just hadn't been assertive enough.

Chase pressured Paige to get with him, and finally, she promised to on his birthday. Her parents had an office over the garage, and they snuck up to it using the back stairs.

They kissed and touched. Chase felt nervous. He couldn't get hard. He had no problem on his own, but suddenly, he was limper than a dead cat. Paige didn't seem to notice, but then she lost her nerve. Or had she sensed his problem and felt sorry for him? He decided she had and grew angry. And a little hard.

She started to cry. He got angrier. And harder.

It became a self-fulfilling loop. More tears, more anger, more arousal.

He yanked her panties off and reminded her that she had promised.

A few more minutes of persuasion and she gave in, though she started crying again.

He discovered he liked this hard-to-get routine. The more they resisted, the better.

High school girls weren't always receptive to his approach. Women even less so. Finally, he took Stacy. He couldn't help himself. Afterward, she had threatened him with arrest, so he killed her.

He felt nothing—beyond the urge to do it again.

Chase knew he was heading down a dangerous path and withdrew from dating to avoid further temptation, criminal charges, and prison. He then decided on a different approach. He became a cop to game the system in his favor and bought apartment 139.

Right now, he was puzzled by a disturbing rumor circulating at work.

Chase knew officers would search the common areas of the Mill sometime today. They would find nothing. Curiously, the lead detective, Martin Kettridge, had talked to a woman who pointed to the mill. She was rumored to be psychic.

What?

He then thought, why am I worried?

Psychics were frauds. The woman had to be some nut job looking for her fifteen minutes of fame. Directing them to the mill was an obvious ploy. Simply a lucky guess. Why had Martin even entertained the crazy bitch? Desperate to solve the unsolvable, probably. Martin didn't have a clue. Never had. He was a lousy detective.

Sure, they would perform a search of the building, but they would never get warrants to look inside individual apartments. Even if they went through his unit, they would find nothing.

He chuckled humorlessly. His preparations were just that good.

Chase descended into the basement, grabbed two beers, and sat in his deck chair. He set a bottle across the table and took a swig from his.

A familiar voice spoke. "Hello, friend."

Chase tipped his bottle in acknowledgment.

"Feeling pretty good about yourself today," Eamon said. A statement, not a question.

"I am. Things have gone very well lately. Wouldn't you agree?"

"I would. You're the man, my friend. Just don't get too comfortable."

"You worry too much," Chase said.

"Somebody should."

"I'm sorry you missed the actual moment I grabbed the woman. It was flawless. Poetic."

"I have no doubt of that. Still, a little more humility on your part would be good."

"Nonsense. Right now, I feel invincible."

"I'll bet you do." Eamon chuckled.

Chase thought the laugh sounded vaguely evil.

It sent an inexplicable shiver down his spine.

Twenty-Six

The answer was Word.

Emma could type notes into an iPad using Word on a screen that resembled a typewriter. She felt confident she could summon the app and communicate through it. Really, it was perfect for her, a program that was ghost friendly.

She snickered. As if there were such a thing.

Now she needed to gain some skill with the device. It wasn't easy. People didn't leave iPads lying about and switched on when they weren't in use. To rush the process, she had taken to diving in while people used their devices, making random swipes and keystrokes to practice. It worked!

The technique also had considerable entertainment value and added new tricks to her haunting repertoire. The reactions ran from startled surprise to outright anger. One guy tossed his iPad on the floor in a fit of pique—a foolish reaction since he cracked the screen. Emma giggled, then admonished herself. It was an unkind reaction and detrimental to her karma.

Occasionally, people set them down for a few minutes, giving her more time to practice. She discovered they were versatile. People could write letters, work from home, watch movies, read the news—her favorite capability.

She felt ready to talk to Lili. If this worked, she needed to make a highly specific request and cooperate on what felt like opposite sides of a cosmic mirror. And she had to hurry. Time was running out for the woman in the cellar.

The disturbance in the Kaplan unit had settled down. As far as she knew, Frank was still there. She sensed his presence. He had gone to ground, and she couldn't blame him. That had been an utterly unpleasant experience and it hadn't been directed at her. It was puzzling. Why had they co-existed with the living until these recent conflicts? What had upset the balance? Was it Lili?

The tension on the other end of the building remained oppressive.

Emanating from the cellar, the rooms beneath the floor remained a blank slate. Maybe just as well. Given the awful pictures of rape and murder she saw on his computer, she knew exactly what that dreadful man was capable of. She felt certain he was assaulting a woman and intended to kill her.

Emma couldn't comprehend what drove a person to grab someone, to hurt them, and then kill them. Didn't understand the thought process. That was in the realm of psychology, and she knew little about mental illness. Another subject she needed to study.

Drifting over to 124, she spent the rest of the afternoon snooping and reading, waiting for Lili to return home. She worked most days. Emma found a business card for her shop with the hours listed. It sounded like an interesting place.

Lili had a veritable library of books on witchcraft and the supernatural. Emma soon learned the event in the Kaplan apartment was probably an exorcism, an attempt to drive Frank out of the building. Poor Frank. What could he have possibly done to deserve that?

Some of the books were preposterous. The authors made stuff up as they went, talking about the realm of ghosts as if they had visited such places, when it was clear they were clueless about the spirit world. Fortunately, some of the living were more receptive to spirits and Lili was evidently one of those people.

Lili arrived home after dark, made a salad for dinner, and then curled up on her sofa, playing games on her iPad. Emma still didn't understand most of them. Often, people played games like Solitaire, a card game she knew. She had moved a few cards while watching games in progress to humorous effect.

Other games were inscrutable puzzles involving red birds, gems, and grids full of numbers or letters.

Emma hovered well above Lili and watched her play a game with numbers. She seemed anxious, edgy. There were moments when she paused and stared into space absently, her finger frozen in mid-air.

To grab her attention, Emma had to change the screen and open the app with the W symbol. She prayed this would work. A woman's life depended on it. She slid across the screen to minimize the number game.

Lili jumped and said, "Shit!"

She shook her head and restored the program. Emma closed it again. Lili stabbed the screen forcefully to reopen her program.

This was going nowhere fast.

Emma pulled a quick slip-slide movement, closed the game, then darted up and opened the Word screen. It caused Lili to pause. Emma performed a second double swipe, trying to type *hi.*

Instead, *hu* appeared.

* * *

Lili sat and struggled with Sudoku, waiting for her Xanax to kick in. Anxious and distracted all evening, she was putting off going to bed, fearing the nightmares that sleep would bring. Something about her apartment felt off, too.

Then her game disappeared.

"Shit!"

She restored the screen only to have it disappear again. A moment later, Word popped open and two letters appeared. Lili looked around and raised a finger to close the screen, then stopped, mouth agape. After a confused moment, an awareness dawned on her.

She looked up and spoke. "Hello?"

hi

Lili felt a thrill run down her spine. This couldn't be happening. Either she was hallucinating or losing her mind—which, given her nightmares of the past few nights, was entirely possible—or she was talking to a ghost through her iPad!

"Who are you?"

emma

No way!

Was that possible? Or was someone screwing with her? That made no sense. Who? Why? Finally, she said, "Emma Kiekhafer?"

yes

So many questions. Where to start? Could she record this somehow? Word would autosave it, but there was no way to prove a ghost had written any of it. Everyone would assume trickery. Lili wasn't sure she believed it herself.

"Talk to me."

need help

The typing was slow. This might take a while. Still, somehow, her iPad had become a modern-day Ouija board. She decided to let Emma direct the conversation for now. The questions could come later. "How?"

problem here

Huh? Lili didn't understand. "In my apartment?"

no, cellar

"What? What about the cellar?"

under 139

Lili waited a minute, but nothing further was forthcoming.

"Emma? Are you still here?"

Nothing.

"Emma?"

She waited an hour for something to happen. What the hell? Had she imagined it? But their exchange was still open in Word.

It wasn't fair.

She didn't know exactly where 139 was and she didn't want to leave and risk missing any messages from Emma.

What had Emma been trying to tell her? A problem with the basement? The same thing she sensed? Or something else?

Hold it!

Basement? There was no basement—the manager had been adamant. What the hell was she talking about? Actually, she had used the word *cellar*. Was it some sort of metaphor? It wasn't enough.

Why didn't Lili just talk to her? Why use an iPad?

Lili needed more information.

She would stay awake all night if need be. But she was exhausted after the terrible dreams of the last few nights and had already taken a Xanax.

Lili sighed and swallowed the last sip of wine.

She closed her eyes, just for a moment, trying to recharge.

Instead, she fell asleep.

⋆ ⋆ ⋆

Emma looked at the iPad, perplexed. Her technique had simply stopped working. No matter how delicately or forcefully she swept over the screen, nothing happened.

It wasn't fair.

She had opened a dialogue with a living person and *poof*, the ability had evaporated. God, she hated this place sometimes.

Then a darker thought intruded. Had she broken another rule? Was the building messing with her? The thing in the cellar? Frank even?

Oh well. She would just keep trying. She would get her message out and have someone look under 139.

In a snit, she went to find someone using an iPad she could torment.

Maybe that wouldn't work either.

Darn.

Twenty-Seven

Martin stared wistfully out the window.

The sun shone down on the sparkling Rock River on the far side of the parking lot. People walked, jogged, and biked along the riverbank, enjoying the warm weather. He wished he could leave and join them. Maybe go fishing. He often did his best work then, picking over the details of the case.

Martin knew the mill search would be pointless when the manager told him the building had no basement. Nevertheless, she agreed to a warrantless search of the utility and common areas, and Martin accepted the offer. It was almost a formality. He expected nothing and found nothing. There were no known hidden rooms or nooks. No disused doors or passages. They had repurposed every square foot of the building.

It was quite a marvel. The company had converted a grim old paper mill into thirty-eight apartments and condos, all of them bright, desirable spaces. The maintenance areas were discreet and clean. He viewed two vacant units and liked what he saw. Besides the condos, there were common areas for meetings and parties. Outdoor patios and grilling areas. A classy place. Martin might consider moving there when he finished helping his kids with college expenses. Right now, he couldn't afford it. In the end, the search felt more like a tour than official police business.

He couldn't imagine Danielle being held in an apartment. Too many people lived in the building. It would be virtually impossible to manage a hostage. Someone would hear something. Assuming Danielle had been abducted, such offenders liked remote locations. Abandoned buildings. Old farmsteads. The mill was simply too busy. They interviewed the neighbors again anyway.

Nothing.

Since the only *evidence* had come from an attractive, sincere fruitcake who happened to live in the building, he wasn't surprised. To his chagrin, word about his source had traveled through the department and he'd faced some gentle ribbing.

He thought of Ms. Paltrinieri on several occasions unrelated to the case. Then he wondered why. She was an oddball and clearly not his type, attractive or not. He had dated little since the divorce. Busy with work. Busy with the kids. Busy with—

Excuses.

He tried the dating services and had some luck, but nothing that felt right. Too many women his age were looking for a husband. He wasn't ready for a commitment. He wanted to start out with a few casual dates and have some fun. Grill out. Go to a bar. Maybe go fishing—

Abby Eriksen knocked and stuck her head in the door. "There's a gentleman up front who would like to speak to you."

"About?"

"He's a diver. He says he found two human teeth and three possible finger bones in the river. He wants to file a report."

His interest was piqued. It could be a tangible lead, but he then thought grimly: if they were human, one of the women was probably dead. Rarely did useful leads arrive without some catch in this business.

Martin followed Abby to the front.

A tall, geeky-looking guy stood outside the locked access door. Maybe fifty with a full head of greying hair, he wore a plain white tee, Levi shorts, and white crew socks. The man was no slave to fashion. Good for him.

Martin opened the door and extended a hand. "Detective Kettridge."

"Dr. Craig Stevens. I'm a dentist, right over there." He pointed out the window to a professional building a quarter mile east by the river. "I'm also a diver and occasionally, I like to explore the riverbed. I have a trip coming up and I took a practice dive to check my gear."

"Let's go back to my office."

Martin led the way, and when they reached his office, Dr. Stevens set a quart Ziploc bag on the desk. Filled with water, it contained two teeth and three nuggets that looked like bones.

Martin held it up, twisting it this way and that. "What's this?"

"The teeth are human. I'm certain of that. A maxillary first molar and mandibular second molar. The bones are phalanges—finger bones—I think. I'm not certain they're human, but with that woman missing, I brought them in to let you people figure it out."

"Did you touch them?"

"No. I was wearing dive gloves, and that's river water in the bag. I hope it turns out to be nothing."

"Can you show me exactly where you were diving?"

"I can do better." He pulled a slip of paper from his pocket. "These are the exact GPS coordinates."

"Wow. Thank you."

They chatted for a few minutes about Martin's fishing photos before Dr. Stevens turned and made for the door. He looked at the bag and said, "I hope that isn't what I think it is."

"Thank you, Doctor. So do I."

Martin went to the computer and typed in the coordinates. They fell about five hundred yards downstream of the mill.

But what were they? Normally, he had just one option going forward. Send it all to the state crime lab. Depending on how busy they were, it might take weeks or months before he received the results.

They couldn't wait. He needed to know right now.

He stepped over to Sam Farber's office.

"Got a minute?" He held the bag up.

"Sure. What you got there?"

Lieutenant Farber was five-eight with broad shoulders, a round face, close-cropped dark hair, and a military bearing. Quiet with a serious manner, Martin knew him to be smart, tough, and a dedicated professional. Their friendship went back to their days in high school together. Martin deferred to Farber's rank, but Sam trusted Martin and often treated him as a virtual equal. Sam's son, Travis, was a cop as well and Martin's godson.

Martin detailed the visit from the dentist and finished by saying, "I don't think we can afford to wait for the results."

"Agreed." Farber held a finger up. "I have a friend at the crime lab."

Farber made a call, explained the situation, made a couple of notes, and ended with an appreciative goodbye.

"Send the bones to the forensic pathologist. We're not sure they're human and apparently, they're not very useful for DNA testing." Sam took the bag and twisted it this way and that. "They require mtDNA testing—whatever that is. It'll take too long."

"The teeth?"

"Probably ideal. They contract with a private lab for overflow testing, so we'll push the teeth through that way. They have rapid DNA capability."

"What does that mean?"

"Forty-eight hours, if we're lucky. Do we have DNA profiles on both women?"

"Yes. We had Megan's, and Danielle Hamlin took a test through Ancestry. The parents shared the data with us."

"Perfect." Sam handed a slip of paper to Martin. "Here's the address for the lab. Run the teeth over there. Let's get going on this."

It was a beautiful afternoon for a drive. Thirty minutes later, Martin pulled up to Bio-Horizon Labs just outside of Madison, signed the paperwork, and asked, "Any idea how long?"

The young brunette at the desk shook her head. "Nope."

He drove home, feeling ambivalent. Maybe they had a lead. If so, one woman was probably dead. For now, Farber wanted to keep the discovery under their hats until the results were in. He didn't want to suggest a break in the case until they had hard evidence. He wanted everyone focused on finding Danielle alive.

On his way home, he turned a ball game on and tried not to think about the teeth and bones.

Or about the person who had been dismembered and tossed in the river.

Twenty-Eight

Eamon O'Keene shuffled along like a zombie.

West along the south passage, right at the end, then east along the north passage and through a little zigzag by the old well room. When he reached the other end, he started over in a routine that never varied. The cellars were his domain and he guarded them jealously.

Eamon had been a mason's helper when the mill was built. A dirt-poor, illiterate Irishman, he was killed by a cave-in beneath the footings when they laid the foundation. They didn't even bother with a body recovery. With no family to answer to, they probably decided he wasn't worth the trouble. It would have slowed construction and that couldn't be allowed. God forbid.

A pauper's burial, really, his grave was unmarked beyond the small cross carved into the brickwork above the spot where he died. He had lived an unremarkable life and died without due consideration or respect. But not right away. His head fell into a small pocket of air near the footing. He suffocated slowly—over minutes or hours, he didn't know—it seemed like a fecking eternity before he died, terrified and alone in his lightless tomb.

Buried alive. The most feared nightmare of all. It happened and everyone knew it.

For some, there was a chance for a reprieve—if you were well-to-do. The phrase *saved by the bell* expressed that primal fear. After burial, the undertaker fed a rope from the coffin to a bell above ground. If an unfortunate soul woke up and realized their circumstances, they could pull on the rope and pray someone heard the bell.

Eamon had no rope and no second chance. He had been murderously angry since.

He didn't pray to any god in his last moments. Eamon wasn't a Christian. His mother was a Cailleach—a fancy word for witch—and he followed the old ways as well. Instead, he cast a spell that bound his soul to the mill forever and ever. To stay and exact revenge whenever an opportunity arose for the awful death he suffered. Three men died before they finished the mill and Eamon had a hand in each one. The foreman who left him for dead? He died when the bracing supporting a new brick wall failed.

That had been fecking hilarious. That wall squashed the dim bastard flatter than a pancake.

Eamon remained stuck underground, though. It seemed fitting since he died under the mill. He sensed the world in the mill above, but had no physical access to any of it.

For a long while, the cellars were interesting spaces to haunt and occupied his time nicely. Wandering the halls day and night, he was the boss, the gaffer. Occasionally, he spooked the people who worked there and created trouble when he could. After all, paper mills were dangerous places to work.

Then some silly wench died in the machinery room upstairs. She had the run of the mill, everything but the cellars. It seemed patently unfair. Why did she get the entire building when he was stuck down here? Worse, she seemed so nice, it was sickening. They called her the ghostly girl of the night shift, the star of the mill. What bollocks!

He discovered her name was Emma. She annoyed and aggravated him incessantly. He threw spells at her, but she seemed little affected by them.

At times, he mused about killing her and taking the place over.

Becoming the gaffer of the entire mill.

But how do you kill a dead person?

He didn't know.

Eamon still managed to cause trouble up above. He influenced the men who killed Frank. They had a secret meeting room in the cellar, and he encouraged them to deal with Frank in the sternest manner possible. And they did. Then they were caught and sent to prison. It was delicious. That had been one of his goals all along.

Poor old Frank? He learned the hard way about the consequences of flapping his gums. Of being a rat.

After Frank's death, they filled the staircase with cement and people no longer came down to the cellars. The closure seemed to weaken his magic powers as well. It was a real hardship. Life became unspeakably boring. Eventually, he couldn't stand the monotony and stopped walking the halls. He took a long nap and was oblivious to everything. For how long? He didn't know. It must have been years.

Then Chase Riddell reopened the cellars.

Soon after, Eamon awoke from his long rest. It took him awhile to rouse and become coherent again. He was rusty and could barely move, much less perform any magic.

But now, he felt much better; felt ready and able to stir the pot and create some trouble.

The crazy copper was the perfect vessel for his conniving. The man was a psycho when he walked through the door and Eamon enjoyed pushing him to ever greater recklessness.

The fool thought he was a bloody genius.

Ha!

So did the twits who shoved big daft Frank into the pulp vat.

While he plotted against Chase, he did enjoy their conversations. He liked American baseball. Watching it. Learning the rules. A pleasant break from the monotony of the preceding years. But Chase also rambled on about how he was saving mankind from women. Eamon hadn't much cared for colleens himself, or bitches as Chase called them, but he considered them too weak, too insignificant to be much trouble, anyway. Chase gave them far too much credit. It was fun to encourage his lunacy, though. After Megan, Chase hadn't been able to control himself, even though he supposedly knew better. Yeah, he was a big bad copper and knew *everything*. He even had rules for being a good psychopath.

Fecking idiot.

His ego would be his undoing. Eamon looked forward to it.

He could sense the drama affecting the rest of the building. Some bizarre event the other night had roiled the atmosphere in the building right down to the base of the foundations. He figured it was the wench upstairs, interfering and working against him. In time, she would get hers.

No matter. Down here, he ruled, and really?

He was just getting started.

Twenty-Nine

Martin pushed a mower across his lawn.

On a sunny Saturday afternoon, it felt good to be outdoors and away from work.

He owned an older three-bedroom ranch on the east side of town with room for the kids, though they didn't stay as often now. Cutting the grass was as domestic as he leaned. A maid service cleaned the house twice a month.

No dwelling on the case here. Sometimes it was best to walk away for a breather.

His phone pinged.

An email. The lab with preliminary DNA results. Wow! Just under twenty-four hours. Evidently, things were slow at Bio-Horizon.

Martin had been nervous about this moment. It would be all or nothing. He hoped for the latter.

No such luck.

The DNA recovered from the teeth matched the profile for Megan Rice.

Shit.

The finger bones would probably match too.

After the fleeting sense of triumph in finally catching a break in the case, sadness washed over him. He had never met Megan Rice, but she had become like a friend. They had delved deeply into her life, looking for clues, and now she was dead. In his mind, Megan had always been a woman, a mother, not a victim. Her death was tragic, and it angered him.

Martin jammed the phone back into his pocket and marched the mower around the rest of the yard, trying to burn off his ire, finishing in record time. Then he realized he had jumped the gun. Megan could still be alive. She could survive without two teeth and a couple of fingers. The odds were slim, but an uncertainty remained.

Given the location of the teeth and bones, he drew a more critical eye on the mill, wondering if they had missed something.

Martin stowed the mower and called Sam Farber with the results. Farber agreed the mill warranted further consideration, but wanted to bring in divers and conduct a new search along the river first. Given the ambiguity, he wanted to continue withholding the story from the press to keep people focused on Danielle. No point in alerting the suspect that they might be on to him either.

Farber closed by saying, "You need to talk to the family though. Soon."

Yes, he did. They had a right to know, but he dreaded it. They had remained firmly hopeful that Megan was alive, and now he would probably crush their hopes in delivering the worst news a family could receive. The lingering ambiguity would be particularly tough on them.

Once again, he considered the possibility they were dealing with a serial killer. Martin cracked a beer, sat at the kitchen table, and googled the term to refresh his memory on the subject with an eye to developing a suspect profile. He hadn't profiled lately and wanted to start with an informed set of ideas to avoid any preconceived notions about potential suspects—a fatal error in any investigation. He also remained mindful the two cases might be unrelated.

Martin started with a review of the common professions and career choices such people made. A fascinating subject by itself. Psychologists typically arranged serial killers into four broad skill groups.

In the professional and government employee categories, serial killers were often cops, security guards, military types, or religious officials. Most famous in the category was Joseph DeAngelo, the Golden State Killer, who had been a cop and served in the Navy.

Serial killers who worked in skilled occupations tended to be aircraft machinists or assemblers, repair people, or automobile upholsterers. In the semi-skilled trades, they might be arborists, truck drivers, or warehouse managers. Finally, those in the unskilled trades were often general laborers, hotel porters, and gas station attendants. The last group seemed vague, overly broad, and included large numbers of people. Too many to be useful.

The mill was an upscale place and seemed an unlikely home for a psychopath in the unskilled trades. Given the criteria he just reviewed, it certainly included people in the professional categories, but he could imagine no way a person could hold a hostage there.

He couldn't go through the mill questioning people based on a profile, not yet anyway. But the names of the people living in the mill were public record. Could they tie each resident to an occupation? They should try and he decided to assign the task to a junior detective, Alex Yang. It was a place to start.

Was he partly focused on the mill based on the dreams of a strange woman he found attractive?

It was possible. He was a normal guy. Once an attraction arose, reason often went out the window. Was he interested in Lili? He nodded to himself, recognizing the symptoms. He needed to suppress those feelings. She wasn't his type, and they had nothing in common. Evidently, he had been single a little too long. Martin resolved to be more dispassionate toward Miss Paltrinieri going forward.

He returned to the task at hand.

How had Megan's remains found their way into the river? If not the mill, what location farther up the river could be a dumping point?

Anywhere, he supposed. Done late at night, discreetly, anywhere. Someone could have dumped her over the side of a boat.

He assumed, based on the small pieces, she had been dismembered and cut up first, though boat propellers may have played a part too.

They needed to organize a new search of the riverbank. Call the sheriff to arrange for divers. Martin also wanted the blueprints for the mill. To make sure there was nothing hidden beneath the building—spaces or tunnels not connected to the floors above. The manager couldn't know the full history of the building. Could be lying, too. Martin could imagine many sins hidden beneath the floors of the mill.

Martin stepped into the shower before going to visit Megan's parents.

He knew nothing with certainty. Megan Rice might be dead, the victim of a homicide. Or still alive and being subjected to unspeakable acts? The idea she had bolted was off the table. There was a better chance Danielle Hamlin remained alive.

But he felt the walls closing in. Narrowing the options.

Until only bones and teeth remained.

Thirty

Lili woke at eight.

Her Xanax-induced sleep had been deep and dreamless.

Grabbing her iPad, she opened Word and left it on the island, hoping for another message—anything—from Emma.

The prospect of talking to a spirit through a tablet was exciting. She had so many questions. The girl died in 1894. How had she kept up on technology and learned to use an iPad? How did she interact with the screen?

Lili made coffee and a piece of toast and sat at the island.

When Emma failed to respond, she donned jeans and a dressy navy blue tee and walked to the foyer to scan the mailboxes.

The slot for unit 139 bore the name Riddell. She didn't recognize the name. Didn't know if they were male or female, but she would find out. The apartment lay at the east end of the main hallway, the door down a separate hall like the Kaplans'. Standing outside the unit, she detected no aura. Sensed nothing at all. She could stake the place out but risked drawing undue attention to herself, at least during the daytime.

Returning to her apartment, she googled Riddell. The name appeared only once locally. The police department website listed Chase Riddell as a patrol officer.

A cop?

He seemed an unlikely source of trouble. She had rather hoped some shady guy lived there and they could settle the case quickly.

Perhaps something was going on beneath his apartment and he was unaware of it. Would he be receptive to a search, knowing the stakes? It wasn't a large police department. Martin must know the guy.

Lili felt a contradiction in her thinking.

If something awful was happening beneath the apartment, how could he not know about it? Wouldn't he hear something?

Everyone insisted there was no basement. Except that Emma said there was a problem in the cellar. Many old buildings had crawl spaces under the floors. Is that what she was talking about?

Unbidden, the dark image of a medieval torture chamber hidden beneath the building popped into her brain. In it, Danielle was strapped to a table and screaming in pain. A profound shudder ran from head to toe. Lili shook her head to clear the vision. God, her imagination was a dreadful curse sometimes. It did remind her of the stakes, though.

Should she talk to Chase Riddell? What would be the harm? He'd want to know. Wouldn't he?

Unless he was the rapist.

No. He couldn't be. She couldn't accept that a small-town cop could be that evil. Or was she being naïve?

She decided to proceed carefully before approaching this Riddell character. Do a read outside the apartment tonight to assess before she took any other steps.

Lili thought about calling Martin but decided not to. The lead was too flimsy. She had nothing but an apartment number via a ghostly Ouija conversation on an iPad. He'd think she was a wacko and she would lose all credibility—if she hadn't already. But she had the sense Martin believed her, at least a little.

She would build a case carefully.

The knowledge that Danielle was being held and raped in that deplorable dungeon gnawed at her. She knew exactly how awful it was. How much longer did she have to live? Moving too slowly could be deadly. Blundering into things could get her killed.

It was all very stressful.

Right now, she had to focus and get ready for work. She wanted to cancel the day, but had too many people scheduled and had no idea when Emma would show up again. Logic suggested it would be later tonight.

She meditated briefly and hopped into the shower.

⋆ ⋆ ⋆

Two a.m.

The building was silent.

After work, Lili waited for hours. She set up her crystal and tried to connect through a séance, hoping to hear from Emma, but nothing happened. Not a peep. Finally, she gave up and left Word open on the iPad so Emma could leave a message if she returned.

Leaning against the wall of 139, Lili closed her eyes and shut off all extraneous thought. She worked a relaxation exercise, wiggling her toes, ankles, and knees, then worked the same routine up her arms.

If someone wandered through, they might assume she was drunk and had passed out. She shrugged. At this hour, everyone was probably sleeping. Unless Chase Riddell stepped out his door, she expected no interruptions.

Relaxed and focused, she fell into a trance. A little later, she felt the familiar disconnect as her mind drifted upward, left her body, and passed through the wall into the apartment.

The living room was a dark space with a strong male quality, the brick walls various shades of brown, the paint colors blue-greys, the decor steel and glass. Every room was spotless, the walls blank. Free weights and a treadmill took up a corner of the living room. Otherwise, not a single piece of art, nor a photograph. Nothing. Soulless. No clues about the true nature of the tenant. She saw no evidence of a stairway to a lower level, though she didn't understand how there could be. Her unit sat on a concrete slab. She assumed the rest of the building was the same—though maybe one existed here, beneath this apartment.

She drifted out, feeling little enlightened.

Maybe she needed to burrow beneath the floor. Try to glimpse the elusive basement. If she found it, could she then connect with Danielle?

She ran into a problem, a barrier of some sort. While free to roam the hallway and the adjoining spaces, she couldn't penetrate the floor. Completely resistant to her probing, it might as well have been steel.

It happened. She wasn't an expert in the art of astral projection and couldn't always visit the places she aspired to. Something to do with purity of thought. Perhaps her motives were the issue—though this felt different, like a force field protecting the basement. That alone made her suspicious.

Or was Emma wrong about the basement?

Regardless, she was going nowhere fast. Time for bed.

As Lili returned to her body, she glimpsed something tenuous. A dark and turbulent thing like a cloud, rushing at her.

What the—?

She was vulnerable in this state, and scrambling wasn't really possible during astral travel, but Lili found a way. She scuttled back to her body, jumped up, and tore down the hallway. Turning the corner, then the next, she quick-tapped her door code, flew through the opening, and slammed the door behind her. She fell on the sofa, gasping for breath.

Shit!

Was she safe now?

A minute passed and the building remained quiet. She couldn't really recall visually what she had seen. It was more like a feeling. An ominous premonition that things were about to go awry.

But she didn't believe in precognition.

Had she imagined it?

Probably. She was tired and susceptible to false impressions.

If there was a basement, it was hidden. Intentionally concealed. Emma might be her only source of information. Lili was still trying to wrap her head around that business. She'd had conversations with spirits in the past, but only while in a trance, as a part of a séance, or during astral travel. Those conversations had a surreal quality to them. Talking to Emma felt as real as texting a friend. Only with a ghost—*on an iPad!*

Still, she was no wiser than yesterday.

Lili tried to dismiss the feeling of impending trouble, clinging to the belief that Danielle was alive and could still be saved. She stripped and fell into bed, frustrated with the lack of communication from Emma and little sense of the situation in or under the Riddell apartment.

Dead tired, she had to work tomorrow.

Premonition or not, she feared Danielle was running out of time.

Thirty-One

Danielle stirred.

Shivering, she felt cold, sick, or both. The continuous stream of adrenaline from the ongoing assaults and constant terror of impending death had left her emotionally and physically ruined. The few hours of sleep had been dreamless and had restored her a little—a respite from the nightmare her life had become.

Her thinking felt confused and disordered. With the continual abuse, the lack of meaningful human interaction, and the loss of temporal awareness, it felt like the seventh circle of hell every moment she was awake. She often slipped into despair but fought it, hoping for a reprieve or a chance to escape.

A new resolve had taken hold while she slept. She sat up, determined to fight back even if she lost her life. Death had become less and less frightening in view of the continuing assaults. Soon, she would welcome it. The experience was dehumanizing. She felt like a caged animal, some feral creature being beaten into submission by an inhuman monster. Women who were trafficked for sex must feel like this. Nothing could be worse than this living horror show.

Other than instructions on what to do—or not to do—the man didn't speak. He never taunted her. He mumbled occasionally, incoherent words that seemed to be directed at himself. Treating her like a sex doll, he seemed otherwise oblivious to her pain and suffering. He seemed so indifferent that she couldn't tell if he hated women in general or just her. She wasn't certain he even saw her as real.

He smiled, though. The creepy, sadistic leer of a control freak who enjoyed dominating her and using her body in any way he desired.

Was it misogyny or something else that drove him? She couldn't know. Did it matter?

He looked vaguely familiar, but she couldn't place the face.

She knew one thing with certainty. Her abuser was a psychopath and would kill her when he grew tired of her. Yet he left her a blanket, water, and a box of crackers. Of course, they weren't for her comfort. They were simply there to keep her alive for his pleasure.

She tried to divine a vague sense of time and felt she might have as much as eight hours before the bastard returned.

Dani performed a careful search of her prison, determined to fight her way out or die trying. Her father had always taught her to use whatever was at hand.

There was a bucket to relieve herself. The bucket was padlocked to the wall. She tried wrenching it loose to no avail.

That left the mattress and the cot. The room was otherwise empty.

Danielle pulled the mattress onto the floor and sat on it, examining the frame of the cot inch by inch with her hands. It was cast angle-iron. The legs were welded to the frame. No bolts or fasteners anywhere. She yanked on each leg, but they felt solid, immovable. She flipped the frame over and wrenched on each leg again with maximum strength and better leverage.

The last leg moved a little. Or was she imagining it? Desperate, near despair, her mind might imagine just about anything, but right now, she had to believe there was a little play in the leg.

She positioned herself at the corner and braced the frame with her feet, focusing her strength into that leg.

It moved. Ever so slightly. Maybe a tenth of an inch.

Dani knew that small amount of play would weaken the weld with sufficient time and energy. Working it back and forth, she concentrated on forceful moves, not speed. She wrenched on it for ten or fifteen minutes to little avail. Maybe she had increased the range of motion slightly. In any other circumstance, she would have given it up as a lost cause, having little patience for tedious tasks.

Today, she had patience to spare. She would get that damned leg off the cot or die trying. Funny how the threat of further abuse and death had honed her concentration.

Dani worked in quick shifts, four to five minutes at a time. Her hands grew sore and tired. After about thirty minutes, the leg moved a quarter of an inch from side to side. Soon, the wobble was greater than half an inch. Her hands felt bruised, but the weld to the frame was failing, the metal warm from working it so intensely. For the first time in days, she felt the merest sliver of hope.

With another excruciating burst of effort, one weld broke, followed by the other. When the leg pulled loose, she lay back on the mattress and cried.

She might have dozed for a bit.

When Danielle startled awake, she was still gripping the chunk of iron.

Shaking her head to clear the fog, she stood and imagined a way to wield that piece of metal to inflict the maximum damage. Now armed, her smoldering rage grew, and she felt fully capable of murder.

The leg didn't feel sufficiently sharp to use as a stabbing weapon—she doubted she had the strength to cut him deeply enough to disable him. As a club, Dani thought she could swing it with ample force to knock him out. Hard enough to bash his miserable skull to a bloody pulp.

Dani flipped the frame again, dragged the mattress onto it, and balanced it, concealing the missing leg. Then she practiced, swinging the makeshift club, learning to handle the heft. She pictured him walking through the door, the element of surprise on her side. Lunging and striking him again and again. Picturing a successful outcome, a technique that served her well in life.

She would knock him out. Kill him if need be. Escape and find help.

Be free and live again.

Dani had to believe she could prevail. She knew she had exactly one shot at this.

The element of surprise. Speed. Resolve—

Danielle heard the familiar sound of his footsteps approaching.

She wasn't afraid anymore.

In a few minutes, one of them would be dead.

Thirty-Two

Martin walked along the river.

The day was hot. Too hot for this kind of detail. The sun shone down mercilessly, the sky devoid of clouds.

Search teams walked both banks of the river upstream of the spot where Megan's teeth were discovered. Another team had searched the trails and paths in Rock River Park, eighty-four acres of park and woodland on the north side of the river and the most likely point of abduction for Danielle.

Those areas had been searched once, but with the discovery of Megan's teeth, Sam Farber insisted they scour them again.

In the river, a diver worked the area where the teeth and bones had been found. The county had six trained divers, but between vacation and other, more pressing cases, they could only spare one officer.

Their combined efforts had been fruitless. Nothing on the banks, nothing on the trails. Martin had no expectations. The trails were busy at this time of year. Any evidence had been trampled underfoot. Still, he was discouraged by their lack of progress and remained troubled by the ambiguity of Megan's status, which, like Schrödinger's cat, left her both dead and alive.

He was reasonably certain they were looking for a serial rapist and murderer who was just getting started or had recently moved to the area. It was possible that Danielle was still alive. The scenario that Lili Paltrinieri described kept coming back to him.

An awful possibility.

He felt time slipping away, and hope for Danielle growing slimmer every hour the search ground on.

He couldn't stop thinking about the mill. Sadly, two teeth and three finger bones weren't much to go on. There was little reason to suspect the building other than proximity to the river and the suggestion from Lili. He shied away from her ideas even though he had a gut feeling she might be right.

He shook his head. It was illogical.

Thanks to Alex Yang and hours of overtime, they now had an unofficial tenant list for the mill. Alex was still at work, running background checks and attaching an occupation to each name. Thus far, the search had revealed nothing significant beyond the usual youthful indiscretions and two OWIs.

As a list of possible suspects, it wasn't promising, but included Chase Riddell, a patrol cop. Technically, he fit the profile. And while the guy didn't seem like a budding serial killer to Martin, he was a bit of an odd duck with a detached affect. Martin also suspected the man had a hidden streak of misogyny from the way he looked at women, especially women of rank. A subtle look, a microexpression of scorn.

He had met plenty of men like Riddell, but they weren't serial killers, just unenlightened men who considered women inferior. Neanderthals.

Still, he couldn't ignore the connection. Then he wondered: how could a patrol cop afford a place in Rock River Mills?

A hundred yards up, the diver emerged from the water and waded to shore, holding several Ziploc bags. Low-tech, they worked well for underwater evidence collection. He must have found something.

He met the diver, Dave something-or-other, at the water's edge. "What did you find?"

The guy slipped his full-face mask off and held the bags up. "A few small bones, a tooth, and about half of a mandible."

Martin looked at him quizzically.

"Lower jawbone."

Martin considered the discovery for a moment and realized the ambiguity had probably been resolved.

Shit.

That piece of bone might be the final nail in Megan's coffin. A few teeth and finger bones were one thing, but a piece of her jaw would seal the deal if the bone proved to be Megan's.

She was probably dead. The pressure to find Danielle never felt greater. Or more urgent. He didn't want to even consider the possibility that the jawbone was hers—or that of a third woman.

Just then, a hot dog driving a boat went flying down the center of the river, violating the *No-Wake* rule.

"Jackass." The diver flipped a middle finger in their direction. "Idiots like that make diving in the river dangerous."

Martin nodded and smirked, amused by the gesture. Dave had a temper. Staring upstream, he noticed a concrete sewer pipe exiting the foundation of the mill. The opening lay below the waterline, but as the wake swept along the foundation, the maw of the pipe was briefly visible.

He stared for a moment, tuning the diver out, and had an *aha* moment.

Maybe that pipe was how Megan got into the river. Did they still have a chance to find Danielle alive—?

"You okay, Detective?" The diver looked at him quizzically.

"Yes. I just had an idea. We appreciate your help. Done for the day?"

"I am. I'll be back tomorrow."

"Good. I'll get that stuff over to the forensic pathologist."

Martin took the bag and they shook hands.

He needed to call the pathologist and plan another visit to Megan's family once the find was confirmed. The case was probably now a homicide. And he needed to check back with Alex Yang to start digging deeper into that list, starting with Chase Riddell.

Danielle Hamlin felt like a time bomb ticking in his head.

And the clock was nearing zero.

Thirty-Three

Chase felt a pleasant tingle in his groin.

It quickly grew to an urgent need. The woman still aroused him deeply. He anticipated a long session today.

With his phone, he set the alarm system and turned the lights off. He clicked the OnGard door brace into place, physically restraining the steel door. He had bolted the receptacle into the floor and it would withstand heavy abuse, even a police battering ram.

In the bathroom, Chase lifted the carpet strip and baseboard pieces, then rolled the flooring back. He popped the latch and lifted the door. It was heavy, and he had insulated the underside with foam to dampen footsteps on the door. A person walking in the bathroom would have no clue it was there. It also helped soundproof his activities in the basement.

Clambering down the stair rungs, he paused and pulled the trapdoor shut, then slid the bolt to the locked position.

He walked to the door, rapped sharply, and said, "Sit on the side of the bed."

He slid the bolt back and pushed the door open. Danielle was sitting on the side of the bed as instructed, looking down, docile. Crushed. He had been explicit and graphic in the first few days of captivity, describing just how badly she would be punished if she resisted.

As he stepped into the room, she leapt up with surprising speed and lunged at him.

Shit!

A weapon in her hand—?

Something solid struck his head with a stunning blow. He lurched back as she wound up and struck again, hitting his shoulder.

Jesus!

She was crazy. What in the hell did she have? He threw his arms up, off balance and on the defensive, thoroughly shocked by the sudden turn of events. He hadn't imagined her capable of such willfulness and violence. She had been obedient until now.

Making feral noises, Danielle swung again and again, hitting his arms and hands, driving him back into a defensive posture. As he tried a counterattack, she landed another blow to his head. The side of it felt wet. Dripping wet.

Blood.

She jabbed his gut high, near the solar plexus, stunning him, then dashed past him toward the light.

He reached to grab her, but she swung the object with considerable force, smashing his hand and fingers.

Oh fuck, that hurt!

Chase was off balance, mentally and physically. He had been so damned sure of himself.

Jesus! She was running for the stairs! If she got out—

A gush of horror and nausea ran through him. He could scarcely believe the turn of events. Chase ran after her, closed within reach, and shoved her shoulders as hard as he could.

She stumbled but stayed on her feet. He remembered she was a runner and very fit.

Damn it!

Was this how it was going to end? One resourceful girl, an inattentive moment, and a stupid mistake on his part? He would look like an idiot. Women were only this capable in movies and on TV and it was a huge lie.

She reached the rungs and scrambled up. Slammed the bolt back and pushed up on the door.

Shit! She was almost out of the basement!

With a desperate flying lunge, he grabbed the nearest elbow and yanked her back. Hard.

Danielle lost her grip. Her foot caught on the rung and snagged as she fell backwards in an arc, her head hitting the concrete floor with a sickening, wet crunch.

Insane with anger, he turned and kicked her, before focusing enough to see she was unconscious, maybe dead. A small pool of blood grew beneath her head.

"Fuck!"

He kicked her again.

"Bitch!"

Her eyes opened and fixed on him. For a moment, he thought she might make it, but no, the light in her eyes was fading, her lips moving silently as the pool of blood spread around her broken head.

He leaned over.

She murmured two words with a hiss: "Fuck you."

Danielle died with an exhaled sigh and a slump of her shoulders, eyes staring at him with final reproach.

Mocking him.

Fuck!

His anger swelled in a giant wave. The bitch had beaten him and ended the relationship on her terms.

He kicked her again and again, but it was a futile act.

She was dead. Was she smiling a little?

Chase tried to regroup but couldn't get past his anger. Danielle was dead, but not the way he'd planned. He wasn't done with her.

Shit! Shit! Shit!

He spun in a circle, trying to get his head around this disaster.

He had to get rid of her. Simple enough, but a chore. Where the hell was Eamon? Great fucking friend. Never around when you needed him. He really wanted a sympathetic ear right now. Chase felt pressure building from all corners.

Three of Megan's bones and two teeth had been found in the river. Unbelievable, really. What were the odds? Still, they wouldn't point back to him.

He had also heard Martin was assembling a list of tenants. The new kid, Alex Yang, was working on it. Why? Building a profile?

The more disturbing story was the psychic living in his building. He knew her name now.

Lili Paltrinieri. He'd checked her out and discovered she lived in 124. Her name had quietly filtered through the department. It shouldn't have, but it did.

Could she be psychic? Was that possible? Could she identify him personally?

He thought it was bullshit, but a fragment of doubt ate at him.

Chase couldn't take any chances.

Suddenly, the anger rose and exploded outward in a primal scream. He kicked Danielle again.

"Fuck!"

As his head cleared, the blame for everything that had gone wrong fell squarely on Lili Paltrinieri. She was responsible. She was messing with his life and needed to pay for it.

He had to settle the score.

And he would.

Thirty-Four

Frank felt fearful.

Something—a violent death he assumed—had roiled the atmosphere in the building. He remembered the feeling from the day Tommy died, though this felt more intense.

After the exorcism, he had been content to lay low. He didn't need the trouble and had concluded that interacting with the living was dangerous. But sitting still wasn't his style. The room felt too confining. He needed to move around to create at least the illusion of space.

A strange, growing undercurrent in the mill made him feel uneasy as well. Emanating from beneath the floor, it seemed to have intelligence of its own, a malign consciousness capable of evil. A beast of some sort. It chafed at him, a constant sense of irritation. The only thing that eased the discomfort was motion, so he wandered his space incessantly. Haunting the tenants provided an added distraction.

Frank purposefully created small eddies in his wake, stirring the curtains. He became more adept at recognizing the movements of the two people who were trespassing in his domain. The guy seemed oblivious to his presence but the woman was acutely aware of the slightest change in her environment, reacting whenever the curtains moved.

Just for fun, he wandered into the bathroom just as the woman stepped out of the shower. He blew on her neck and stared into the mirror, trying to project his image onto it, which appeared faintly on the steamy glass. Suddenly, she screeched, grabbed a towel, and ran out of the room.

Ha!

When the woman burned the paper that looked like money, he blew it out.

That was funny too.

And probably a bad idea. He was being reckless. No point in pushing the evidence of his presence. That was just inviting trouble or another exorcism.

But he couldn't stop. When he did, the disturbing vibrations returned to the fore, making him jumpy and uncomfortable.

Frank wanted to believe that if the exorcism guy showed up again, he would scare the bejesus out of him and chase the bastard off. The two living souls here would just have to live with him. After all, he was here first.

He wanted to fight for what was his, though really, he worried about another exorcism.

And he was afraid of the beast in the basement.

* * *

At rest in the skylight outside the door of 222, Emma felt a powerful surge of negative energy pass through the mill.

Someone had died. Violently.

She knew the feeling well, a sensation similar to the ones she felt after Frank was murdered and Tommy died in the machine. But when she drifted around the various hallways of the building, nothing looked amiss. No crowds of onlookers, no police, no ambulance, no medical people rushing in.

The disturbance was strongest around unit 139. More so inside. The apartment itself was quiet, the door in the bathroom floor closed and concealed. Still, whatever the cause of the disturbance, Emma felt certain it originated in the cellar beneath the apartment.

It had to be the missing girl. While she had no direct evidence of it, Emma knew she was dead.

Over the past few days, things had been peculiar. Besides her inability to manipulate the iPad, she'd had difficulty reading and minimal power to move objects. Whatever the rules were in the mill, they made little sense and changed without notice. There were no books on the subject. No ghosts to talk to. She could only assume this experience was unique to her. Frank had his own reality. Same for Tommy. Strangely, he had never caused any trouble, evidently choosing to maintain a low profile.

Some other force was rising. But who? Frank? The guy in the cellar?

Emma believed that might be the answer. That for some reason, the man had woken up and was looking for trouble. Did he hope to challenge Emma directly?

She had to try talking to Lili again. Maybe resort to something more primitive. Like a scrawl on a mirror or a trail of breadcrumbs to 139. Or should she just risk talking to her? But when she went to 124, the apartment was empty and Lili was gone. She was probably at work. Emma would come back later.

Still, it felt like someone or something was conspiring to keep her from communicating with Lili.

Perhaps she was breaking some unwritten rules by doing so.

Or maybe she just needed to try harder.

⋆ ⋆ ⋆

His plans were proceeding perfectly.

Eamon had to chalk one up for the colleen in the cellar, though. She might be dead, but she had exited on her terms. His 'friend' was now extremely angry and easily prodded into ever more desperate acts. Eamon had some ideas about where to direct that malignant energy. He hadn't had this much fun since Frank died in the pulp vat and those four goons went to prison.

The annoying little wench upstairs was causing trouble as well. He'd taken a shot at her, trying to neutralize her by disrupting the energy fields in unexpected ways, using some of dear old Mum's magic. His mother had been a miserable whore, but she knew how to throw a good spell.

He couldn't leave the cellar yet, but with magic, he could extend his reach beyond the ceiling overhead, though his skills were still rusty. He needed to practice more before he could take on dear little Emma, but wanted to believe he had a shot at getting out of the cellar.

Then he decided to throw down the gauntlet and challenge her directly.

What the hell.

I'm coming for you, bitch.

Ha!

Meanwhile, Chase was coming unglued, obsessing over some woman who was supposedly psychic.

She probably was. Eamon believed in such things.

Why not? He was dead, yet here he was, stirring up trouble.

He had suggested to Chase that grabbing the psychic woman would reduce his risk of exposure. And he would strike a blow for men everywhere by taking her and teaching her a lesson.

Being the devil's advocate, he had also suggested that when the coppers came for him, he should fight back and go out in a blaze of glory. The fool was actually considering it!

Shit would hit the fan soon, one way or another.

Eamon planned to sit back and enjoy the show.

He just wished he had some popcorn.

Thirty-Five

Lili woke with a start.

She literally jumped out of bed, ending the horrendous sensation of falling off a cliff. The descent had lasted forever.

Putting her head in her hands, she tried to ground herself, feeling unnerved and adrift.

Twenty-four hours had passed and she had accomplished nothing. Work had been busy, and she'd spent a fruitless evening waiting for a message or some sign from Emma. She knew nothing more about the business in 139, not even an inkling. As far as she knew, Martin and the police hadn't acted on her tip. The sensation that something was about to happen had passed.

That only increased her anxiety. What was she missing?

She had finally taken a Xanax and passed out, but the drug hadn't worked for long. Her sleep was disturbed by an endless procession of dreams in which she was falling, followed by a bizarre voice yelling at her in the dark: *I'm coming for you, bitch.*

She didn't know what that was about. It scared and unnerved her even more. As just one more element in a crazy quilt of nightmares, it might mean nothing, but after seven hours of disrupted sleep, she felt barely rested and ill-prepared for work.

There was a loud knock on her door as she sat down with her coffee.

"Lili!"

Raleigh. Great. Just what she wanted this morning.

She pulled the door open and said with some edge, "What's up, Raleigh?"

"Frank's back."

"Seriously?"

"Olivia thinks so," he said with a none-too-subtle roll of the eyes.

Ass.

"So the exorcism didn't work," Lili said, mostly to herself.

"You know how I feel about that nonsense."

"Then why are you here?" Lili snapped. She had little patience for Raleigh today.

"She's been seeing Frank more and more. Says he's following her." Raleigh scratched the side of his head in a goofy "aw shucks" routine. "Can you come and do something?"

She didn't feel like doing Raleigh any favors, but worried about Olivia.

"Sure. Around eight, after work." She agreed just to get him out of her face. A bad feeling had been stealing over her since waking. A black mood. The feeling time had run out for Danielle.

A dread that persisted until she left the building.

⋆ ⋆ ⋆

Lili knocked on the Kaplans' door at eight sharp.

Raleigh showed her in without a word. Olivia paced by the fireplace, the atmosphere tense and moody.

Pointing to the dining room table, he said, "You can set up there. I'm going to stay and watch if that's okay."

"No problem. I just need you to keep quiet."

Lili set out her crystal ball, the spare. The new one hadn't arrived yet. She felt distracted, trying to fathom why Frank had returned despite his earlier promises; angry that Emma had disappeared at the worst possible moment. Had things become so unsettled that Frank couldn't help it? Mostly, she fretted it was too late to save Danielle.

With all that stress, she didn't need Raleigh's attitude and Olivia's neediness. She began to think they deserved Frank.

But that was a crappy thought. Part of the irascible mood she had been unable to shake all day.

They settled in. Raleigh on the sofa, his face set in an impatient frown. Lili and a nervous Olivia faced each other at the table. Lili lit three white candles, set out a food offering of two dinner rolls, and silenced Olivia with a finger to her lips.

Lili, holding one of Olivia's hands, allowed herself to relax. Cleared her mind. It was difficult, given the atmosphere in the room, the tension in her body. Ten minutes passed and Raleigh started to say something.

"Shh!" Lili held a forefinger up in reproach.

She tuned him out. Let herself slip into a hypnotic state until her consciousness was hovering just inside the crystal. The grim, grey overlay of the factory resolved out of the mists. The room looked empty.

"Frank? Are you here?"

Silence.

But she sensed a slight disturbance at the periphery of her vision. He was present but avoiding her.

"Frank. Talk to me. I mean you no harm."

The slight disturbance continued, and Lili remained silent, exerting no pressure on him, giving him time to trust her.

A minute later, he spoke in a soft, low voice. *Then leave me alone.*

Olivia's light grip remained unchanged. She hadn't heard it. Good.

"We want to, but why are you bothering Olivia again?"

Olivia's grip tightened.

Restless. Uneasy.

"Because people are living in this space?"

Yes. No. He had moved closer, but remained little more than a shadow.

"The exorcism?"

Yes.

"We won't do that again." She then wondered if that was the reason Emma refused to talk to her. Was it fear of an exorcism?

Might have to. Something else is here now.

Someone else was here? What was he talking about?

"Emma?"

No. Basement.

Holy crap! Frank felt it too. But what basement? There had to be hidden spaces under the floors. How could she convince Martin of the danger?

"Eamon O'Keene?"

Scared.

Then he was gone. He simply evaporated. "Frank?"

Silence.

"Frank?"

Frank was afraid of something?

Shit!

What could a ghost be afraid of? What would she tell Olivia? Lili felt an apprehensive shudder pass through her. Her skin broke out with goosebumps. She thought of the old phrase, *someone walking on my grave,* and understood the feeling implicitly.

She came back to earth and, with little thought, blurted, "You two need to get out of here for a few days."

Raleigh leapt up from the couch. "What?"

Olivia grabbed her hand. "What did he tell you?"

"Frank's acting up because he's afraid."

Raleigh marched over to the table, his face an angry scowl. "Frank the ghost is afraid? Are you crazy? Get out!"

He blew her candles out and shoved them in her bag while she hurriedly packed up the crystal ball. He nudged her toward the door. "Bye, Lili! Don't let the door hit you in the ass."

He slammed the door as she scurried down the hallway.

She could hear them fighting as she retreated to her apartment. Poor Olivia! Lili texted her door code to Olivia in case she needed to leave for a while. Tonight, Lili would welcome the company.

Jesus!

She was now sure of only one thing.

Raleigh Kaplan was a complete asshole.

Thirty-Six

Chase knew he was out of control.

Taking Danielle had been a delicious but inordinate risk. Now she was gone. The satisfaction and pleasure in taking her had been ruined when she disobeyed him and tried to escape. He couldn't believe he had been outsmarted by a girl, but then realized he hadn't. She had help. That fucking psychic woman had somehow contrived to help Danielle. It was the only plausible explanation.

The story of Megan's death had also broken. A diver had found more remains—a jawbone identified through dental records and other, unnamed bones. It felt like the jig was up. How long before they started looking at the mill more seriously? Still, there was little chance any of it would trace back to him.

He needed to chill out and keep his composure.

It was difficult given the setbacks of the past few days. Danielle's unexpected death. The discovery of Megan's remains. Alex Yang's probe of the Mill residents.

Chase had worked his overnight shift and then spent the day disposing of Danielle. When necessary, he could stay awake for days to accomplish any task. He knew how to apply concealer and makeup to cover up any signs of fatigue, like grey skin or rings under his eyes. He usually looked great, but last night had been a challenge. His hand was bruised where Danielle had hit him and he struggled to keep it hidden. Luckily, the area on his scalp where she drew blood was concealed by hair. His aches were a none too subtle reminder of the beating he took from a girl.

Bitch.

Disposing of a body wasn't difficult and he wasn't squeamish. As a hunter, he was accustomed to gutting and dismembering animals. There wasn't much difference between a human body and a deer or bear carcass.

He threw the body parts into five-gallon plastic buckets filled with warm water and lye. The sodium hydroxide would dissolve the body parts in about six to eight hours, leaving a harmless, untraceable liquid that he then poured down the drain. A liquid that would disappear in the river.

Bone fragments and teeth remained after the process and last time, Chase had tossed them into the drain, assuming they would disappear into the riverbed. Who could have guessed someone would go diving and find them? He needed a new plan for Danielle's bones and teeth.

All the while, his friend kept bothering him.

You were reckless, mate. You're gonna get caught.

"Yeah, thanks for stating the obvious, buddy."

On and on it went. It was so fucking annoying.

But what if Martin did figure it out?

Chase had taken some steps to set up an escape. A secret path out of the basement into one of the apartments. Money deposited in an account under an alias. A car stashed nearby with another five grand hidden in the seats, registered in the name of his dead Aunt Karen. He had prepared for most contingencies but didn't have a definitive plan to relocate with a new identity.

Truthfully, he never expected to reach a point where he might be implicated. He was too damned smart and had been feeling invincible. These setbacks had caught him off guard. He'd underestimated the blowback from the incompetents around him.

While he finished up with Danielle, he considered the options with a depressive slant.

It felt like the end was closing in.

How did he go so badly off the rails, so far from his well-laid plans?

He feared escape might be futile. In the tech era, flight was essentially impossible without an exceptionally well-considered escape plan, executed *before* the police realized a suspect was running.

Facial recognition, closed-circuit cameras, phone tracing were exceptionally difficult to beat—he would need a new identity, and he had nothing in place beyond the vehicle, some cash, and a fake ID.

Was he already under surveillance?

Chase took a deep breath to relax.

He didn't think so. He knew what to look for and had seen no evidence of it.

If the worst came to pass, suicide was an option, but he also considered exiting in a blaze of glory. If need be, he could mount a last stand. He had plenty of weapons and ammo stockpiled. Plenty of provisions, too. Eamon had tried to convince him that fighting was the noblest course, but Chase decided that was a load of shit. There was nothing noble about being dead.

He hoped none of it would come to pass. He had to remember that nothing pointed to him.

Nothing.

Once he had fully disposed of Danielle, he would lay low for a while. A *long* while. Six months, a year, whatever it took for interest in the case to wane and the investigation to go cold.

Except that he kept thinking about that psychic bitch. It gnawed at him. What could she know?

Nothing.

If they were on to him, an entry team would be at the door. He hadn't been fingered. That was the obvious and sane conclusion.

Taking her would be a mistake. They would tear the mill apart.

He had to chill out. Get his confidence back.

These fucking nerves would be the end of him.

Finished with Danielle, he pulled the Stoli from the freezer, poured three fingers, and sat in his deck chair. Took a long draw of the ice-cold alcohol and closed his eyes. Felt it sink into the pit of his stomach, the warmth spreading through his body.

The sensation settled his nerves.

A grumpy Eamon suddenly chimed in. "Where's mine, you wanker?"

"Didn't know you were here." Chase poured a finger and set the glass across the table.

"Got her all cleaned up?"

"Mostly. She's slowly dissolving in the buckets."

"You fucked that up, didn't you?"

"Yeah, thanks for the support, buddy," Chase said with a snarky edge.

"What are you going to do when they come for you?"

"They're not coming. They have no clue."

"Keep telling yourself that, matey."

"You're not much fucking help." Chase swallowed the rest of his vodka and slammed his glass down. "Later, dude."

Eamon merely laughed.

Chase slammed the trapdoor shut, rolled the flooring out, and replaced the baseboard and carpet strip.

A shower, a couple hours of sleep, and he would go in and work his shift.

Regain his composure. Carry on normally.

Most of all, stop listening to his friend in the basement.

That idiot was nothing but a downer.

Thirty-Seven

Martin sat in his office.

Lately, it felt like he lived there.

Based upon accumulating circumstantial evidence and a persistent gut feeling, his focus now fell exclusively on Rock River Mills. While the floor plans revealed no rooms or stairs beneath the building, he believed crawl spaces hidden by the renovations might exist. If so, the engineering consultant would know about them.

He perused the mill website, finding the number for Apex Engineering in Madison, the general contractor. A company operator provided a cell phone number for Dominic Garcia, the chief engineering consultant on the project.

Martin wanted to interview him in person to watch his face and body language. He punched the number into his office phone and a moment later, a man with a deep voice answered. "Hello, Garcia."

"Mr. Garcia, this is Martin Kettridge with the Ash Grove Police Department. I have some questions about Rock River Mills. It's a matter of some urgency. Could we meet somewhere this afternoon to chat?"

There was a long pause until Martin said, "Mr. Garcia?"

"Sorry, I was just thinking. There's a travel center just west of the interstate in Woodlawn. Could we meet there?"

Martin looked at a map. It was about thirty minutes away. "Sounds good. About an hour?"

"Sure. I'll be wearing a blue shirt with an Apex Engineering logo."

⋆ ⋆ ⋆

Martin pulled into the travel center an hour later. A glorified truck stop, the coffee brewing smelled good and the donuts looked fresh. He needed a boost right about now and had no issue with the stereotype about cops and donuts. Who didn't love donuts, especially Krispy Kremes?

While he waited for his order, he spotted Dominic Garcia sitting in a booth near the cash register. Thin, with a narrow face and dark hair, he looked about forty. Martin imagined women found him quite attractive.

He stood as Martin approached. The guy was tall, maybe six-three.

"Thanks for meeting me on such short notice," Martin said as they shook hands and sat down.

"No problem. I'm curious to know what's so urgent."

Dominic seemed congenial enough, but had a wary air about him, gripping his coffee mug with two hands.

Martin sipped his coffee and jumped right in. "I know that sometimes, you guys find things on a project that might delay construction. I also know that sometimes, you opt to cover them up and move on. Usually, it's borderline stuff; no harm, no foul."

Martin watched Dominic carefully, sensing he was on the right track. "I don't care if that was the case at Rock River Mills. I don't care what you guys papered over during the renovation. I have no intention of making any waves—unless you guys did something blatantly illegal."

Dominic Garcia eyed him for a long moment, weighing his response. Martin could see the wheels turning.

Finally, Dominic said, "There were some rooms and hallways beneath the building that were deemed—unimportant. They didn't appear on the original blueprints and weren't structurally significant."

"How did they go undetected during the design phase?" Martin maintained eye contact and took a bite of his donut. This sounded promising.

"We found them by accident when we replaced the flooring in some of the ground floor units. Most of the building rests on a concrete slab. The slab and foundation were sound, so we had no reason to expect anything but crawl spaces beneath the areas where the floors had been framed with wood. The hallways looked like leftovers from the original construction and had been closed off. There were stairs at one time, but the stairwell was filled with concrete and covered with flooring. As I said, they were deemed unimportant and had no impact on the finished apartments."

"How many units had wood-framed floors?"

Dominic paused and drank from his mug. "Four. We laid new subfloor followed by hardwood, ceramic tile, or luxury vinyl in all four. There's no access to those hallways from anywhere in the building."

"None?"

"No."

That didn't sound promising. Martin felt a good lead slipping away.

Dominic eyed him intently. "What makes this so urgent? What do you suspect?"

"A possible connection to a criminal case. I can't discuss the details. I wonder, could those passages be used for—criminal activity?"

"I don't see how." Dominic scratched his wrist and looked out the window. "As I said, there's no access."

"Which apartments had wooden floors?"

"I honestly don't remember. I can look it up when I return to the office."

"I would appreciate it if you would." Martin suspected Garcia knew something and was holding back. "What was the extent of the hallways?"

"They run the length of the building, two corridors, just inside the foundations. There are a few rooms on the east end of the building as well." Dominic then asked, "What sort of criminal activity?"

"Abduction. Murder."

Dominic stopped mid-sip. "That missing woman?"

"I can't comment on an ongoing case."

Garcia stared out the window and rubbed his neck. He turned, his lips pursed. "Then there's something you need to know."

Martin raised his eyebrows with a questioning look as he bit into his donut.

"One of the tenants knows about the basement spaces. One of your guys."

Martin felt his hackles tighten. "Who?"

"Chase Rider—Riddell. Something like that."

Shit.

"How does he know?"

"During the renovation, some of us went to O'Malley's quite a bit. I met him there. He acted like we were best buds, but I found him a bit odd. One night, after winning a sizable football pool, I drank too much and told him about the basement passages."

Martin nodded. That Chase knew about the basement was more than coincidental. Martin looked at his watch. He had dinner planned with his kids and it was getting late. "Thanks for the meeting, Dominic. I've got to run."

"Good luck, Detective."

Martin strode to his car, weighing the conversation with Dominic. Yesterday, he'd considered Chase unlikely as a murderer. He was disturbed that his intuition had failed him because Chase Riddell suddenly looked very interesting.

In fact, he looked like a suspect.

Thirty-Eight

Lili woke at seven.

Her sleep had been dreamless. The lack of nightmares only confirmed her worst suspicions.

Danielle was dead.

Lili lay there with no interest in getting out of bed, feeling a sick, sinking sensation in her gut.

The woman had been kidnapped, raped, and murdered, and they had failed to save her.

Or had she imagined it all? Was she actually suffering from mental illness? Having a psychotic break?

So strange had the past few days been, she no longer knew which reality was true.

A fork flew off the island and clattered on the floor.

What?

Evidently, she wasn't alone.

"Emma?"

A moment later, a spoon followed suit.

She jumped out of bed. Lili grabbed her iPad, logged into Word, and laid the device on top of the island. Over the next ten seconds, three numbers appeared.

1 3 9.

Lili said, "What about 139?"

she's dead

Lili paused. As much as she sensed Danielle was dead, this confirmation made her feel ill. Quietly, she said, "I know. We were too late. Where have you been?"

Slowly, the words appeared.

couldn't talk sorry

Then it occurred to Lili that Emma might know who took Danielle. "Who did it?"

the man 139

"Chase Riddell?"

i think so couldn't see

She couldn't see? What did that mean? Had Emma been blocked from looking under the floor too?

But Lili was awed and distracted by the realization that she was talking to a ghost through an iPad. She had so many questions, starting with the big one.

"Why won't you talk to me?"

tired later

The app closed by itself a second later.

Tired? Ghosts could wear themselves out? She never considered that ghosts needed to rest, had no idea how much effort or energy was required to interact with the living. Why not? It made sense. Staring into space, Lili attempted to parse the experience with Emma and the gut-wrenching confirmation that Danielle was dead.

Emma thought that Chase Riddell was probably the killer and Lili believed her.

Suddenly, her anger erupted in a red rage. A virulent, blind anger. She had firsthand knowledge of the many ways Danielle had suffered before she died. Maybe Chase Riddell did it, maybe he didn't, but if she confronted him, she would know.

Lili hopped into her jeans and a black tee, and strode down to the lobby and pressed the bell for 139. When no one answered, she walked to the unit and banged on the door.

Still no answer. No sound at all from inside.

Leaning her forehead against the wall, she probed the apartment, but only sensed things she already knew. Dani was dead—a residual energy that seemed more like the power of suggestion than fact. And something dark lurking in the basement. A feeling she didn't understand. A presence that even Frank was afraid of.

The mysterious Eamon O'Keene?

Lili suddenly realized she had lost her mind.

Angrily pursuing a man who may have raped and murdered one woman, possibly two? She had forgotten about the Megan Rice story until the media revived it with the recovery of some of her remains. What was she going to say if he answered?

She peeled away from the wall and made a rapid but nonchalant retreat to her apartment, grateful he hadn't answered the door.

Lili then recognized that lashing out was the outward expression of the fear and horror she had experienced in her nightmares. Still, was she suicidal? That was entirely the wrong way to handle things.

Better to call Martin. He might think she was crazy. She didn't care, feeling compelled to do something. Still, an annoying voice in her head suggested that she had lost the plot.

Martin answered, sounding distracted. He agreed to see her at 11:30.

As she prepared to leave for the police station and work, someone knocked on the door.

Now what?

She had an anxious moment, wondering if Chase Riddell had come looking for her. Or maybe Raleigh wanted to bitch at her again.

Checking the peephole, she let out a sigh of relief.

Olivia.

Lili pulled the door open. “What’s up, sweetie?”

“Raleigh’s being an ass and we’re fighting.” Olivia held up her laptop. “Can I take you up on your offer to stay for a few hours?”

“Sure. I have to go work, but you’re welcome to stay.” Lili vacillated for a moment, then decided to say nothing about Danielle or the appointment with Martin. Poor girl had enough on her mind.

Lili walked around, gathering her things. “Help yourself to the wine and snacks.”

“Oh, thank you.” Olivia’s shoulders slumped in relief. She walked over and settled in front of the TV.

Lili checked her look in the mirror, and added, “Stay the night if you need to.”

Grabbing her phone, she rushed out the door, worried she’d be late.

One way or another, she would get justice for Danielle Hamlin.

Even if she had to arrest Chase Riddell herself.

Thirty-Nine

Martin scribbled on his blotter.

Random notes, circled names, connecting lines and arrows, most pointing to the word *Mill*.

Normally a calm, methodical thinker, his mind was racing out of control.

After the meeting with Dominic Garcia, he was obsessing over Chase Riddell—parsing every interaction, every detail of his record, trying to find the missing observation that confirmed he had been working with a serial killer.

Alex Yang had discovered nothing of critical import about any of the Mill tenants. Martin had requested more intensive background checks, starting with Chase Riddell. It was too early to share his suspicions with anyone beyond Lieutenant Farber, so he simply suggested they needed to eliminate Riddell first, given his position with the police department.

So far, Martin knew Riddell's parents were dead and that he was an only child. He hadn't served in the military. Had no criminal record. He was evidently funding his lifestyle with money inherited from an aunt.

There was no anecdotal evidence from his childhood like a fascination with fire, torturing small animals, or bed wetting—the classic triad of childhood issues behind the men who become serial killers. Of course, the obvious clues often surfaced only after the arrest.

They had nothing.

Then Dominic called with the list of units with wooden floors. One of them was 139—Riddell's unit. He knew about the basement space beneath his apartment. A coincidence? Not a chance in a million.

Martin swiveled to look out his window and sighed.

More and more, the finger pointed to the mill and Chase Riddell. Circumstantial evidence. The ramblings of a psychic. A plausible suspect. But not enough to convince a judge to sign a warrant. Even his knowledge of the basement wasn't sufficient probable cause.

Meanwhile, Danielle might be dying while he struggled to build a case.

Alex called. He had stumbled on to something interesting. Chase's paternal grandfather had served three years in prison for two separate assaults. The accompanying rape charges had been dismissed. Back then, rape charges rarely stuck. A family pattern or background noise? No one really knew. The jury was still out on the link between sexual violence and genetics.

Having initially downplayed Riddell as a suspect, his apparent lack of insight troubled him. His instincts were usually impeccable. Evidently, he had allowed a bias toward a fellow officer to interfere with his judgement, even though he already suspected the man was a misogynist.

But he understood the blind spot.

Serial killers could be charming and intelligent and often fooled the people closest to them. Spouse, family, friends. John Wayne Gacy ran a successful business in the Chicago area. Had a wife and two stepchildren. He was active in the community. The man also murdered thirty-three boys.

Still, Riddell might be intelligent, but he was hardly charming.

Martin decided to call him to schedule a meeting, hoping to get a read on him under the guise of discussing a case they had worked on last month. The call went to voicemail, so he left a brief message, hoping it sounded sufficiently casual.

Lili called. He wasn't in the mood for her ramblings but opted to take her call anyway. The unexplainable attraction was still there. She really wasn't his type. Or was she? No, his interest felt more like desperation, a poor basis for a relationship.

"Hello, Ms. Paltrinieri. How can I help you?"

"I have vital information about Danielle. Can I come in and talk to you?"

It probably wasn't helpful. Likely a waste of time. Still, he said, "Sure. Eleven-thirty work for you?"

He tapped the red icon and shook his head.

What could the woman possibly tell him that he didn't already know?

⋆ ⋆ ⋆

Lili parked in the lot just after 11:30.

The day was warm, sunny, and pleasant, but noting it seemed frivolous. Danielle was dead.

Martin met her at the locked entry door and they walked back to his office in silence. He was better looking than she remembered. Nicely dressed too. Probably married, but he wasn't wearing a ring.

Regardless, he had been condescending and dismissive toward her and wasn't someone she should even think about.

She wanted someone in her life, but online dating was frustrating. Men lied about everything on their profiles. Their age, their weight. Their jobs. The guys she did date were confused by or disinterested in her fascination with the paranormal. Most only seemed interested in sex—

Stop!

She needed to look and sound serious. Credible.

Motioning to a chair, he said, "You have new information?"

She sat down and locked eyes with him. "I know you think I'm a lunatic, but bear with me. Please."

He nodded with a tight smile. "I'm listening."

"I believe Danielle is dead. Something awful happened in the building last night and I'm certain it happened under apartment one-thirty-nine."

"What did you see?"

"Nothing—in person. You know how I operate."

"A feeling then?"

Lili nodded. "And I spoke with one of the spirits in the building who confirmed that a man had been holding Danielle under one-thirty-nine."

"I doubt a judge will give me a search warrant based on a feeling and a séance," he said dryly.

There it was, the cop sensibility. He didn't believe her. Lili focused a glare on him. "Do you know who lives in that apartment?"

"No. Should I?"

His expression seemed guarded. Did he know?

"Chase Riddell," Lili said.

He frowned and an indeterminate microexpression crossed his face. Anger? Disbelief? She had hoped he'd be receptive to her information. But apparently not when it involved another cop.

"Chase Riddell is a member of the police department. Are you seriously suggesting that he's a dangerous felon?"

His affect was off. He didn't believe what he was saying.

"I brought what I felt was critical information to you. How you handle it—"

"Noted. I'll take it under consideration. Thanks for coming in." He stood and showed her the door. He was blowing her off.

Asshat.

Like she needed his help.

Forty

Chase was exhausted.

As he dozed off in his recliner, his phone rang.

Recognizing the number as Martin's extension, he ignored it.

A new voicemail popped up a minute later. Martin wanted to meet with him to review a case. The message sounded innocuous.

It also sounded like a lie.

Shit!

Chase panicked, worried they were on to him.

Meeting with Martin would be a mistake. Going in for his shift tonight? Also a bad idea—until he knew more. He felt like hell; needed sleep and time to regroup. To stop freaking out. Danielle's death had thrown him off balance and he was having trouble getting straight again. He also felt bruised and sore from their altercation.

He looked out the window. No cops, no squads. No strange vehicles lurking nearby. Not like they could hide. He knew every unmarked vehicle in the department.

Taking a deep breath, Chase relaxed and called in sick for his shift.

Was he a suspect yet? Probably not, but if they were coming for him, he had to decide on a course of action. Imagining the worst, he felt stuck somewhere between an impulse to flee and preparing for a fight to the death.

Mostly, he obsessed over the psychic woman. Eamon had implied his biggest problem was the psychic bitch who lived in 124. If they weren't yet looking at him, it was imperative to deal with her before she convinced them he was a suspect. A preemptive strike before she talked. Make her disappear.

If they were on to him, then he had a score to settle.

There was no time to plan, no time to watch and observe. He would have to wing it. A basic smash and grab.

His doorbell rang.

He ignored it.

Then someone knocked on the door. Twice. Sitting in his office, he wanted to look but didn't. Any movement would alert whoever was outside to his presence. His phone was nowhere in sight, so he grabbed his laptop to check the entry cam. He feared his time was up, but realized if the SWAT team was at the door, they'd announce themselves. Loudly.

By the time he logged into the door cam, the hallway was clear.

Nothing important, evidently. Good.

Chase relaxed and ran a background check on Lili Paltrinieri using an online service. Wisconsin Court Access did not reveal any marriage records. There were no entries listed under *Other Names at This Address.* The apartment was titled solely in her name. She was single and almost certainly lived alone. Of course she did, he thought. She was a freaking weirdo. Probably had cats.

Perfect.

He vacillated. He should run and forget about the woman. But she was a loose end, and his obsessive nature wouldn't let it stand unresolved. There were principles involved. He couldn't be bested by a woman—any woman—but especially some wacko who claimed to be psychic.

Jesus!

Chase retrieved the trunk and a roll of duct tape from the basement, then grabbed his Taser—just in case. Left everything by the door and rechecked the windows and the peephole. He walked to the lobby to grab his mail while checking the hallway. It was a normal, quiet weekday in the building. No cops evident anywhere.

A slim redhead walked past him as he retrieved the mail. Not his type exactly, but interesting—once he'd dealt with his immediate problems.

Returning to his apartment, he grabbed the trunk and walked casually to 124. Checked the hallway again and knocked. Slipped his gloves on. Hearing footsteps approach the door, he felt prepared for every possibility.

If a man answered the door or she had company, he could abort.

Sorry, wrong apartment.

He realized he hadn't looked at any photos of the woman. But he felt confident again—it was her apartment. Who else would answer? This would go perfectly. Why did he continually doubt himself?

The door swung open slowly. He saw a petite blonde standing there, a questioning look on her face. Hmm. Not much of a psychic if she didn't recognize the looming threat he represented. The apartment looked otherwise empty.

Chase focused on the target and punched her hard in the solar plexus. As she caved forward, he pushed her back and grabbed her arm, turning and pulling her into a chokehold while he gently closed the door with his foot. As she recovered and struggled against him, the reduced blood flow to her brain rendered her unconscious and she fell limp.

Laying her on the floor, he first wrapped a piece of duct tape around her head and mouth. Within seconds, he had folded, taped, and stowed her inside the trunk.

Perfect.

Chase checked the peephole. The hallway remained clear.

He stepped out, closed the door quietly, and walked nonchalantly back to his apartment, pulling the trunk behind him.

Safely inside, he set both locks and snapped the OnGard door brace into the plate bolted to the floor. SWAT wasn't coming through that door.

But the sense of victory he felt in successfully grabbing the psychic faded rapidly. Now it felt like he was off the reservation. Martin suspected, or worse. Taking this woman had been foolhardy. What did he hope to gain? Revenge for revealing his role in the disappearance of Danielle Hamlin?

He didn't know that she had done any such thing. But he had heard her name at work, and Eamon said she had ratted him out. Still, taking her would increase the pressure. A second disappearance at the mill? They would tear the place apart.

Really? What the fuck was he thinking?

He had been listening to his friend far too much, had allowed himself to be talked into one rash act after another.

Now, he had to assume the worst. Plan for the worst.

Chase stepped down the rungs to the basement with the barely conscious woman over his shoulder and carried her to Danielle's room.

There was only a mattress and the bucket. The cot was gone. Lesson learned. This bitch wouldn't be around long, anyway.

He had made some preparations for this moment. Had planned for every contingency—except for Danielle's escape attempt.

Retrieving the prepared plywood boards from the hall closet, he screwed them to the window frames. The boards were like hurricane protection but mounted on the inside of the windows to keep flash bangs and tear gas out. The apartment was virtually impregnable now.

His elaborate defenses had only one purpose: to slow them down. They were coming for him. He felt certain of it. He had broken his well-considered rules and now risked paying a steep price unless he acted quickly and intelligently.

Stepping down into the basement, he walked about a hundred feet along the north hall to a room where he kept his weapons—the armory. He had stocked the room with a dozen handguns of various calibers, four shotguns, an AR-15, three rifles, and thousands of rounds of ammunition. He checked each weapon and the magazines to ensure that every gun was locked and loaded.

He also had cases of canned and dry food. Gallons of water. Flashlights. Batteries. Night-vision goggles. A Kevlar vest. Just in case.

But when they came for him, he would likely need none of it.

Nope.

He was running right after sunset.

Forty-One

Lili gritted her teeth, fuming.

Martin had given her information zero credence. The other day, he seemed more receptive to her ideas. He just blew her off today.

Because Chase Riddell was a cop? Was that it? She decided Martin wasn't so good looking after all. Oh well. If the police refused to take her seriously, she would investigate and expose Chase on her own, despite the potential risks.

She went to work but had difficulty concentrating. Danielle's death weighed heavily. Her anger at Martin simmered. She had two people scheduled early, then a break before appointments at five and six. Too jittery to concentrate, she canceled the later sessions, closed the store at four, and drove home. Her anxiety level had been rising all day. Had something new happened?

Striding to her apartment, Lili opened the door and felt a strange undercurrent in the aura, a darkness, like a shadow. What—?

But the place was empty.

"Olivia?"

No answer. The bathroom door was open. She must have gone

back to Raleigh.

Good.

Lili gave it no further thought. She could only think about Danielle. And Chase Riddell. He killed her. She just knew it. Maybe she just needed patience while Martin and the evidence caught up with her. But he knew something. His manner was ambivalent—conflicted. What if the cop escaped—?

The phone interrupted her disjointed thinking.

Raleigh. Just what she needed. She tapped the green icon anyway.

"Put her on, Lili." He sounded grumpy.

"Huh?"

"Put Olivia on. I know she's there."

"No, she's not. I thought she went home."

"She hasn't, and she's not answering her phone."

Lili flashed to the faint disturbing sensation felt as she walked in and feared for Olivia. Then she saw Olivia's laptop sitting open on the coffee table. Increasingly alarmed, Lili said, "Could she have gone to the store or something?"

There was a brief pause. "No. Her car's in the lot. I know she's there, Lili, stop—"

"No, she's not! Get over here now! Hurry!" Lili felt panic closing in, apprehension that something terrible had happened. Could Riddell have taken Olivia? Would she be his next victim?

A moment later, Raleigh knocked on the door.

"What's going on, Lili?"

"I don't know. I left and went to work. When I came home, she was gone. I noticed a disturbance in the aura of the room when I walked in."

Raleigh shook his head in confusion. "What are you saying?"

"Look, she left her laptop. I think somebody might've taken her."

"What? A feeling? Did a ghost tell you that—?"

"Wait. I have a camera we can check." She had installed one in case of a break-in, but also wanted to make sure management wasn't entering her apartment illegally. At her last apartment, she caught a shifty maintenance guy going through her bedroom drawers.

Lili grabbed her laptop and set it on the island. Raleigh edged in next to her as she logged into the program. When the feed came up, she hit 3X reverse.

People moved quickly backward like cartoons. The two of them talking. Raleigh backing out of the apartment. Soon after, Lili backing out. Another pause and a man pulling Olivia out of a trunk. Olivia backing away from the door—

Holy shit!

She ran the feed forward at normal speed.

Olivia opened the door. A man stepped in, punched her in the chest, and twisted her into a headlock until she passed out. He taped her up, folded her body into a trunk, and wheeled her out the door. Casually. It happened in seconds.

Lili gasped in horror. Raleigh looked too stunned to speak.

Finally, Lili said, "Who was that? Do you know him?"

He shook his head, still in shock.

A millisecond later, her rational brain kicked in. They needed to report this now.

A spoon went flying onto the floor, but Lili ignored it. She had no time for Emma.

Grabbing her phone, she tapped Martin's contact, thinking he would react the quickest. Finally, she had actual evidence.

She wasn't positive that Olivia's abductor was Chase Riddell, but she would bet her life savings it.

A second later, Martin answered. She explained the situation in a rushed but lucid manner. Martin asked only a few questions before he said, "We're on our way. Do nothing, say nothing until I get there. Understood?"

Lili nodded and said, "Yes."

She turned to Raleigh and said, "They're on their way."

"Oh Jesus, I can't believe this is happening."

"I think the guy in one-thirty-nine did it—the cop," she said, rubbing her shoulders. Lili wasn't certain of it, but spoke simply to fill the void.

"What?"

"I think he took Danielle as well."

The moment she spoke the words, she realized her mistake. Raleigh morphed into an angry, predatory hunter in seconds. He pushed past Lili and rushed out the door. She had forgotten he was ex-Special Forces.

Shit!

"Raleigh! The cops said to wait!"

But he was gone.

⋆ ⋆ ⋆

Martin looked out his office window.

Three kids were fishing. Heat rose off the asphalt parking lot in shimmering waves.

He regretted being brusque with Lili earlier, but he couldn't risk revealing his hand, couldn't publicly entertain an accusation against Riddell just yet.

Lili's insights had rattled him. Identifying Riddell as a suspect could be a lucky guess. But how did she know about the basement under 139? Was there something to this psychic stuff?

No matter, it was hardly grounds for a warrant.

Chase Riddell hadn't returned his call. Then Abby advised him Riddell had called in sick for his shift.

Pressure was building, the need to do something, to push this to a conclusion. Everything adding up, the coincidences and circumstantial clues, a feeling the case was about to break.

Was Riddell thinking about running?

Martin decided to rattle the man by going to his apartment. Meet him face-to-face, certain he would see the truth.

His phone rang.

Lili.

Words flew at him. "Martin! He took Olivia! He grabbed her from my apartment—"

"Whoa, stop! Tell me again. Slowly."

She did, though it took a moment for the gravity of her words to sink in: Lili Paltrinieri had video of a man she believed was Chase Riddell abducting a woman from her apartment. Riddell had clearly gone off the reservation. Finally, something they could act on.

Martin told Lili to stay put and ended the call, thinking about where to start. The chief was out for the day but Sam Farber was in. Perfect, really. He was the SWAT team leader and Martin knew he would handle the situation carefully and professionally. Better than the chief, certainly.

Martin ran to his office and reeled off a recap of the phone call.

Farber looked stunned. "Chase Riddell is the suspect?"

"Probably."

"And this came from the psychic woman?"

Martin nodded.

As Farber picked up the phone, he said, "Get squads around the building and establish a silent perimeter while I alert the team. Get over there and look at the video. We're going slow and quiet until you confirm the details of her story."

Made sense. It would only take a few minutes and, given the source, confirming the story first seemed prudent.

He briefed Abby. She started pulling squads into discreet positions on the streets adjoining the mill with explicit instructions: no sirens; stay out of sight; await further instructions.

Martin holstered his gun, grabbed his sport coat and Kevlar vest, and ran out to his car. A warrant was probably no longer necessary. If Riddell was the man on video, exigent circumstances applied, and they could enter his apartment immediately.

It was interesting how some cases unexpectedly drew to a close. But what did another abduction mean for Danielle? Was she already dead?

Halfway to the mill, a call came in about a disturbance in the building. A man was yelling and banging on the door of unit 139.

Jesus!

What was that about? So much for a stealthy approach.

Martin instructed another squad to handle the call.

He was dying to see that video.

Forty-Two

Emma watched events unfold with horror.

Watched the psychopathic cop grab a woman from Lili's apartment, throw her into a trunk, drag her back to his unit and into the cellar. Her ability to pursue them ended there. She couldn't intervene herself and feared for the blonde woman's life.

Emma knew her. She lived in the apartment where Frank had been stirring up trouble. Was Frank up to something? Was he helping the cop? Did the man in the cellar have a hand in it?

That guy was a mystery. During her time in the mill, no one had died in the cellar and yet, he had always been there.

Oddly, she now knew his name. It just popped into her head in the last day or two.

Eamon O'Keene.

Some itinerant Irish laborer killed during construction years before her accident.

Did he have exclusive access to the cellar because he died down there? Was that how things worked? He got the cellar, she got the mill, and Frank and Tommy got the leftovers? It sounded weirdly plausible.

It also felt like those barriers were breaking down.

It had been a strange day. She had talked to Lili earlier, a moment when the iPad worked. Then she grew tired and felt compelled to rest. She hadn't been able to resist the urge. Worse, she had felt herself come and go recently—she could think of no better way to describe it. She simply went blank for periods of time. Over the past few days, life had been unpredictable. She also had occasional difficulty reading books and moving objects.

Emma had a sense of bigger forces at work. She was missing something, and events were spiraling out of control. Given the poisonous atmosphere in the mill, she felt off-kilter anyway. She chalked it up to stress and the disturbed energy fields around her.

But were the others conspiring against her, trying to run her out of the mill? She felt certain Eamon was. Maybe Frank. Tommy even. It made sense. They were probably jealous of her.

The thought made her angry. The mill was hers. She was the famous one, the ghostly girl of the night shift.

Then she recognized the paranoid nature of her thinking.

She had spent time in the past few days studying psychology texts to gain insight into the things Chase Riddell was doing. She didn't understand his behavior or motivation. In her short life, she'd had little exposure to criminality or evil. The afterlife had been a shock. Theft, greed, wanton sex, murder? She had witnessed all of it—right here in the mill.

This place was like a master class in the seven deadly sins.

She concluded that Chase Riddell aspired to be a serial killer. People like him had rough childhoods and bad mothers. Again, concepts she had trouble understanding. Her mother had been an angel. Her father, though, was an animal. Only now, reading these books, did she realize he had been molesting her with his monthly *examinations.* She hadn't understood what he was doing was wrong, even though it made her feel awful. Then she suffered additional traumas in dying violently at such a young age. Having her dreams ripped away. Being forced to stay and watch Jacob carry on and have a life with someone else.

Really, much of her life had been a nightmare.

She might have something called post-traumatic stress, though it was unclear if she, as a spirit, could suffer from a mental condition like the living.

But she also learned that feeling people were out to get her was a symptom of paranoia.

Unless they were.

Were they? Or was she overthinking the events of the past few days?

She didn't think so. A woman had been kidnapped. Frank had been acting out and trying to chase the living people out of his space—

Emma stopped. How did she know all of this? She had never been this in-tune with the mill before. What had changed? More and more information was becoming available to her, and she didn't know how or why. Another strange quirk of her life here and an ever-changing set of rules.

She decided to embrace it. She would be better prepared to meet any challenges from Frank and Eamon. Emma needed all the help she could get. She wanted to reclaim the mill as her own. To do so, she had to put the others in their place. If they objected, she'd drive them out.

The deviant cop had to go first. He was the biggest threat. His criminality seemed to be the trigger that incited Frank and Eamon to act up. Saving the blonde woman and ensuring the psychopath was caught were the first steps toward regaining full control of the building.

Emma did the ghostly equivalent of pacing, waiting for Lili to return home. Would they be able communicate? Would the iPad work? She had to find a way. Maybe she would have to risk actually speaking to the woman.

When Lili walked through the door, she appeared to sense something amiss. Then the man from 114 arrived. They stared at a computer. Emma hovered above.

Somehow, they had a movie of the abduction. Good. They knew the woman had been kidnapped.

But did they know where the woman had been taken? Emma needed to tell Lili now.

Random forks and spoons had been laid out on the quartz-topped island. She shoved a spoon and it fell, clattering on the floor.

Oh good.

Her tricks were working, but Lili ignored her, grabbing her phone, and making a call.

Then the other man left.

Emma pushed a fork onto the floor.

Lili responded by laying her tablet on the island and opening Word.

Finally.

"Emma? Are you there?"

When she slipped across the screen, she was able to type.

yes help

"What? Is it about the woman who was taken?"

yes 139 took her

"Do you know where?"

cellar

"How does he get down there?" Lili asked.

bathroom hurry beware of eam

As Emma typed, the room grew hazy, and she felt herself slipping away, again. The iPad no longer worked, and her surroundings faded to black. This seemed to happen whenever she talked with Lili. It had to be that dumb Irishman interfering. Why? What was his game? This was the reason that talking to Lili was too risky. It just left her open to further dangers and interference.

Then a voice spoke to her. A voice with an Irish accent.

I'm coming for you, bitch.

Whoa. He was challenging her head-on.

At least she had gotten her message out first.

As for Eamon O'Keene?

To hell with him.

This was war.

Forty-Three

Lili paced to and fro.

Barely able to manage her anxiety, it felt like time was crawling. Where in the hell was Martin?

A fork fell to the floor.

Lili rushed over and opened the iPad. After a brief conversation, Emma quit abruptly with a cryptic warning.

beware of eam

"Emma?"

Silence.

"Talk to me!"

But she was gone, again. What the hell was eam? Did she mean Eamon?

A knock at the door.

Oh sure, now Martin shows up, after the conversation with Emma is over.

Martin stood there with a wild-eyed Raleigh.

"Do you know this guy? He says he knows you."

Lili nodded.

"Can he stay here? Otherwise, I'm going to arrest him."

"He can stay here. I just talked to—"

Martin raised his hand to stop her. "I need to see the video."

Lili directed him to the laptop on the island and hit *play,* the feed cued to twenty seconds before Olivia opened the door. Martin watched with obvious horror as the man punched Olivia, neutralized her, and folded her unconscious body into the trunk.

Shaking his head, he hit pause and said, "Wow. That explains a lot."

Martin was still staring at the screen when Lili said, "Believe me now?"

He nodded absently. "Who's the woman?"

"My wife, Olivia," Raleigh said.

Lili pointed. "Is that Chase Riddell?"

"Yes." Martin held up a finger and tapped a contact on his phone. After a brief conversation, he said, "I've got to go. The SWAT team is here. Thank you, Ms. Paltrinieri. That recording is valuable evidence. An officer will stop by to make a copy."

Lili spoke quickly. "Riddell has her in the basement. He gets down there through his bathroom."

Giving her a skeptical eye, Martin said, "How do you know that?"

"I talked to Emma."

A non-committal, tight-lipped nod. He didn't believe her. Lili, ready with a snarky retort, opened her mouth to speak, but Raleigh barked, "What about my wife?"

"We're going to get her back. You two stay here." Martin tapped a finger on Raleigh's chest. "Especially you. We've got this."

Martin turned and strode out the door.

Raleigh, agitated and pacing, suddenly turned to Lili. "I need a favor while we're waiting."

"Sure, anything. God, I'm so sorry."

"Thanks." Raleigh looked focused. Dangerous. "Grab your crystal ball and stuff and come to my apartment."

"Huh?"

"Come on. Hurry! I want to talk to Frank."

"I thought you didn't believe in ghosts?"

"I never believed my wife would be abducted either." Raleigh marched off.

Lili grabbed her stuff and followed, if only to do something besides worrying alone in her place, pacing and gnawing on her fingernails.

⋆ ⋆ ⋆

Martin replayed the video in his head while walking to the lobby to meet with Sam Farber.

In thirty seconds, virtually all of his questions had been answered. The punch to the solar plexus, the choke hold, the tape and rolling sports trunk. It explained exactly how Danielle had been taken and the lack of evidence. Chase Riddell was clearly a psychopath. Smart, high-functioning, and dangerous. How had he missed it? He had detected something off about the man, but not this. He shoved the thought away. There would be ample time to berate himself later.

It occurred to him that Lili may have been the true target. Why? He couldn't imagine. Right now, they had clear, exigent circumstances, and SWAT could enter with force.

He met Lieutenant Farber in the hallway leading to Riddell's unit.

"What's the plan, sir?" Martin asked.

"The team has set up covertly around his unit and we're pulling the squads closer to the building. The apartment is a fortress. The windows are protected with plywood on the inside and the entry door and frame are steel, set in brick. We may not be able to breach it."

"Any sign of Riddell?"

"Nothing yet. No attempt to escape that we're aware of."

"That seems unlikely. He just took a hostage," Martin said. "He might be holed up in the apartment with the woman, Olivia Kaplan. More likely, he's in the basement."

"Do we know how he gained access to the basement?"

"Not for sure. It's possible he built his own access through the bathroom floor," Martin said.

"How do we know that?"

"An educated guess." He was curious about Lili's knowledge based on the supposed word of a ghost. What if it was true? Was Lili truly psychic? Getting evidence from a dead girl would surely upend his world view.

Sam side-glanced him. "Your psychic?"

Martin nodded.

Farber shook his head and said, "Assuming that Riddell is monitoring police frequencies, we'll communicate with cell phones."

"Good idea."

Sam turned to Abby. "Try his cell."

A moment later, she said, "It went to voicemail, sir."

"Send him a text and an email. Tell him we want to talk."

Abby shook her head minutes later. "No response."

Farber sent two officers to knock on Riddell's door, hoping to open a dialogue, but he didn't answer.

Farber turned to Martin. "Five minutes. As soon as we've evacuated residents at that end of the building."

When the entry team was ready, they followed Farber along the hallway. Martin wandered down to observe from a safe distance.

Four guys took up positions. One on either side of the door, one holding back, all three armed with Colt M4 carbines, the fourth armed with a battering ram. The lieutenant signaled to breach the door.

The battering ram hit the door with a resounding clang of metal on metal. The door didn't budge.

"Again!"

The officer swung harder. Nothing.

After four additional hefty whacks, Farber called them off. The damaged door remained closed, mocking them.

Martin walked over to the lieutenant. "Now what?"

"I don't know. We could use a torch on the door, but it might be easier to go through the windows."

"Sounds like we're here for the long haul. There's a conference room just off the lobby. Should we set up a command center there?"

"Do it," Farber said and strode off.

Fifteen minutes later, the command center was up and running in the conference room. Someone had fired up the coffeemaker and the building manager sent donuts in. The office provided the blueprints for the building. As for the basement, they only knew there were two corridors inside the foundations that ran the length of the building with rooms on the east end. Martin knew the room numbers of other apartments with wood framed floors but had no clue how they were connected. The best path was clearly through Chase's unit to utilize his access to the basement.

He turned with a questioning look when the lieutenant walked in.

"We'll try a hydraulic jamb spreader, but I don't think it'll work," Farber said. "Because of the window height, we're trying to locate a hydraulic lift to wheel into place. It's probably our best bet. I can't wait until the news breaks that the suspect is a cop."

"Tell me about it."

Martin wondered if Riddell had an escape planned. No matter. They had a tight perimeter. Even if he had a way out of the basement, he wouldn't be able to escape the property.

Why was Riddell refusing to negotiate?

Did he really want to go down shooting?

That didn't bode well for the hostage.

Forty-Four

Chase heard faint pounding above.

Someone at his front door.

Let the games begin.

Sitting underground, in the armory—his command post—he eyed the three monitors with views of the apartment and basement. He brought up the camera hidden in the hallway, surprised to see a stranger pounding on his door, yelling his head off. Who the hell was he? Did the psychic chick have a boyfriend? If so, why did the guy suspect him?

Shit!

If that random dude knew he was the perp, the jig was up.

Then a patrol cop, Andy Szymanski, came and pulled the guy away from the door after a heated confrontation.

His phone pinged.

Let's talk – Sam.

Chase muted his phone.

SWAT arrived. Four guys and a battering ram. They planned a forced entry. Running the standard playbook.

Good luck with that.

He snickered.

Only dynamite would open that door. They might try. More likely, they would breach the windows. Either way, it would take time, and they were operating under pressure. They had to know he had a hostage. At first, taking the woman felt like a mistake. Now, it looked like a stroke of genius. As long as she remained alive, they would be hobbled by her presence.

Then they had to breach the bathroom floor. The door was three inches of solid wood, double bolted beneath. After that, they still had to penetrate a hundred feet of hallway to his armory. That room had compelling views of the north and south passages. He had multiple cameras watching the entrance and the passages as well.

He could snipe at them and bottle them up, hold them down for hours, but he wouldn't wait that long. Unless he held a gun to her head or engaged them in sustained gunfire, the SWAT team wouldn't rush him, hoping to keep the hostage alive through a non-violent resolution. That was always the goal; he knew the game plan perfectly.

Chase moved the woman to the adjoining room and left her on the cold concrete next to the well. She was conscious, and he had retaped her mouth, having no desire to listen to her whimper and cry. Too bad he didn't have time to teach her a lesson or two. She wasn't his type, but why look a gift horse in the mouth?

Getting out was the primary concern. He could drag her along. As a hostage, she remained useful until she wasn't. Then he could have some fun before he killed her.

Earlier, Chase had considered a fight to the death. He sure as hell wasn't going to prison. A cop convicted of rape and murder wouldn't last five minutes. Even in protective custody, he would never be safe.

But he wasn't ready to be dead and he had a solid escape plan.

As they closed in, they would tighten the perimeter. When they breached the basement, he would fire some rounds to force a stalemate. They would want to talk. He would demand a negotiator. Let them think he was ready to deal.

Everything would stop until the negotiator arrived.

All of this was necessary to stall while he waited for darkness to fall.

Then he was gone.

⋆ ⋆ ⋆

Eamon was having the time of his life.

Chase, the fecking genius, had run amok. He had kidnapped another colleen and brought the full weight of the coppers down on him. Chase believed he'd nabbed the psychic, but Eamon felt sure he'd grabbed the wrong woman. No matter.

Exerting maximum influence to direct the outcome, Eamon gave Chase confusing and conflicting ideas. For a genius, the idiot had remarkably little resolve and was easily swayed. The idiot was so unnerved by his failure with Danielle, he appeared to have gone over the edge. Eamon had suggested Chase stay and fight to the death. Kill the woman, kill as many cops as he could, rain down hellfire in a grand finale before he died and became a martyr to real men everywhere.

The wanker almost bought into that crazy idea.

Ha!

Now, the fool was bent on escape. That worked, too. Eamon was less interested in death and carnage in the cellar and more intent on destroying Chase Riddell. Eamon finally understood why. The man reminded him of the bastard foreman who left him for dead. Similar appearance, same arrogant know-it-all-fuck-you attitude.

If a few coppers died, that would be frosting on the cake, but he preferred the prick alive. Just like the twits who killed Frank. Then he could go to prison and spend the rest of his miserable life reflecting on what a dumb fecking bastard he was.

That vision gave Eamon great pleasure. This was more entertaining than Frank's murder.

Eamon knew every detail of the cop's escape plan and would strive to trip him up.

Once he guided this mess to a conclusion, he would turn his attention to another, equally pressing matter. He continued to feel pressure from above. Emma, the little whore, wasn't content with her place above ground. She seemed intent on interfering with his fun, encroaching on his space, opposing his plans to move out of the basement.

He wanted to kick that little bitch out and stake a claim to the building.

Become the gaffer of the mill.

All of it.

And he had just the plan.

Forty-Five

Raleigh paced in his kitchen.

He felt ready to burst. Primed to kill.

Lili had set up on the cherrywood table. Lit candles. Set out dinner rolls. It was an odd ritual. How could something like that work?

"I need peace and quiet for this to work. Sit down over there." She pointed to the sofa.

Reluctantly, he sat, but continued to fidget.

Lili turned to him. "What do you want from Frank? So I know what to ask."

"Is there a way into the basement from this end of the building?"

"Why do you want to know?"

"Just ask him." He stood and resumed pacing. He couldn't sit still. "You said anything, Lili."

"Okay. Just sit down. Your fidgeting is throwing me off."

Raleigh forced himself to calm down. He had to pull it together; needed to remain cool to get Olivia back.

Once a captain in the Third Special Forces Group, he had been a formidable soldier. Now rusty physically and mentally, he hadn't trained in several years. Still, he believed the instincts and muscle memory from years of training remained and would see him through.

He didn't trust the cops to handle this. They were dealing with one of their own. Olivia was probably a secondary consideration. More than likely, they would get her killed. Minutes before, he had surreptitiously crept down the hallway to monitor their progress.

What a joke! They were sitting in the conference room, drinking coffee and eating donuts. Doing nothing. It sounded like their attempt to breach the door of 139 had failed. Par for the course.

It wasn't their fault. Small town cops just weren't trained for this type of tactical situation. And he recognized the rogue cop appeared to be cunning and well-prepared. It wouldn't do to underestimate his opponent.

The old adage applied here.

If you want something done right...

Yep.

Raleigh was certain Riddell planned to kill Olivia, convinced he was the same psycho who had taken Danielle and Megan.

No matter. Soon, the bastard would be dead.

If he could access the basement, he would sneak up on Riddell, kill him, and get Olivia back.

Despite his military training, he felt considerable anxiety. He feared for Olivia's life. Feared the possibility of failure. He stood and paced again. So absorbed was he in that thought, he almost forgot about Lili sitting there.

A moment later, she spoke. "Frank? Can we talk?"

Silence.

Raleigh sat on the sofa and gripped his hands, twisting them until they hurt. The pain helped him focus and, oddly, relax. His heart and breath sounds seemed unnaturally loud. Lili sat, trance-like, eyes closed, hands set on either side of the crystal ball.

Finally, she said, "Frank? Is there a way into the basement from here?"

More silence. How was this not a con?

Then Lili nodded. She sat for a few more minutes before opening her eyes and looking at Raleigh.

"Frank says there is, under the kitchen pantry. Why do you want to know?"

"I don't trust the cops to handle this. That guy is one of theirs. They're going to dick around getting things in place. Bring a negotiator in. It will take hours. In the meantime, that freak could rape her. Then he'll kill her. If there's an entry in my pantry, there might be others. He could get out. I'm not letting any of that happen."

Lili stood and said, "You're going to get Olivia killed."

He tuned her out; couldn't entertain any thought of failure. "You should probably go back to your apartment, Lili."

"What you're planning is stupid. And crazy."

"I know what I'm doing. I'm not going to wait around for the cops to fuck things up."

Raleigh knew exactly what he needed and where to find it: a maintenance room at the back of the building. He ran out the door and out the rear exit, across the patio to the exterior entrance of the storage bay. The door stood wide open. No one in sight. He found what he wanted almost immediately.

A chainsaw. No time for finesse now.

He checked the gas and oil levels, then ran back to his apartment.

He quickly cleared the floor of the pantry of various bags and boxes, potatoes, onions, bottles of beer and wine—sweeping everything out onto the kitchen floor. A wine bottle broke. Oh well.

Raleigh primed and fired up the saw, pushing the cutting tip of the bar into the hickory flooring. About three inches in, he felt the resistance lessen. He was through the wood layers. The basement had to lie below.

The noise of the saw was deafening, the cloud of oily exhaust choking, but Raleigh never faltered. He cut a rough two-by-two-foot hole in the floor and watched with satisfaction as the chunk of wood fell into a dark space below. A waft of dank air hit him.

First hurdle crossed.

Raleigh suited up. Black pants and soft-soled boots, a black tee, and a Kevlar vest. Opening the gun safe, he grabbed a Glock 19 and the AR-15, a knife, a Taser, and a Maglite. He dropped extra magazines into his pockets. Blackened his face and the tops of his hands with makeup. He wished he had night-vision gear, but he had broken the last set and hadn't bothered to replace them. Too late now. Donning a helmet, he checked his presentation in the mirror, then closed the pantry door to prevent extraneous light from shining into the basement, potentially giving him away. He had a painter's ladder in the pantry. As he lowered it, he worked the legs open, reached down, and set it on the concrete floor.

Excellent.

Now he could exit quickly if need be.

He climbed down and waited a minute for his eyes to adjust, listening for any activity in the basement. It was silent beyond the normal, expected sounds: random bangs, footsteps, creaks and such.

Raleigh flashed the Maglite downward in brief spurts to establish his bearings. He stood in a short hallway that ran north and south with openings at each end. He eased up to the north passage. It led east under the mill for about one hundred feet and was dimly lit at the far end. Going to the south hallway, he saw it was considerably longer than the other.

South was the obvious choice since apartment 139 was at the far end of the building.

Was Lili right? Was he crazy? Overly arrogant in thinking he could handle this alone?

No.

A psychopath had taken Olivia hostage. It might take the cops hours to get things in place. Then, while they fucked around negotiating—burning up additional time—he would grab Olivia and lead her to safety. Yes, she could be frivolous and annoying, but he loved her deeply and couldn't imagine life without her. Raleigh saw no choice but to go in himself.

He started down the south passage. Silently. Carefully.

What could go wrong?

He pushed the thought away.

Now was not the time for negativity.

Forty-Six

Lili grew impatient sitting by herself.

Emma wasn't talking, and when she tried to catch Martin's attention in the conference room, an officer shooed her away and sent her back to her apartment. The police had set up in the hallway leading to 139. Otherwise, she saw no activity. Maybe Raleigh was right. The cops would dither until Olivia was dead.

Finally, she could sit no longer. She grabbed her iPad and the bag with her crystal ball and candles and walked across the courtyard to the Kaplans' unit.

She knocked. When Raleigh didn't answer, she entered the code and stepped into their apartment, wrinkling her nose.

Yuck.

The room reeked of gas, exhaust, or something. It was otherwise quiet. Raleigh was nowhere to be seen.

"Raleigh?"

Silence.

Then she saw the open closet and gun safe. Whoa. Raleigh had some heavy artillery. She knew he had been Special Forces or something, but his collection of guns was impressive.

"Raleigh?"

Opening the pantry door, she flicked the light on and peered down into the dark hole in the floor. It gave her the creeps. She peeked and spotted the ladder. She could climb down, but as she hung her head into the space, Lili lost her nerve and pulled away.

Something down there gave off a bad vibe. Eamon? Riddell? Residual energy from Danielle's death?

She had no clue.

Lili felt compelled to do something, but what? Talk to Frank? He probably knew no more than she; he couldn't see beyond the walls of this unit.

Emma was the obvious choice, but their communications had been unreliable in the apartment. Maybe location mattered. She had sensed Emma's presence most often around 202 and the hallway outside 222, but Lili feared the cops would toss her out. They had already cleared the apartments at the other end of the mill. Lili decided to risk sneaking upstairs, hoping to contact Emma. To do something. Anything.

Lili slipped out of the apartment, scuttled around the corner toward the west exit, and climbed the stairs by the door.

The upstairs hallway was clear and quiet.

Lili dashed over and sat, leaning tight to the door of 202. The entryway was inset by eighteen inches, effectively hiding her from prying eyes in the hallway. She brought up Word on her iPad, set the crystal out, and lit a candle.

She felt as taut as a spring.

Not good.

Following a routine, she closed her eyes and worked to settle her anxieties, wiggling her toes and working slowly up her legs and body.

As she reached for her crystal, the iPad came to life.

help me

* * *

Martin stood on the riverbank behind the mill.

SWAT was preparing to enter the apartment through the windows.

It was the easiest way in but inherently dangerous. Riddell might be hiding behind barricades, waiting to ambush the entry team. More likely, he had taken refuge in the basement. He knew the geography. Based on the security in his apartment, he was probably well prepared to mount a vigorous defense.

But what was the endgame?

Negotiate for the best deal on the charges? That wasn't happening. Take as many cops out as he could? Sow maximum chaos? Was he suicidal? Was the hostage even still alive?

They would soon find out. Hopefully, Riddell would speak to a negotiator, but his refusal to communicate so far did not bode well for that approach.

The south face of the mill had been built on a slope overlooking the river. The windows were tall, double hung, and wide enough for easy entry, but the sills were twelve feet above ground, too high for direct access. They were the only windows in the apartment.

Sam Farber had commandeered a scissors lift and several ladders from Bob's Equipment Rental three blocks over. They were feeling pressure to end this standoff before it turned into a circus. News crews were arriving en masse. The lieutenant had closed the street in front of the building to keep them away until they resolved the situation.

How did they know already? A tenant, probably.

The team wheeled the lift along a walkway and under the center window, then stabilized it with outrigger supports. Two officers stepped on board, armed with a battering ram and two Colt M4 assault rifles. They raised the platform into position, level with the windows, and signaled their readiness. Two more cops, armed with carbines, raised a ladder up to the lift platform. Indoors, another team stood ready to attack the apartment door as a distraction.

With everyone in position, Lieutenant Farber gave the signal to proceed.

One cop cut the screen. With one powerful stroke of the battering ram, the other cop took out the window, the frame, and the plywood. He stepped aside while his partner tossed a stun grenade into the apartment. A loud blast and brilliant flash followed.

Grabbing their weapons, barrels aimed forward, they charged in, shouting, "Police!"

Sam, trailed by two officers, scaled the ladder and went in. Martin could hear them working quickly through the apartment with occasional shouts of "Clear!"

A minute later, Sam appeared in the window. "Nobody here. We've opened the front door."

Martin walked around to the building entrance, down to the apartment where the lieutenant was waiting.

"So he's in the basement then. Did you check the bathroom?"

Farber nodded. "Come, take a look."

One glance in the bathroom and Martin understood. The vinyl flooring had been rolled back, exposing what looked like plywood subfloor. Looking closer, he realized it was a trapdoor, though the joint between the door and the surrounding subfloor was nearly invisible.

Martin shook his head. Unbelievable.

I talked to Emma. He gets down there through his bathroom.

Lili's words. How could she have possibly known? He wasn't ready to believe the woman talked to ghosts, but this was some spooky shit.

"Have you tried opening it?"

"There's no obvious handle. We're bringing some tools in. We'll try to pry it open with a Halligan."

Martin wandered around the apartment while they set up and worked on the door. It was spare, but tastefully decorated. It lacked any personal touches. No photographs of family or friends. When he saw the tower computer in the office, he called Jason, their computer forensics specialist.

"I need you at the Mills, unit 139. Bring your stuff."

Sam Farber leaned into the office and said, "We can't budge it. It's secured underneath."

"What now?"

"I have a big saw on the way."

Forty-Seven

Emma lurked in Lili's apartment, reading.

It was all well and good to declare war on Eamon, but in a practical sense, she had no idea how to proceed. He seemed to be one step ahead of her, directing events in the building and leaving chaos in his wake. The disruptive currents in the mill grew ever stronger and more unpredictable. She popped in and out of consciousness with little to no warning.

She decided Eamon was using some kind of magic to hobble her. Cheating, really. Reading about magic and witchcraft had clued her to his strategy, but she didn't know how to counter it. Emma spent hours studying the subject, but how useful would any of it be in practice?

Binding spells? Hexes? Revenge curses?

It sounded impressive.

But it was obvious she couldn't just toss spells about and effectively counter Eamon's magic without considerable practice. She recognized her disadvantage. He knew far more than she did and she had no time to learn.

Did Lili know magic? She had the books, she was psychic, and she had strange powers—like the ability to float through walls. Maybe she was a witch, too. If so, Emma had been wise to maintain a respectful distance. Still, could Lili handle Eamon? She hoped so. But would she? Whose side would Lili take?

Emma needed to talk to her, hoping Lili had the power to confront Eamon. Convince her to act on her behalf.

Could she trust her?

Right now, she felt naked and exposed, surrounded by people with too many advantages.

She sensed Eamon moving around the building. Or was she just imagining it? Emma had become increasingly distrustful—though she felt it was wise to assume people couldn't be trusted. People were base animals, looking out only for themselves. Her father, the men who killed Frank, many of the people she knew. All evil people who acted on impulse in their own best interests.

Why should she trust Lili?

It was simple, really. She had no choice. She had to trust *someone.*

Drifting through the hallways, searching, she found Lili outside 202.

Clever girl. She must have intuited how much time Emma spent there. Plus, it was kitty-corner to 222 and the skylight where she normally rested. A big assumption, though. Maybe it was a warning that Lili was moving in on her.

So much doubt and distrust lately. Her thinking had been increasingly paranoid. While she needed to remain vigilant, she had to relax. Hopefully, with Lili's intervention, they could neutralize Eamon and send him back to the cellar where he belonged.

Would a binding spell work? It sounded promising, but she felt driven by desperation, afraid of his magic.

Lili had her iPad at the ready. Emma jumped in, sliding back and forth, manipulating the virtual keyboard.

help me

Lili started. "Huh? What can I do?"

Emma liked Lili's voice. She wished she could talk again, wished she had a proper voice. It was a genuine hardship. When this mess was over, maybe they could be friends. Maybe together they could exile Eamon from the mill forever.

She felt strongly theirs was an existential battle. One of them would lose and be cast out. Though uncertain whether it was actually true, she had become fixated on the idea after reading about witchcraft. Maybe she was being a little melodramatic? She also thought about exorcism. As unpleasant as that experience had been, she had no qualms about unleashing those forces on Eamon, though worried the process would hurt her too. Maybe binding would be enough.

stop eamon

"The guy in the basement? How?"

bind him

Lili looked up roughly in Emma's direction. "What? Like a binding spell?"

yes

"I don't really do magic. You're a ghost; can't you bind him yourself?"

This wasn't going well. Emma felt a quiver of doubt. Definitely not a witch. Did the woman even know what she was doing?

no can you try

"I suppose, but I've never performed a binding spell."

first time for everything

The cocky answer belied an anxiety that Lili was unwilling or unable to help.

"What about my friend Olivia? The blonde woman?"

Emma realized she had lost sight of the issue—at least from Lili's point of view.

Or had she? Wasn't Eamon the one goading the psychopath along? The police would handle Chase Riddell. Getting rid of Eamon would only assist with that cause, and she hoped Lili understood as much.

shes okay

She had no idea how Olivia was doing, but sensed no harm had come to the woman. Still, why was she lying? It felt wrong, but she was worried and afraid, desperate to have some support in her fight with Eamon.

in cellar with eamon

That was true. Probably.

"She is? What can I do?"

If she got closer to Eamon, she might be more effective.

go there bind him

"In the basement?" Lili looked fairly horrified at the idea.

Then Emma felt herself slipping away. Darn! She quickly typed a message—

yes fading i

In a last desperate effort, she tried to speak to Lili.

Not even a whisper came out.

Then she was gone.

Forty-Eight

Raleigh crept along the south passage.

Tight against the inside wall to present as small a target as possible, he sidestepped in the dark. It was quiet, other than the muffled sounds coming from above: footsteps, plumbing, doors closing, a dog barking. It smelled vaguely damp.

The old instincts were kicking in. Just like riding a bike. But he felt a weird unease he couldn't explain. It wasn't the darkness. He had been in plenty of dark places in Afghanistan. It was something else. Maybe Lili and her strange ideas were rubbing off on him.

After all, he was down here based on intel from a ghost.

Jesus!

About twenty feet up, he found a small alcove on the inner wall. Suitable spots to hole up if gunfire broke out. Good to know. Hopefully, there were more. He had worried about cover, but hoped his training and skills would allow him to sneak up on the bastard and neutralize him without firing a shot.

He leaned in and rested. The tension sapped his energy. He was out of shape. Fit maybe, but not to the level he had attained in the service.

Raleigh took a deep breath and continued edging along the wall. Another twenty feet up, he found another alcove.

Excellent.

His eyes were fully attuned to the dark. There was a faint wash of light about sixty feet farther along the passage. He dared not use the Maglite.

Fighting the urge to rush, he stepped up the pace while maintaining a silent approach. Time was running out. He feared Olivia would die if the police blundered into the basement—or he dithered too long.

Suddenly, someone stepped out in front of him, about twenty feet away, perhaps from another alcove. In the dark, he couldn't tell if the guy was armed or not, but he looked vaguely luminous and held something in his hand. Was that a gun? Or a trick of the light?

Gun.

All that passed through his mind in a millisecond as his finger closed on the trigger of the AR-15. He fired a tight pattern of three at chest level.

The figure evaporated.

What the fuck?

He flattened himself against the wall. Moments later, a head and a gun appeared farther up followed by a burst of gunfire.

Jesus!

One round glanced off his vest. A stunning blow that winded him and nearly knocked him down.

He fired another burst and scrambled back to the last alcove to regroup.

A man yelled, "Get out of here or I'll kill her!"

Raleigh fell back out of the line of fire.

Fuck!

He had lost the element of surprise. And who or what was the thing in the passage? Was he imagining things? Freaking out? Was he that rusty?

No. He had definitely seen something. Something strange. Not quite human.

What the—?

Raleigh tried to sidestep the thought, but a name popped into his head anyway.

Frank.

⋆ ⋆ ⋆

Chase watched the show from his armory.

He had multiple cameras covering the apartment, including the bathroom. They came in as expected, through the window with flash bangs. They would repeat the tactic once they breached the door in the bathroom floor. He heard a chainsaw somewhere in the far distance but wrote it off as irrelevant. It had to be outside.

How had they zeroed in on him so quickly? They must have suspected him before he snatched the psychic bitch. And how did they know she was gone? He didn't get it. Didn't matter, it was a moot point now. SWAT was here and they were coming in.

He continued to weigh his options. As long as he was moving, running, he stood a chance of getting out of this. He couldn't decide about the psychic. Take her or kill her? Most likely, she would be a burden with little upside.

The biggest hurdle was getting away from the building. But he had a plan and a few aces up his sleeve to avoid capture. Once he was clear, he would go southwest. Get lost in one of the big cities out there—

Eamon whispered in his head. *There's someone in the passage and he's armed.*

"What? Who? A cop?"

Don't know. Not a copper. He came in the other end. He has several guns.

He sensed Eamon leaving. It felt like a breeze. Seconds later, a burst of gunfire came from the west end. The wrong end of the passage.

Shit!

The dude was right.

Chase grabbed the AR-15 and glimpsed down the passage. He saw a shadowy figure, aimed, and fired back.

The guy scrambled sideways out of sight.

Who the fuck was this lone ranger? Had to be the boyfriend. An unexpected wrinkle. Just his luck, the guy was armed to the teeth. One of the unknown unknowns in this mess. And he had no cameras facing that direction.

He yelled, "Get out of here or I'll kill her!"

Chase ducked back into the armory. Shit, things were getting hairy. It was almost time to leave.

He checked his watch. After seven. It would be dark soon. He just had to hold things together a little longer. While he liked the idea of having a hostage, it wasn't practical. She wasn't his type, anyway.

He needed the cops to breach right now. All their attention and energy would be directed to that task.

Really, what the fuck was taking them so long?

His escape route lay behind him through the well room. A secret door into the closet of apartment 106. Hidden and braced with two four-by-fours, he had cut and prepared the opening soon after he moved in, before the unit sold. The exterior windows sat at ground level and a dense briar hedge ran along the outside wall. He could creep behind it and get close to the river. Create some kind of diversion to cover his escape. Once he was in the river, he had a snorkel and a route out of town mapped.

He believed escape was possible.

And he would.

He was just that good.

Forty-Nine

Martin and Sam debated the idea.

Sitting in the command center, they discussed calling in the FBI. Sam had mentioned it first, but to Martin, it felt unnecessary. They had solved the abduction. They just hadn't resolved it—though that was an area where the FBI excelled. He had called their best negotiator, Janine Archer, who was on her way. He hoped that worked out. Even without the psychic confirmation, he was almost certain Danielle was dead. This woman, Olivia Kaplan, still had a chance. Maybe. It was dangerous to assume anything in a hostage situation.

Martin said, "It's your call, of course. I think you have things in hand—"

The muffled *pop pop pop* of gunfire from somewhere in the basement startled them both.

"Who the hell is shooting?"

Sam jumped up, looking perplexed. "I don't know. I thought it was just our guy and the hostage down there. Checking his weapons, maybe? Trying to warn us off?"

A second burst of gunfire followed. Then a third.

Nobody wanted to speak about the alternate possibility. But surely Riddell wouldn't kill his hostage before they breached the basement, would he?

One of the SWAT guys walked in wielding a large circular saw. "Open it now?"

Farber jumped up and strode toward the apartment. "Yep. We need to get down there to assess."

Martin wondered if they were too late. The gunfire had shaken him. What was going on down there? Their SWAT team was well trained, but this kind of entry was inherently dangerous. They would scope the basement, then hit it with flash bangs before an entry. Chase would know all of this and plan accordingly. In the worst case, Farber could be sending people into a shooting gallery.

How had they reached this crazy juncture? How had Chase passed his psych evaluation? This promised to be a huge black eye for the department—but he regretted the thought at once. A woman was dead. One was missing. One had been taken hostage. All at the hands of a psychopath who happened to be a cop.

What a nightmare.

The saw was loud and angry, even at a distance.

Martin wandered over to 139, curious, watching the team in action.

The saw quit abruptly. A muffled bang followed.

The team leader popped out of the bathroom a moment later. "It's open. Dark and quiet right now."

"Any contact?"

"Nothing. We're dropping a camera down now for a better look."

"Good," Sam said. He and Martin watched as a monitor lit up and displayed the camera feed as they rotated and scanned the scene. It revealed a room with a TV, deck chairs, and a table. It looked like a backyard hangout lit by a wash of light from above. The adjoining room appeared empty, too, no threats evident.

Going quiet, they went to hand signals to communicate.

The team members donned their night-vision gear. A stun grenade went into the opening and a muffled boom followed. Sam Farber and four members of the SWAT team dropped into the room below.

Martin heard a quiet, "Clear."

So far, so good.

* * *

Lili sat outside 202.

Parsing Emma's words. Trying to plan her next moves. Gathering her courage to go into the basement and confront Eamon.

Then she heard cops farther down the hallway, knocking and telling people they had to leave.

Time to move.

Rushing down the stairs and into the Kaplans' apartment, she locked the door, leaned against it, and fretted about going into the basement. Did she have the nerve?

Lili vacillated. Paced the living room. Sat and chewed on her nail. She wanted to help Olivia and Emma, but going into the basement felt unspeakably dangerous.

There was a killer in the basement. Raleigh was down there as well and heavily armed. And there was Eamon. An unknown, and probably dangerous.

She heard muffled gunfire. Three quick rounds. Silence. Three more. Then another three.

A gunfight.

Shit!

Had Raleigh prevailed? It was too scary to contemplate the alternative.

There was a loud knock on the door.

"Police! We need to clear the building."

They continued rapping for thirty seconds before they gave up and moved on. Would they come back with the door code? She couldn't take the chance.

Shutting the lights off, Lili grabbed the bag with her stuff and found a flashlight in the gun safe, one of three. She flicked it on. It was dazzling.

She navigated the mess in the kitchen, ducked into the pantry, and turned the light off.

Remembering the ladder, she put a tentative foot through the hole in the floor and found the top step. She whispered, "Thank you, Raleigh."

A way in—and a way out. Quickly, if need be.

Lili climbed down—deciding she would go no farther than the bottom of the ladder—and looked both ways, trying to get her bearings in the near darkness. She considered calling Raleigh's name quietly, but thought better of it. Any sound might draw the wrong kind of attention.

The air stirred like icy breath on her neck. A creepy feeling, causing her skin to contract like crepe paper. Lili froze. She wasn't alone.

A voice spoke in her head. A male voice with an Irish accent.

Hello, Lili.

She startled and almost bolted up the ladder, but forced herself to stand her ground. She stood, rigid with fear, took a deep breath, and quietly said, "Who are you?"

Eamon O'Keene. At your service.

A sensation like a cold, wet finger slid down her spine. She had sensed his presence down here before. According to Emma, he might be the devil himself. She fought the urge to run.

"What do you want?"

I have information. Vital information.

God, he sounded creepy. No other word for it. As pleasant as he attempted to sound, she sensed an inner darkness. A cold, bitter wasteland.

"Is Olivia okay?"

She's fine. Don't worry.

"How do you know that?"

A long moment passed.

"Hello?"

Finally, he spoke.

Don't trust Emma, she's—

A saw started up somewhere and echoed through the passages. She missed his last words.

"Eamon?"

No answer. Had he slipped away? No matter. Lili decided Emma was right.

Don't trust Emma?

Clearly, it was Eamon who was dangerous and couldn't be trusted. Whatever he wanted to say, she suspected it would be lies and misinformation. Better not to listen.

To bind Eamon most effectively, she needed a possession of his, but she had nothing. Would words alone work?

She held the amulet in one hand, her crystal in the other, and recited the only binding spell she could remember: "I bind you, Eamon O'Keene, I bind you from doing harm. I bind you, Eamon O'Keene, I bind you from doing harm. I bind you, Eamon O'Keene, I bind you from doing harm."

Lili kept repeating the spell until she felt the force of it leave her fingers, seeking the target at the speed of light.

Time to get out. Her skin was crawling.

She was concerned for Emma's well-being, but why did she refuse to speak? First Frank, now Eamon. Everyone could speak but Emma. What was she missing? What was Emma hiding?

As she climbed out of the basement, she heard more gunfire.

Fifty

Raleigh hung in the alcove, reassessing.

The advantage of surprise had been lost and the bastard was threatening to kill Olivia.

Should he back up and take the other passage? That might restore an element of surprise, but he hated to waste the time. SWAT would burst in soon. Pressure from the cops on the other end would create the needed diversion. Enough to throw the psycho off.

Maybe.

It also created new dangers. The cops didn't know he was down here. He could become a target.

The passage was near dark. If he lay down and low-crawled, he would be virtually invisible unless the guy had night-vision gear. He hadn't been wearing any earlier, had he? Raleigh ran the encounter through his mind, visualizing every moment. Guy, dark hair, about five-eleven, wielding an AR-15, but no eyewear.

Good.

He peeked along the passage occasionally, but the guy wasn't showing himself. Why? Was he otherwise occupied? Hurting Olivia?

Raleigh tried to shake that awful image; felt the window to save her closing rapidly—

A commotion somewhere overhead. Heavy footsteps. The cops were coming. He had to act and hope SWAT gave him cover for the final twenty feet without getting Olivia killed. The racket above should work.

He slung the AR-15 over his shoulder, lay down, and low-crawled silently to the next alcove, keeping the Glock 19 pointed forward.

So far, so good.

The noise overhead stopped. The quiet seemed preternatural.

Not good.

The din of a saw ripped through the silence. Had to be the cops at the other end. Evidently, they had the same idea he had about getting in.

Loud and angry, it was perfect.

He stood and charged with fast, light steps. The circular saw echoed down the passages, covering the little noise he made.

Ten feet from the doorway, he stopped and pulled in tight, his back to the wall as he crept forward. He holstered the Glock and eased the barrel of the AR-15 around and forward, ready to fire.

There were no changes in the dim light from the room. No hint of activity. It was just enough light to spot his opponent and shoot him. No half measures now. No questions. Just aim and kill.

Three feet from the doorway, the barrel of a gun snapped around the corner, pointed right at him. A Sig P226.

Fuck!

Raleigh dropped like a rock as the gun barked. He felt a bullet smack the top of his helmet, knocking it off as he squeezed the trigger and fired a burst at the doorway. But the angle was too acute. Some of the rounds scrambled the brick work while one ricocheted back and glanced off the opposite wall.

"Shit!"

He scuttled backward but the gun did not reappear. The guy was dealing with threats on two fronts.

Good.

Raleigh shoved the rifle aside, grabbed his pistol in one deft motion, and trained it on the doorway. There was no room to handle a long gun. The extra microseconds in bringing the rifle to bear could be the difference between life and death. The Glock was a better weapon at close quarters with plenty of stopping power and fifteen rounds in the magazine.

But the gun still did not reappear. Curious.

He was committed. No turning back. Hopefully, the bastard was too distracted by the impending arrival of the cops to fully engage him. With SWAT coming in, Olivia was valuable. That would keep her alive, unless they bungled the operation.

The guy must have a camera somewhere. How else had he seen him coming? He hoped it was aimed more at head and torso level. That was the usual case.

He scuttled forward in low-crawl, using his elbows, closing in on the doorway.

Raleigh trained the gun forward, up at a slight angle, ready for anything. The angry growl of the saw echoing along the dark hallways provided perfect cover for his approach.

He imagined his ultimate moves while remaining alert for any countermeasures: a quick shove forward, a roll, an instant assessment of the room, aiming the Glock and killing the rogue cop.

The Sig popped around the corner. Raleigh pulled up slightly and fired three quick shots.

The gun went flying—blown right out of the hand holding it.

Nailed it!

A quick smirk. His eye was still deadly.

Raleigh rolled and leapt to his feet, pivoting toward the opening and bringing his pistol to bear, fully primed and feeling murderous.

That bastard cop had microseconds to live.

Fifty-One

Chase couldn't wait much longer.

The guy coming in the other end had convinced him the sooner he ran, the better. The sun had set. Darkness was falling.

Where in the hell was SWAT? Jesus. He knew they were incompetent, but this was ridiculous. He needed the diversion. Best to have them concentrating their energies on gaining access to the basement and trying to flush him out while he slipped away.

Suddenly, Eamon was back.

The other guy is moving in. Thirty feet.

Then the saw started up.

This was fun. Cops coming at him one way, some lone wolf the other. He expected them to pry or chop their way through the door, but they took a more direct approach. Someone had found a big heavy-duty circular saw and they were making quick work of his door.

Twenty feet.

Eamon's voice was clear over the din. Chase eased over to the doorway, staying out of the wash of light from the monitors to avoid giving himself away.

Ten feet, right on the inside wall. Fire along the wall.

Chase grabbed the Sig P226. A great weapon, accurate and deadly at this range.

He's going to pop around the corner. Take him now.

Chase snapped the gun around the corner and fired. He heard something clatter to the floor. A helmet?

Nailed him!

The moment of elation evaporated when several bullets slammed into the edge of the doorway. Chase recoiled from a spray of brick fragments.

"Shit!"

Things were getting hairy. He didn't need the added distraction of this asshole while SWAT threatened from the other end.

He whispered tersely, "Eamon! Where the fuck are you?"

The saw roared on, his heartbeat thumped, but no Eamon.

Chase heard a snicker. *Problem, mate?*

"Where is the bastard?"

Hmm. Let me look.

"Don't take all fucking day," Chase whispered, feeling the pressure wearing on him. This weekend warrior could pop through the doorway any moment. It would almost be like a duel. Who had the faster reaction time? He wished he had time to drag the bitch out here and use her as a human shield. He should have kept her closer at hand.

He's crawling up with a pistol. Shoot down at a forty-five-degree angle.

Chase did a quick calculation of the angle and stuck his gun around the corner as he squeezed the trigger.

Three lightning-fast shots ripped the pistol from his grip.

"Fuck!"

After a quick assessment of his hand—yes, all the fingers were still there—he grabbed a Glock 22, swiveled, and fired three rounds as the guy did some fancy rolling move and brought his gun to bear. Chase fired a microsecond faster. The rounds hit the guy and threw him backward, slamming his head into the brick wall.

He dropped like a rag doll.

Threat eliminated.

The saw quit, followed by a loud bang as the heavy square of wood hit the floor.

Chase checked the monitor.

A camera dropped downward and scanned the room.

Here they come.

A minute later, a flash bang dropped, followed by five SWAT members wearing night-vision gear.

He waited until they cleared the first two rooms and set their sights on the hallways. The camera appeared in the opening at the end of the north passage. With the AR-15, he fired a long burst, then scrambled over to the south hallway and fired a second volley.

Silence.

Mostly. He felt almost deaf, his ears ringing from the gunfire and the rush of blood pumping to his brain.

Sam Farber yelled out, "Chase, let's talk."

He waited thirty seconds and yelled back, "Get a negotiator down here. I want Janine Archer."

"On the way! Hold tight. How's the hostage?"

"She's fine."

"Good! Let's keep it that way."

The clock was ticking. The negotiator would arrive soon. Janine Archer was meticulous and would want a full briefing. Most of the energy would be directed to facilitating her efforts. They had confirmed he was in the basement and willing to talk. The officers outside would relax and focus on crowd control. Meanwhile, SWAT would plan their next moves in case negotiations failed.

No matter. He wouldn't be here.

With the cloud cover, it was nearly dark.

Time to run.

The guy in the hallway remained inert. Probably dead. Chase debated what to do with the woman. He didn't have time to fuck her. Given the trouble she had caused him, she wasn't getting out alive. He had an idea.

He stripped, dumped his clothing on the floor, and dressed in the dark, lightweight gear he had laid out for the upcoming swim, wincing from one of the injuries Danielle had inflicted. He clipped two stun grenades to his belt and slipped the Glock into a waterproof swim bag, along with two spare magazines and dry clothes. Slipped a wicked switchblade into his back pocket. If he needed more weaponry, he was in trouble and probably wouldn't make it.

He grabbed his snorkel and hit the main breaker to kill the power, rendering the armory pitch black. He peeked around the corner. There was a thin wash of light from the end where SWAT had set up. Good thing he didn't need the hallway. They would never see him leave.

Chase went into the adjoining room, clicked his flashlight on, and stared at the frightened woman on the floor. He tossed his phone into the two-foot diameter drain, picked up her squirming body, and sat her on the rim of the opening. Clipping the tape from her hands, he shoved her in with a satisfying splash. It was a shame, but she really wasn't his type. Served her right for ruining his well-laid plans.

"I hope you can swim, bitch."

He turned the light out and slammed the door. Someone would find her.

Eventually.

Fifty-Two

Olivia was exhausted.

Hours of sheer terror had depleted her adrenaline reserves. Fear of rape. Fear of death. Fear of the unknown.

Lying on the cold stone floor, she was chilled beyond feeling. The room was so dark she imagined things. Ghostly creatures flitting in and out of view. The vague sound of running water. Faint steps overhead.

Gunfire.

After a while, she felt delirious, her thinking skewed and foggy. Her heartbeat thumped in her ears like a subwoofer.

She imagined rescue. Raleigh. The police. Firefighters. But she focused on Raleigh. He was capable. Special Forces. He would fight to find her. She just knew it. Yes, he could be an insufferable ass, but he loved her deeply and she loved him just as much.

Maybe she slept for a while.

How much time had passed?

Hours?

Days? That seemed unlikely.

The door opened. A flashlight lit up and blinded her. A man picked her up, set her down, and ripped the tape off of her wrists. Her vision improved and she realized she was looking down a well or something, water visible about ten feet down.

A jolt of terror ripped through her. She tried to scream, but tape still covered her mouth. Before she could react, he shoved her and she fell into the dark, hitting the water with a splash.

Overhead, he muttered something.

Then the lights went out.

* * *

Emma felt the tide turning against her.

Determined to best Eamon at any cost, she had sought Lili's help to cast a binding spell on him, but so far, nothing had changed. Instead, he seemed to be growing more powerful and audacious. She sensed him expanding his range above ground, encroaching on her territory in apparent violation of the rules, though Emma was no longer certain there were rules. They seemed to shift without rhyme or reason, and had become increasingly skewed against her.

Gunfire had broken out somewhere below. A black, corrosive wave of energy arising from the cellar followed in a painful distortion of the energy fields. Some new wrinkle in the disturbingly complex atmosphere of the Mill. Had someone else died?

Whatever it was, it had to be Eamon's fault.

He had to be stopped.

Emma had no idea how. Instead, she felt herself coming unglued. She trusted no one and increasingly doubted her own senses.

She had been counting on Lili, but the binding spell appeared to have no effect on Eamon. Maybe Lili wasn't so powerful after all. Or was she? Emma recognized a new potential threat. What if Eamon won her over to his side? What if Lili bound her instead? In the current scheme of things, Emma still didn't know if Lili was friend or foe.

She had her own problems. As the tension ramped up, her awareness waxed and waned in erratic cycles. She felt disconnects in her thinking and moments of confusion. It was frustrating. How was she supposed to maintain a cogent presence to counter Eamon's malign influence? Maybe Lili was still working on a binding spell and would hobble him yet.

Would it make a difference?

She should be the more powerful of the two based on her ability to navigate through most of the building, by her status as star of the night shift. That wasn't how things were working out.

Emma went looking for him—a task not even possible a few days ago—but Eamon seemed to be nowhere and everywhere at once. How? Had the rules ever been real? Or had she and Eamon simply conformed to self-imposed boundaries? He stayed in the cellar because he died there. She stayed in the mill for the same reason, though she didn't understand the dynamic between her and Frank. Or Tommy.

As she searched, the atmosphere slowly changed.

She felt freer. Lighter. More present.

Was it Lili? Had the binding spell finally worked?

It seemed so.

She sensed the Irishman fighting the spell and then she intercepted something more tangible.

A train of thought.

Chase is going to run. He's going to run downriver. Must tell the coppers.

It belonged to Eamon. Could she read his mind? Or had she imagined the voice?

But it felt like a new skill. Something Lili had given her?

It was real. Peering inside his head, Eamon's machinations were exposed and unfolding before her eyes.

Eamon had coaxed Chase Riddell further into crime and convinced him to grab the blonde woman. Riddell was plenty evil on his own, but Eamon had driven him to new lows, growing stronger in the process. But his goals seemed contradictory. As he pushed the cop further into lunacy, he also appeared to be setting him up to fail. Reveling in the violence and yet, trying to end it. Emma couldn't comprehend the strategy.

He was plotting an outcome to his advantage, though. The bastard was conniving to talk with the police by drawing on their board or using an iPad, in effect, stealing her ideas!

Somehow, he felt aiding in the capture of Chase Riddell would improve his standing and make him more powerful. Maybe it would. She didn't know, but his goal was clear: to push her out and become boss of the mill.

Phooey!

Not if she had a say in it.

She knew his game plan. If the binding spell controlled him, he was exposed—an advantage she would use to beat him at his own game.

If she could just figure out how.

Pondering the question, she watched, astonished as Riddell escaped with impunity. He skulked through an apartment and jumped out a window.

He was gone and no one seemed to know.

Except her. And maybe Eamon.

Question answered. She knew what to do. Tell Lili and steal Eamon's thunder before he had a chance to tell anyone.

Eamon himself had given her the answer: *he's going to run downriver.*

She rushed off, looking for Lili.

Right now, only one thing mattered.

That she had the first word.

And the last.

Fifty-Three

Chase slipped into the adjoining room.

A long narrow space, it had a rough dirt floor. In the far corner, a ladder rested against the brick wall beneath apartment 106.

As he reached the ladder, Chase said, "So, my friend, I guess this is goodbye."

He heard a hollow chuckle that seemed to emanate from everywhere.

"What's so funny?"

You're going to jail, matey.

"What?"

Eamon spoke with a sing-song lilt.

Forever.

"I thought you were my friend."

I'm not your friend, you wanker.

A mocking laugh followed.

"Fuck you!" Chase hissed.

Enjoy prison, fool.

Chase climbed quickly, trying to shake off the sense of betrayal he felt. He had never been able to trust his friends. Bunch of backstabbing bastards. Why should this time be different?

Releasing the sliding bolts from the supports, the hatch fell open. He listened for a moment, but the apartment was quiet. Chase crawled up into the dark closet onto a narrow ledge and slipped his gun from the waterproof bag. He really hoped no one was home. Having to shoot them would be loud and inconvenient.

He eased the closet door open. The apartment was dark.

Good.

Chase crept into the living room, over to the window. It was dark out, the parking lot lit by halogen lights on tall black poles. Red and blue lights flashed everywhere. He smiled. This was a big deal. He was a big deal. A successful escape would make him bigger than life. He would become a legend. A bona fide serial killer, three kills to his credit. For now, anyway. Once free, he'd start up again somewhere else.

Positive mental attitude. It was the secret to life.

The windows were double-hung, and one was fully open. The bottom half of the window lay below the top of the manicured hedgerow that ran along the front of the building, hiding heat pumps, air conditioners, and utility meters.

He had to go west. He could make out squads at that corner of the parking lot, holding the perimeter. Otherwise, the area was clear. All attention was focused on the east end of the building and his apartment.

Perfect.

Chase slit the screen and slid through, onto the ground, stopping to catch his breath. The soil was dry. Rock hard. A faint scent of dead fish wafted off the nearby river. He walked slowly in a crouch along the wall, invisible to anyone on the other side of the hedge, all the way to the corner. A hundred feet closer to freedom.

The foliage was dense, but he caught glimpses of the two squads, parked at right angles, one looking east over the asphalt parking lot, the other pointed south, toward the river. The cops seated within looked bored. They didn't expect any activity. The bad guy was in the basement.

He was about to fuck up their day.

Chase paused for a minute and caught his breath. Slowed his breathing to a calm state. Eyed the terrain. It was fifteen feet across a sidewalk and the lawn to another hedgerow. Behind that, a brick wall on the property line that ran down to the river.

He saw no one by the road. No one by the river. It was mostly dark on this side of the building, as he knew it would be.

Fifteen feet of open ground. He could do this.

He pulled the pins on two flash bangs and tossed them toward the front of each squad car.

They landed precisely and exploded.

Perfect.

He dashed across the open space to the hedgerow and forced his way through it, snagging his clothes and scratching at his skin. Concealed, he turned back to look. The cops in the squads still looked disoriented. There was no activity for a moment. Martin then ran out the front door of the mill. No one was looking toward the water.

Chase scrambled along the wall to the river. It was rough. The hedge was closer to the wall—nothing to hide here—and he fought it all the way. Kept his right shoulder hard to the bricks, trying to avoid visibly disturbing the hedge, but all attention remained concentrated where the flash bangs had gone off. Chase slithered the last five feet to the river's edge like a snake.

He drew a deep breath and slid under the water. Swam out twenty feet and poked the tip of the snorkel above the surface. Took another breath and swam with easy strokes to avoid disturbing the surface of the water with eddies or a wake.

The river was cool but tolerable and inky black.

Perfect.

Freedom was close at hand.

It felt peaceful beneath the surface after all the chaos in the building. An adept swimmer, he reached the small island in the middle of the river in about five minutes. The island was bisected by railroad tracks, a trestle crossing the river diagonally on the mill side, sweeping northwest beyond the property wall. On the far side, an old rail bridge crossed the river. The island was otherwise undeveloped, a rocky outcrop of limestone covered with tenacious spruces and scrub pine. He paused, catching his breath.

The path was clear.

As he rounded the west end of the island, he was no longer visible to the mill or the north riverbank.

A mere six miles to a car. A disguise. Money.

He was almost free.

Fifty-Four

The command center was quiet.

Martin sat, briefing the negotiator, Janine Archer. The night shift lieutenant, John Tisak, was rushing in to take his place unless Sam finished in the basement first. Then the two lieutenants would coordinate, and Martin would gladly hand it to them.

Abby positioned squads as they arrived, coordinating with the officers in the field, holding the perimeter, and working crowd control around the building. Two other officers, Kate Alford and Andy Szymanski assisted, handling updates by cell phone to keep all communication off police radio frequencies.

Two loud blasts outdoors disturbed the calm. Facing the entrance, Martin saw bright flashes through the front door from the parking lot.

Flash bangs?

All activity in the room stopped.

Martin jumped up, scanning the room. "What the hell was that?"

Silence. Everyone looked equally puzzled. Abby shrugged.

He ran out the front door and looked down the parking lot. The officers were just emerging from their squad cars, looking confused and disoriented. Had they accidentally set one off? But he remembered hearing two.

He yelled, "Did you guys do that?"

One cop shook his head. "Nope. Never saw them coming."

Martin stopped and looked around, thinking, trying to figure it out.

It had to be a diversion. Did Riddell have an accomplice?

Then he connected the dots. "He's out! Search that end of the property! Now! Everything!"

Martin typed a message to Sam Farber on his phone.

I think he's out. Unsure about hostage.

He received a reply as he returned to the command center.

We'll take his position to check for hostage. Organize a search until Tisak arrives.

Martin looked around the room. "I think Riddell is out. Alford and Szymanski, go help search the west end of the building and the property."

He rolled up the blueprints and tossed them aside. "Abby, get me the county map!"

She carried it in from the hall. Five-by-nine feet on a dry erase board, they laid it across two tables.

"Send squads here, here, and here," he said, looking to Abby and pointing to various intersections in town. "Then get the sheriff on the line."

Looking the map over, he pointed to the river. "He probably went into the river. I want a squad downriver on each side. Have them set up here, and here. Watch the river carefully and await further instructions. Call in the K9—"

Martin stopped and stared at the top edge of the board. On it, someone had scrawled:

He's running out of town

It was creepy and inexplicable. He pointed and spoke tersely. "Who did this?"

The officers stared, dumbfounded. The name Lili Paltrinieri popped into his head.

Seconds later, they heard gunfire below.

⋆ ⋆ ⋆

Lili emerged cautiously from the pantry.

The apartment was quiet, but two loud reports like firecrackers broke the silence.

She felt a peculiar sensation of motion—some swirling shift in the aura of the mill, but not a ghost or spirit. Something more tangible. She didn't understand it.

A commotion ramped up outdoors, people shouting and running about.

Where was Raleigh? Olivia?

She wanted to talk to Emma. Maybe she could explain the odd aura. But mostly, she was concerned for Emma's well-being. Had the binding spell worked? Had she neutralized Eamon?

The power structure between the ghosts in the mill was baffling. Was there such a thing? Emma implied there was, and it appeared to define her conflict with Eamon. If they had more time to talk, Emma could explain it—though if she needed Lili's help against Eamon, she probably wasn't the one in charge.

Lili grabbed her iPad and checked the peephole before opening the door.

The hallway was clear.

Bolting down the hall, she ran up the stairs by the exit, two at a time. She saw cops with flashlights through the exterior door, searching around outside. She hoped they hadn't seen her. Who or what were they looking for?

Had Chase Riddell escaped?

She ran to 202 and sat tight to the door in the corner to evade prying eyes. Laying the iPad on the floor, she leaned back, controlling her breathing, trying to relax. Willing Emma to talk to her.

The commotion outdoors continued. She heard gunfire below but shut it out, attempting to reach a meditative state—to open to conversation with a ghost.

"Emma?"

Her iPad vibrated and a message appeared.

cop escaped

"He's out?"

yes going east

"Where?"

downriver tell cops

"Is Olivia okay?"

think so yes

Oh, thank God.

"Did the binding spell work?"

Nothing.

Lili, willing the iPad to respond, picked it up and shook it. Like that would help.

Tersely, she said, "Emma? What about the binding spell?"

Minutes passed, but the device remained silent. She was dying to know if the spell worked—

tell cops

Lili started, recalling Emma's words.

Did Martin know Chase Riddell was running? Was that the commotion outside? She had to find Martin. Make sure he knew. No way was Chase getting away.

At least Olivia was safe.

Lili ran down the stairs to the first floor, hurrying along the wall, pausing in doorways, peeking ahead as she went. She wouldn't be stopped and turned around. The hallway was reasonably quiet, but she heard muffled gunfire below. If Chase had run, what were they shooting at?

The lobby looked clear. The conference room was just off to the right. Lili threw all caution to the wind and ran through the doorway into the room. As a cop stood to stop her, she swiveled around and saw Martin.

"He's out and running! I know which way he's going!"

Fifty-Five

Sam Farber's phone vibrated.

A text from Martin.

I think he's out. Unsure about hostage.

Sam groaned.

How did that happen? Shit!

If Riddell was fleeing, he had probably left the hostage behind. Alive, hopefully.

Just to be sure before they moved, Sam bellowed, "Chase? The negotiator is here!"

Silence.

Sam had assembled a small team because of the confined spaces. Kyle Russo, Matt Jorgenson, Brooke Neske, and his son Travis, were his best officers. Each had at least three years on the SWAT team and the highest consistent scores in marksmanship.

While they were waiting for the negotiator to arrive, the team had searched the first three rooms but found little of interest. The first room really did look like a backyard hangout: beer and vodka in the fridge, dirty glasses and empty bottles, deck chairs and a table, a large flatscreen on the wall. There was a lateral hallway off the second room with a door in the middle of the far wall. Two hallways extended west under the building.

After a camera scan, they breached the middle door.

Dark and grim, it looked like a bedroom, a bedroom from a horror movie furnished with only one item: a four-poster king bed with steel rings and restraints on each bedpost. The walls and ceiling had been soundproofed.

Ugh.

Sam tried to stay focused to avoid contemplating the vile acts perpetrated on that bed. Beyond that space, they found a closet sized room furnished with only a mattress and a bucket.

A jail cell.

No sign of Danielle Hamlin or the hostage.

Damn it!

Sam shuddered and briefly hoped Chase Riddell gave him an excuse to shoot him. Really. Why not save the taxpayers the cost of a trial? But the feeling passed. As righteous and satisfying as instant justice might feel, he could end up in jail himself.

With their cameras and night-vision gear, they scoped the long hallways. The south passage was pitch black. A bundle lay on the floor near a doorway about a hundred feet down the tunnel. It looked like a dead body.

Probably not the hostage. It couldn't be Riddell. Who else was down here?

Then he remembered the gunfire earlier and the wide-eyed crazy guy, Raleigh Kaplan. Had he tried to handle the situation himself? If Riddell had found a way out, it seemed possible Kaplan had found a way in.

The north passage had some ambient lighting and a doorway partway down on the left. Perhaps additional rooms or a connecting passage between the hallways.

Sam assumed Riddell had set up down there. With cameras, he could monitor both hallways and respond accordingly. Sam sent a text to the SWAT command vehicle requesting two ballistic shields which arrived a minute later. Bulletproof with armored viewing ports and built-in spotlights, the shields would protect them as they rushed the center position. Once they confirmed Riddell had fled, they would focus on finding the hostage.

On Farber's signal, they lined up in position: Brooke and Travis by the south hallway, Sam, Matt, and Kyle facing the north passage. They had communications headsets but agreed to minimal conversation.

Sam yelled one final time. "Chase!"

Silence.

Sam gave a hand signal. He and Brooke tossed flash bangs down the hallways to temporarily blind any cameras. After the charges detonated, Brooke and Travis marched down the south hallway at a brisk clip behind their shield.

Matt and Sam led, going down the north side, holding the shield, guns trained down the passage, walking in a fast shuffle. Kyle followed closely, the group arranged in a tight triangle. Brightly lit by the shield lights, the hallway was stark grey and empty; silent, the atmosphere tense. A walk into the unknown.

A gun could appear without warning.

Suddenly, a man appeared and charged at them. He seemed to materialize out of thin air. What?

Sam yelled, "Freeze!"

The guy kept coming and Sam felt a microsecond of confusion. The attacker looked almost luminous.

Was that a rifle he was holding? No time to consider—

Sam fired three quick rounds, center mass, with his service Beretta.

The guy evaporated.

What the hell?

He and Matt stopped and looked at each other, dumbfounded, while Kyle whispered, "What the fuck?"

Moments later, shots from the other passage broke the silence.

Sam whispered, "Brooke?"

"Something charged at us and disappeared."

"Any danger?"

"No idea."

Sam waited a full sixty seconds before giving the go-ahead.

They stepped forward, guns leading. The odd experience had shaken his normally calm demeanor. Did Riddell have some sort of 3D imaging system in place to throw them off? Nothing else made sense.

He focused on the doorway to the left, about forty feet up, starkly outlined by the harsh beams of the spotlights. Slowing the pace, he eased forward, alert to the slightest movement. What if Riddell hadn't fled? Was he laying a trap?

The shields weren't foolproof. If he aimed at their legs—

Something jumped through the doorway and rushed them. A bulbous face—just a face—that resolved into a horrendous glowing maw filled with teeth like a killer shark.

What the fuck?

A hologram?

Had to be.

But it looked so real.

He and Matt both gasped in shock in the instant before they both fired on the specter and the image evaporated.

A simultaneous ricochet rang out and Matt Jorgenson went down.

Sam heard gunfire from the other passage and yelled, "Pull back! Pull back!"

He and Kyle Russo grabbed Matt by the vest and dragged him as they retreated to the entry room.

Shit!

One team member down and no sign of Riddell or the hostage.

This wasn't going well.

Fifty-Six

Frank was coming unglued, literally.

It felt like he was disintegrating, spreading bits and pieces of him all over the place. Illogically, he also felt more focused. He had finally met Tommy who was feeling the same unnerving sensations. Tommy had escaped through a newly opened door in the closet of his apartment, amazed to be free of his prison for the first time.

All this had happened because someone or something had created a huge dissonance in the Mill.

Dissonance?

Weird word. Frank had no clue what it meant.

It was a curious business. For over eighty years, Frank hadn't had contact with anyone, living or dead, and had no access to the rest of the factory. Then came the psychic. And the exorcist. Now, everything had changed.

He and Tommy were hanging out and feeling like a couple of teenagers, ecstatic to be free at last.

Finally, he had a friend. First time ever and they were plotting mischief. No words were spoken; none were needed. They could somehow read each other's thoughts and act as one.

He paused.

Really, it made no sense.

Then the muddled sensation returned, stronger than before. Worse than unglued. Coming apart. Decomposing.

Tommy was feeling it, too. As he faded, he stared at Frank with a look of abject horror.

Frank reached out, but his hand and fingers faded, and Tommy disappeared.

He closed his eyes, knowing it was over.

Maybe he was finally going to heaven.

* * *

Chaos reigned. Eamon was loving it.

He had broken out of the cellar and embarked on a scorched earth campaign. Partly to sow mayhem, but mostly to kick the little whore off her throne. He had been having the time of his life until someone yanked him out of the upper floors by throwing a binding spell at him. No warning. Nothing. It had to be the red-haired colleen, the psychic. He was fighting to counter it with limited success, but felt certain the spell was Emma's idea.

Hmm.

So she knew how to play dirty, too. Interesting. That annoying little wench wasn't such a goody-two-shoes after all. Somehow, she and the psychic were working together, ganging up on him. Maybe Chase was right. Women were conniving, evil creatures who didn't deserve to live. But Eamon understood the ridiculous irony in that philosophy. Without women, there would be no men.

And no, Chase wasn't right. The dimwit had kidnapped the wrong woman. If he'd done a proper job, the red-haired wench would be stuffed in the well, not throwing spells at him.

Still, he had a fine moment in his last encounter with the fool who had felt some pathetic need to say goodbye.

Eamon had laughed and said, *I'm not your friend, you wanker.*

The look on the idiot's face had been priceless.

Eamon racked his brain, trying to remember how his mother had countered binding spells. He hadn't used magic much since he died and felt hobbled by a spreading brain fog, some aspect of the binding. He feared it meant Emma was gaining the upper hand. Getting the better of him. That wouldn't do.

Then the lantern in his brain lit up.

To be fully and tightly bound, the spell had to be cast through an object: a possession, preferably something personal, like a lock of hair. She couldn't possibly have such a thing, which meant he was bound by words only. Thus, words alone would reverse the spell.

Really, that type of binding spell only worked against someone who lacked the knowledge and skills to fight back.

He recalled the Gaelic incantation that would break the binding and protect him against further spells. Eamon spoke the words slowly, reverently.

As he spoke the last word, he was free.

Lovely.

Back in the game.

Now he was on a tear, harrying the coppers who had invaded the cellar.

He had started out with a ho-hum scary face. Hmm, a little lame.

Then he turned himself into a hideous glowing shark.

Ha!

That scared the shit out of them and sent them running!

He attacked anyone and everyone he could find. Popping up here and there, drawing gunfire and scaring the snot out of the tough guys who looked like soldiers. One of them was a colleen. That seemed odd. And one of them was down.

Unlucky ricochet.

Eamon smirked, knowing they would be back for more.

While it was fun to mess with the coppers, his primary goal was to send little Miss Emma over the edge.

He had discovered her weakness. She wasn't all there mentally. Nope. Emma was a few bricks short of a hod. Had bats in the belfry. Not the full shilling.

To exploit her weakness, he began tossing random thoughts at her, letting her think she was privy to his deepest, darkest thoughts.

Then he fed her the big lie: *Chase is going to run. He's going to run downriver. Must tell the coppers.*

If he could drive her over the edge and make her look bad, the red-haired whore would stop trusting her. Then the coppers would stop listening to the psychic.

Eamon didn't know why he hadn't thought of fighting for the mill sooner. He wasn't very smart way back then and had simply accepted the status quo.

No more.

He was much sharper now, stealing energy and ideas from Emma and the psychic. Learning the ropes as he went. Growing quickly.

Eamon saw his chance to get ahead.

The past week had been ridiculously fun. Better than badgering those twits to kill Frank.

And really? He was just warming up.

Under his control, the mill would soon become a regular circus.

First, he had to settle a few scores.

Starting with Emma and the red-haired wench.

Fifty-Seven

Martin perused the county map.

Greg Eckert, liaison for the sheriff's department, stood next to him.

Occasional gunfire barked below. Who or what were they shooting at? Was Riddell still down there? Did he have an accomplice? Were the flash bangs in the parking lot some sort of feint? He'd sent a text to Sam Farber but received no reply.

The map, imprinted on a large dry erase board, was constantly updated with squad locations in and around Ash Grove.

Martin concluded his update. "I think he'll stay in the water and swim out of town."

"How'd he get out?"

"We don't know. I have officers searching the grounds and the apartments."

A disheveled city cop popped in. Todd something-or-other. Not the brightest guy. His pants torn, his hair sticking up, he looked like he had just run an obstacle course.

"He got out through a closet in 106, slipped out the window and must have followed the hedge to the end of the building. The flash bangs were a diversion. We think he went into the river."

Martin suppressed the obvious sarcastic retort and continued to marvel at the level of preparations Riddell had made. How much he'd anticipated. He knew psychopaths could be intelligent and organized, but this was stunning. And yet, he had been careless. Otherwise, they would have never caught on to him.

Such irrational thinking was an enigma to Martin.

Lili burst into the room.

"He's out and running! I know where he's going!"

Martin waved her in when Abby stepped over to block her path.

"It's okay, Abby. Come over, Ms. Paltrinieri. Talk to me."

Despite how strange and off-balance things were, he couldn't help but notice how attractive Lili looked in her haphazard state. "How can I help you? We're a little busy here."

"He's running."

"We know—"

"I know which way he's going," she gushed.

He looked at her skeptically.

"Downriver."

"How do you know that?"

"Emma."

To avoid drawing undue attention from the other officers, he murmured, "You're talking about your ghost friend?"

She nodded.

"We're watching the river carefully."

"Good. Can I stay and watch?"

Martin hesitated. The lieutenant would wonder why he let a civilian sit in the command center when he arrived. Why not? She was assisting the police. He shrugged and pointed to a chair in the corner. "Sure. Have a seat over there."

⋆ ⋆ ⋆

Chase lurked in a dark, sheltered area under low-hanging trees at the edge of the island, breathing deeply and scouting the area before tackling the next leg out of town. People had gathered farther downriver, but were focused on the action at the Mill. The flash bangs probably drew them closer, and they were looking in that direction, not at the river. His snorkel had drawn no attention.

Rested, he swam a hundred feet to the railroad bridge on the south side of the island, hugging the shore and staying in the shadows. Then climbed up and sat on the bank, hidden in a cleft between the bridge abutment and a rocky outcropping.

Catching his breath, he opened the swim bag and changed into dry clothing, hiding the wet stuff under the bridge. Chase crawled up the embankment and took a quick peek along the old bridge. The tracks were empty and dark.

All clear.

The trees and brush on the island concealed him as he climbed onto the railbed. In a crouch, Chase scooted across the bridge, hidden behind the rusty cast iron sidewalls. Cloudy and dark, the weather was perfect for an escape. He cleared the far end and ran like hell.

The city had corralled the tracks with ten-foot timber walls so passing freight trains wouldn't spoil the view from the homes where much of the town's wealth resided. The walls also cut the ambient city light. In black clothing, he was invisible. It was so dark he had to watch his step. The rails and ties were just a vague grey pattern beneath his feet. He didn't need to break an ankle.

Only one main road crossed the tracks in town and did so as an overpass. As he ran under the bridge, hugging the shadows, he saw no activity above.

Perfect.

Still ahead of any pursuit. They were probably focused on the river. It was a plan he had considered: learn to scuba dive and swim down river. Too much time and trouble, he decided. This was working just fine anyway.

Chase felt barely winded after the swim, like he could run forever. The promise of freedom was a great motivator. A half mile later, he crossed the city limits into open country. He dropped into the gully next to the railroad bed, stopping to bury the snorkel in the ground cover. No point in leaving any hints to aid his pursuers. He rather hoped they stayed focused on the river—or better yet, the basement, searching for the hostage.

Brush lined the embankment, concealing him as he ran. The few country roads he crossed were quiet and dark. He could slow down, walk, but he didn't. Every mile he ran widened the search area exponentially. After four miles, the area expanded to sixteen square miles. It would take time to put people in place to start a search. When they finally widened the search area, they would be looking for a man. He had that covered, too.

Chase Riddell would walk into the barn, and Karen Lathrop, his dead aunt, would drive out of it. He had makeup and knew how to use it. A wig that concealed his brow ridge and framed his face. A suitcase full of girly clothing. And he had practiced the hardest part, the voice. A fake ID completed the transformation. He hadn't had time to set up a full identity. He could worry about that later once he got out of this mess.

Ironic, really. Another thing men did better. They could easily pretend to be women. For women to pretend to be male? Ha! The voice, the stature? They couldn't do it. No wonder they were determined to force equality. They'd never earn it. They were worthless beyond their basic biological function as brood mares.

Everything was going so well.

He would make it.

Chase just knew it.

Fifty-Eight

Martin briefed the night lieutenant.

John Tisak was fortyish, tall and stocky, and dressed in uniform. He tended to be humorless. Competent but unimaginative. He and Martin got along well enough. His wife was trouble. Cute, but a terrible tease at parties and department functions.

Martin pointed out the squad positions with the roadblocks and checkpoints on the main roads out of town. He detailed the squads sent down both sides of the river, armed with flashlights and powerful searchlights. K9 units were assisting.

Tisak nodded and said, "Looks solid. Good work."

"Thank you, sir."

"Where's Lieutenant Farber?"

"Still in the basement, trying to locate the hostage."

Tisak shook his head in evident disbelief. "I never saw this coming. You?"

"Not even a little, sir."

Martin looked at the map, keeping every option open, every probable route covered. The railroad tracks bothered him. If he was running, he might consider going southwest on the tracks. Catching a freight train and riding out of Dodge. Or not. The tracks were more exposed than the river.

Martin pointed to the tracks crossing Estabrook Road and spoke with raised eyebrows. "I wonder if we shouldn't put a car there, just in case?"

"Do it." Lt. Tisak turned and walked out the door, heading toward the men's room.

Lili then walked over and gently tapped on his shoulder.

* * *

Lili fretted and gnawed on a fingernail.

She had become increasingly convinced Emma had lied to her. She couldn't say why. They hadn't spoken. There was no tone of voice or body language to decipher. Yet the persistent feeling dogged her and grew stronger. The message felt like a lie. Emma had some agenda she wasn't privy to.

Should she say something? Martin would decide she was totes crazy. Shit, who wouldn't? Plus, another officer had arrived and he looked like the boss. Martin acted deferentially toward him.

What could she say?

Yes, I talk to ghosts and sometimes they lie to me.

Uh-huh.

As the conviction grew stronger, a railroad bridge appeared in her mind. A man running along the tracks. Then he was running in the dark of the countryside.

It was happening right now! Chase Riddell was getting away!

Lili suddenly realized Emma had lied about Olivia too. A spasm of fear ran through her. Was Olivia dead?

She knew in that moment that Emma *wasn't* her friend. Never had been.

When the other cop stepped out, Lili walked over to Martin and whispered, "I think she lied to me."

"Who lied to you?"

"Emma."

He lowered his voice. "Emma? The ghost?"

Lili nodded.

Martin glared at her and hissed, "I don't have time for this. You need to leave."

As she feared, he assumed she'd lost it. She had to go all in. Raising her voice, she spoke with a sarcastic twist. "Hello, people. Chase Riddell isn't in the river. He ran out of town on the railroad tracks!"

Martin looked at her like a lunatic on the loose. Everyone in the room stared, mouths agape, including Tisak as he strode back into the room.

Quietly, Martin asked, "He's already out of town?"

She nodded vigorously. "Yes."

⋆ ⋆ ⋆

Emma felt like she was being torn to shreds. Lili had cast her binding spell and it controlled Eamon somewhat, just not to the extent she had hoped. She didn't feel stronger. Quite the contrary. She felt weaker and less substantial. Stretched too thin. Fading like an old pair of jeans.

It wasn't fair.

She couldn't find Lili. Couldn't concentrate on her predicament.

Meanwhile, Eamon had gone missing, back to the cellar maybe. Someone was doing their level best to scare and confound the police down there. Eamon? Frank and Tommy? They were also at large somewhere in the mill. To what end, she couldn't imagine. And the killer was gone.

The entire building had gone berserk.

Emma still believed Eamon was the instigator, that she was the target of all this mayhem. She fumed at the thought of losing her place in the mill and being outdone by some conniving Irishman.

She should have been truthful with Lili about Olivia. It was wrong to lie and bad for her karma. But she had been desperate and really, she still didn't know if she could trust the woman. Random thoughts swirled and threatened to overwhelm her. She prided herself on being smart and savvy; now she was thoroughly at sea.

Afraid, lost, alone, she tried to parse the confusion; thought back to all the books she had read in the past week. Psychology. Spirituality. Philosophy. Somewhere in all that material was the wisdom she sought.

She needed to meditate.

Emma let the worries slip away. Forgot about Eamon. Frank. Tommy. Forgot about Lili. The mill. Everything.

Everything except Jacob. Beautiful, handsome Jacob.

A strange calm settled upon her.

It morphed into a dreamlike state. A place of peace and serenity.

The answer dawned bright and clear.

Emma suddenly saw the bigger picture. The deeper truth.

She had thought of the mill as purgatory since her accident. Now, she concluded her sentence was up. This reshuffle was part of the plan. Let Eamon, Frank, and Tommy fight for control of the mill. She was finally leaving. The angels were coming for her and would take her home. To Jacob.

But would they? Jacob had married another woman. Grown old and died with her.

No. She was going to heaven. She had done her time, and God owed her.

She would get exactly what she was due. That was the promise.

The Bible said so.

Really, purgatory for a little whoopie in the woods? God was a grumpy old curmudgeon at best.

Time to go. She had to be ready.

Emma drifted up to her skylight and lay down to rest.

Closed her eyes and smiled wistfully.

Waited for the angels to arrive.

Fifty-Nine

Olivia could no longer tread water.

Her arms weak, her legs refused to pedal.

With a final desperate burst of effort, she wedged her legs against the cold concrete wall to keep her nose above water.

She tried to conserve energy by relaxing with her head back, breathing in and out in a measured way, but the water was cold. Shivering further depleted her energy.

The terror she felt hitting the water was gone. Fatigue had set in and left nothing but a dull certainty she would soon be dead. She felt no fear. Death was coming like a runaway train and there was no stopping it. She had only one regret: she couldn't tell Raleigh she was sorry. They had fought the last time they were together. A stupid fight about a ghost named Frank who might not even exist. She couldn't bear the thought that their last living interaction had been an angry one. He was an obnoxious know-it-all pain in the ass, but she loved him deeply. He was her soul mate.

But a slim, desperate hope remained.

Raleigh might still come for her. She'd heard gunfire. But how would he find her in this cold, dark hole?

Surprisingly, the water felt warmer now. She felt warmer, too. Almost hot. The sensation was lulling her to sleep.

It was so strange—

⋆ ⋆ ⋆

The bullet had struck Matt in the neck.

There was surprisingly little blood. No arterial involvement. He was lucky.

When they reached the last room, EMTs appeared in the opening above. Sam waved them down the iron steps and they went to work on Matt.

He tried to ignore the glaring improbability about the shooting. Sam could imagine no trajectory in that narrow passage that would cause a bullet to ricochet back, deflect off the side wall, and past the ballistic shield. Except no other explanation made sense.

Could Riddell have an accomplice? It seemed unlikely. Besides, he was supposedly out and running. They hadn't seen a gun.

Mostly, he dwelt on the hostage, fearing she was dead. Riddell seemed intent on inflicting maximum damage in his wake.

As the EMTs stabilized Matt and lifted him out, the group stood in a circle, discussing strategy. They agreed the running men and the ghostly faces were a special effect unleashed to throw them off. Now that they understood the ruse, they wouldn't be distracted and could move quickly to locate the hostage.

"Travis and Brooke, take south passage at a fast walk. Stop twenty feet short of the middle doorway," Sam said. "Kyle and I will go the other way. We'll scope the room and breach if it's safe to do so. Questions?"

They shook their heads.

"After we've breached, move up and check the fallen individual for vital signs."

He turned to Kyle. "Stay tight to me and keep your head down. We're going in fast. Ready?"

Kyle gave him a tight-lipped nod.

Sam took a deep breath and signaled the south group forward.

Silently, he and Kyle fast-walked down the north passage toward that dark doorway, guns aimed and ready. Laser-focused for anything.

Almost anything.

A beautiful woman appeared and floated toward them. Sam tried to ignore the image, but her beauty was breathtaking. Mesmerizing. She was vaguely luminous, even in the glare of the lights.

"It's not real," he whispered into his mic.

Christ, she was beautiful though—

The face suddenly morphed into a hideous avenging angel with teeth and long nails.

Jesus!

How in the hell was Riddell orchestrating these holograms?

A question to be answered later. Confident it was merely an illusion, they pushed forward, and the image evaporated as they blew through it.

That wasn't so bad—

Something flew at them.

Wham.

A brick slammed into the shield.

Sam yelled, "Down!"

He pulled Kyle into a protective crouch behind the shield as a second brick hurtled down the hall and smashed into the hard plastic.

Seconds later, two more bricks hammered them like cannon fire.

"Brooke? You okay?"

"Yep. What's going on over there?"

"Flying bricks!"

"Nothing here."

Where were the damned bricks coming from? There was no one visible in the tunnel ahead, and yet, someone or something was hurling bricks at them. As far as Sam could tell, they were flying right out of the frigging wall!

Two more bricks. Three. Four—it was turning into a barrage.

Jesus!

He had a crazy thought, remembering a story he read long ago about a place in the UK called Borley Rectory. Supposedly the most haunted house in England, the poltergeist-in-residence liked to throw things. Like bricks or stones. He hadn't believed the story. Now he wasn't so sure.

This defied explanation.

A brick flew over the shield and smacked the top of his helmet.

"Fuck!"

They should bail, but a hostage remained whose life might hang in the balance. And the person down in the other passage. What if he wasn't dead?

They had a job to do. Undeterred, he nudged Kyle. "We have to find the hostage. Tuck in and keep the shield up!"

As they closed on the dark doorway, duck-walking, the hail of bricks abruptly ceased.

They stopped and listened.

Silence.

In his headset, Brooke whispered, "In position."

Sam slipped to the edge of the opening and took a peek.

It was pitch black.

He stepped back, tapped Kyle's hand, and grabbed a quick breath. Coiled tight, they aligned the barricade forward and sprang through the opening. With a proactive sidestep against further bricks, they pressed their backs to the wall and swiveled, performing a quick search.

Empty. No Riddell. No hostage.

Quietly, he said, "Clear."

Riddell had been there, though. He had lined the opposite wall with an assortment of guns and rifles. Quite a collection, really. There was a table filled with various computers and monitors, but they were dark.

Where was the hostage?

Sam stepped to the other archway as Brooke and Travis approached.

Brooke said, "Who is that?"

"Shit! That's Raleigh Kaplan," Sam said. "He's the hostage's husband. How the hell did he get down here?"

Blood had pooled beneath a gunshot wound to the leg. Sam knelt and checked for a pulse. Kaplan was still alive.

Speaking into his mic, Sam summoned EMTs. He nudged Brooke. "Go bring them in. Nobody comes in without a helmet. Bring Alford and Szymanski and two more shields. Kyle, stay here and cover their entry. Keep your shield up and watch the west end until they arrive."

Satisfied the immediate area was clear, Sam eyed the door on the back wall and gave Travis a nod.

Travis tried it and shook his head. Locked.

Sam held the shield up and signaled to Travis to open the door.

One swift kick splintered the door and knocked it flat. In a practiced maneuver, Sam entered the room as Travis stepped aside and fell in behind the shield. Travis had wanted to be a cop since childhood and they had practiced moves like this when he was a kid.

A game then. Not a game now.

The room was pitch black. No scary faces. Just darkness. They swiveled and scanned the room using the shield lights, peering through the armored port.

It was mostly empty. Five-gallon pails lined a side wall. A curious two-foot-diameter hole sat in the center of the floor.

They eased over to it and Travis aimed the shield and lights downward as Sam brought his pistol to bear.

A body.

The hostage, Olivia Kaplan.

She looked dead.

Sixty

Chase ran like a marathoner.

Not too fast. Not too slow, his breathing loud but measured as his legs and feet slashed through the long grass. The ground was a hardtack of dried mud, perfect for running. The air smelled of fresh cut hay and manure. As he approached, the crickets quieted, then revved up again as he swept by.

The night was otherwise quiet. No sirens anywhere. No flashing lights.

They still had no clue.

Chase had plenty of time to think. Too much, really.

He had never truly imagined having to run. Had he stuck to the one-woman-a-year plan, they never would have figured it out. But no, he had taken Danielle and tossed his sane, carefully considered plans into the trash. Taking Danielle had been stupid, impulsive, and much too soon. Especially after Megan. He blamed his friend in the basement.

During their talks, Eamon had encouraged and egged him on. Convinced him he had the intelligence and skill to pull it off, that his rules were too rigid.

Why had he listened?

Because Eamon had been so compelling in his admiration for Chase. It sounded incredibly stupid in hindsight. Crazy even? Maybe he deserved to get caught—

No.

He sneered at that ridiculous notion. It was Eamon's fault, plain and simple.

In the end, the guy was a fraud.

I'm not your friend, you wanker.

He had been played by an invisible friend—or a figment of his own fractured mind.

Facts alone that should've given him pause. Maybe he wasn't well. And now, he had tossed his life into a burning dumpster.

Blown it to bits.

He shrugged the thoughts off as self-destructive. Personal reflection was a waste of time. New Age bullshit. He was still at the top of his game. Thank God he'd planned this escape routine. Just in case.

Chase paused at a level crossing on a dark road, looked both ways, and slowed to a jog.

Thanks to his superior intellect, he had a second act coming. It helped that Martin was an idiot. Chase had always known that. Sam Farber wasn't much better. Another advantage.

He was running free with no one in pursuit. Now four miles out of town, the search area had grown to sixteen square miles. They couldn't possibly imagine him traveling this far, this quickly. They were almost certainly still focused on the river.

Someday, they would make a movie about him.

He imagined the next steps. Once inside the barn, he would shave his head and facial hair, strip and change clothes. Wear some girly frock. Apply makeup. Don the wig. The car was a nondescript older Honda in good condition, legally titled in the name of the dead aunt.

He would start over from scratch. It seemed a daunting task, and yet he grew more excited with every step. He wasn't going to prison. After a reasonable amount of time and caution, he could continue his sexual exploits.

The night remained dark, the world a dim grey tapestry to his acute night vision. As the air cooled, some low fog had developed, hanging weightless in the fields.

Perfect.

A fitting backdrop to his version of the *Great Escape.*

A mile behind him, a squad stopped on the tracks, red lights flashing.

Shit. They were getting warmer. Chase pulled tight into the brush and watched. A spotlight lit up the tracks, pointed the other way toward town. And it stayed that way. They were covering their asses. Unimaginative drones.

He relaxed and jogged forward a hundred yards before climbing back up to the railbed and slowing to a walk. He was tired, but the night was black and he was dressed in black.

Invisible.

The track curved gently to the south. They would never see him again as he vanished around the bend.

Thinking ahead, imagining the future, he thought about Phoenix. Warm weather, a vast city—he could get lost there. Find work off the books. Resume his hobby. There had to be a million beautiful women. If he picked on the loners, they might never be missed. He just needed to refine his game. This had all been a useful learning experience.

Chase then saw the railroad signal in the distance that marked the spot where he would turn, leave the tracks, and run east to his destination. The signal shone a bright, steady green.

An omen.

Clear sailing ahead.

Sixty-One

"Shit! Let's get her out of there!"

Olivia Kaplan had jammed her body sideways in the well, her nose and taped mouth clear of the water. But she wasn't moving, and her skin was cyanotic. If she was alive, she had little time.

Pointing to a closed door on the far wall, Sam said, "Clear that. Riddell's probably gone, but let's be sure."

Travis made quick work of clearing the adjoining room. Sam waved him over as he tied a rope around his ankles in the tangled beams illuminating the dark room.

Brooke Neske popped into the room a moment later. Behind her, EMTs had gone to work on Raleigh Kaplan. More team members armed with shields arrived to help protect their flanks against further attacks.

"We're doing this quick and dirty. Lower me down. I'll grab her and you guys pull us up."

Sam lay down at the edge of the well. "Ready?"

The officers nodded in unison and took hold of the rope as he slipped headfirst into the well, using his hands to control the descent. When he reached the woman, he checked for a pulse.

Faint but present.

Thank God.

Her skin was frigid, though. He pushed her legs into the cool water as he tipped her body upright. He could feel the water moving. River water.

Sam slipped his arms around her slight frame in the cramped space, locked hands, and yelled, "Got her! Pull me up!"

A moment later, hands gripped his legs and held fast while Brooke pulled Olivia out and laid her on her back. The only obvious injury was a developing bruise on her forehead.

Sam called over to the EMTs. "Can you guys check this woman out?"

"Yep. This guy's stable. We're waiting for a stretcher to haul him to the surface."

His female partner slid over and quickly checked her pulse, temperature, and pupils. "She's dangerously cool, hypothermic. We need to warm her up."

"Can I carry her out?" Kyle asked.

"Yes. Definitely. The quicker the better."

After they applied a neck brace, Kyle picked her up and positioned her in a firefighter's carry and strode down the south hall, sandwiched between two officers armed with protective shields. Kyle had big shoulders, worked out like an Olympian, and made the carry look effortless.

Travis arrived with two new team members and a stretcher for Raleigh.

Sam said, "I'm going up. Brooke, you and Travis go along the south passage back-to-back with shields and clear it."

"Yes, sir."

"Then clear the north passage."

Sam couldn't wait to get out of there.

The basement gave him the creeps. And he wanted dry clothing.

As he reached the ladder leading out, Brooke spoke in his headset. "South side clear!"

"Okay—"

"—but Travis is missing."

"What?"

"He broke off to look at something and I haven't seen him since."

Damn. Now what? Sam called to Travis using his headset.

Silence.

Sam turned and ran back down the passage toward Brooke. "Where?"

"I'm not sure." She stole a glance down the south passage. "Somewhere down there."

"Shit. Let's go find him."

* * *

Eamon sighed.

The funfest was nearly over.

Chase had fled. It was only a matter of time before the police nabbed the stupid bastard.

Emma had disappeared, but not like Chase. She had simply evaporated. Gone. What the feck was that about?

Frank and Tommy had vanished as well. It was inexplicable.

Poof!

All of them. Gone.

What was happening?

He now had the mill to himself, but was he winning? Or losing?

He didn't know.

Two coppers remained, searching the basement. He lured one of them into a trap with an illusion. A section of the basement that had been closed off, originally intended as a connecting tunnel to another building. Someone decided it was too much trouble, or money, and sealed it up.

He created a door that lasted exactly ten seconds.

Just long enough to snare his victim before it reverted to brickwork.

No way out. No one could hear him yell.

All with a flick of the finger. His magic skills were improving.

Oh no!

The ground collapsed, burying the poor bastard in yards of soil. Now they'd never find him.

The coppers searched the basement for hours but couldn't find their compatriot. He lay trapped and dying in the dark. Eventually, the body would smell bad. Maybe they would find him then.

And maybe, Eamon would have a new friend. They could talk baseball.

Right now, he was exhausted. It had been an insane couple of days, but he didn't feel like resting. He returned to his hallways in the cellar. Strangely, even though the entire mill was his, he still felt more comfortable down there.

Eamon smiled and resumed his ceaseless wandering. Down the south passage. Turn at the end. Back along the north passage.

It was a routine. A comforting routine.

Something to do until the next bunch of twits came along.

Sixty-Two

Lieutenant Tisak glared at Martin.

"Who is this woman? Is this the supposed psychic you've been talking to?"

"Yes, sir," Martin said, meeting his glare. "She's been assisting the department. As it happens. I think she's probably right. She's been persistently right about Riddell."

"Are you suggesting we redirect all our people there?" Tisak pointed to the tracks.

"No. One or two squads. I'll cover the tracks as well. Now that you're here, I'm free to assist in the search."

"Fair enough."

"Good. I think we should extend the search outward. He might've run farther than we think."

"Agreed. Get going. I have a helo on the way. I'll have them run the tracks." Tisak glanced at Lili. "Your friend needs to leave."

"Can I go with him?" Lili asked.

"No. Detective Kettridge will see you to your car." Tisak added with little sincerity, "Thank you for your help, miss."

Typical. Tisak hadn't believed a word of it. Then again, Martin hadn't believed at first either. He wasn't fully certain he did now, though he was a fan of the famous Sir Arthur Conan Doyle quote: *Once you eliminate the impossible, whatever remains, no matter how improbable, must be the truth.*

At least he was willing to entertain the idea. How had that unimaginative twit Tisak made lieutenant?

Martin waved Lili ahead, grabbed his vest, and followed her out into the night.

"Where's your car?"

"Thanks, but I'll walk," she said without turning.

"You sure? Do you have somewhere to go?"

"My shop." She stopped, turned, and took his hand in a casual grip. "Thanks for listening."

"No, thank you. Really. I meant what I said about you being right. I don't understand how, but you were." His hand tingled where she'd touched it. She remained a distraction. "Can I drop you off?"

"No. The walk will do me good. Just catch the bastard. And let me know about Olivia, please."

"I will."

Martin watched her walk away. She really was very attractive. Somehow, she had gotten under his skin. And she probably thought he was an idiot. He had been so dismissive in the beginning. And she had been mostly right. He shook his head and focused on the present. Performing a rough calculation, he decided Riddell could be four to five miles out of town if he was running.

Martin looked at the GPS display and picked a rail crossing almost six miles out on Marsh Road.

He sent the destination to Abby, who promised to send two squads to assist. He closed with: *Keep me updated on hostage situation.*

Five minutes later, he stopped on the tracks. The night was calm, the clouds low, the lights of Ash Grove a glowing reflection off the clouds in the distance. Fog nestled in the hollows and clung to the ground in random patterns. Looking both ways down the tracks, the darkness was near absolute. Then he saw the helicopter coming up the river and turning in his direction, its bright light focused on the ground.

Martin shone the car spotlight down the track toward town, and thought he saw movement at the edge of the brush, brief and fleeting. Probably an animal.

The tracks were clear.

He turned the car and pointed the light southwest along the tracks.

Nothing.

He backed off the tracks, parking the car out of sight. Killed the lights, grabbed his flashlight, and stepped out. The air was comfortable and damp, alive with the sounds of crickets and tree frogs. Quite a racket, really. Martin sat at the edge of the road and watched the helicopter approach, the brilliant light illuminating the railbed. The pilot was taking his sweet time. Martin maintained focus on the tracks.

Still nothing, though the fog wasn't helping. Martin wondered if the pilot had a clearer view. The reinforcements arrived. Martin sent officers walking the tracks for a mile in each direction.

His phone pinged. A text from Abby. Olivia had been found alive, but unconscious. They had also found Raleigh, near death, hanging on by a thread. There was no sign of Danielle Hamlin. Inexplicably, Travis Farber was missing in the basement. No news on Chase Riddell.

Danielle was almost certainly dead and buried. Or in the river. He felt tired and deeply saddened, knowing her last days must have been a horrendous experience.

He sent a text to Lili and quickly answered the questions she shot back.

The helo worked back and forth, performing a grid search on either side of the tracks, drifting slowly to the southwest. Martin stood on the rail crossing and scrutinized the ground beneath the beam.

Time ticked away. Their quarry continued to elude them.

How had Lili known so much about Chase Riddell? He could argue luck and coincidence, but knowing about the bathroom trapdoor? Well beyond an educated guess. Spooky. An unsolvable mystery.

Then the radio burped to life for the first time tonight.

Against good advice, the lieutenant chose to break radio silence, announcing that the command center had moved to the police station and ordering everyone to new positions. They had an unconfirmed but promising sighting of Riddell, east of town, along the river.

Martin wasn't sure he believed it.

A minute later, Abby advised him to return to the station.

Figures.

He was being pulled off the pursuit. Punishment for having Lili in the command center, or sending people in the wrong direction, or who knew what. Maybe it was warranted. Despite the conviction that Lili had been right, it was looking like he fucked up. Sent resources in the wrong direction, perhaps enabling or facilitating Riddell's escape. That was the hidden message in being recalled to the station. He had been deemed useless to the search. Tisak was just that petty.

He sat for a minute, musing. Riddell had almost certainly gone to ground somewhere. They wouldn't find him until he emerged and continued running. Tomorrow or the day after, someone would probably catch him.

The sheriff's department and state patrol were now involved, BOLOs had gone out, and the search had moved beyond their purview.

With a sour feeling in his gut, Martin climbed into his car and turned back toward town.

Sixty-Three

Chase looked over his shoulder.

Still no evidence of a pursuit. No lights. No sirens. Nothing but crickets and the pleasant, still night. The inky darkness was bliss, like a cloak, protecting him, favoring him. He couldn't have asked for a better night for an escape. By the time they realized he was outside the perimeter, it would be too late for checkpoints or other measures.

Less than a mile to the barn.

Not home yet, but close.

Once he left the farm, he had an escape route mapped and memorized along secondary roads until he crossed the state line. By tomorrow morning, he would be in St. Louis. Denver by nightfall. Twenty-four hours later, he would disappear into the urban sprawl of Phoenix. He just had to watch his driving speed. He had previously checked the car for burnt-out bulbs and other red flags.

Meanwhile, Sam and Martin would realize he had outsmarted them.

Fuck 'em.

He laughed.

Up ahead, he saw a couple of cars crossing the tracks on the next road up, Marsh Road. The driveway to the barn exited on Marsh Road. Normally, there was little traffic on it, day or night.

A car stopped on the tracks. What the hell?

Chase stopped and knelt, head down. Someone flipped a spotlight on and trained it down the tracks in his direction. It was a squad car.

Shit!

A minor setback.

The plan was still good.

They were probably waiting for the midnight freight to roll through to the south. Probably thought he planned to hop it.

Good.

He would leave the railbed early, cut east, and approach the barn from the north. There was plenty of cover; he would be invisible from the road and the tracks. He just needed to be more careful. The planned route had been carefully explored. This way, he worried mostly about getting snagged by barbed wire in the dark or twisting his ankle in a tractor rut, though both were unlikely. He couldn't remember any fencing behind the farm and no one had worked the fields in years.

Chase ran across the gully and leapt over the broken-down barbed-wire fence that marked the edge of railroad property while the spotlight swept the field on the other side of the tracks.

He heard a helicopter in the distance, then saw a bright searchlight scouring the ground beneath it.

The area north of the farm was wooded. Mostly mature pines, the ground was soft and padded with needles, the air rich with a piney scent. Beneath the canopy, it was dark, the undergrowth difficult to see. He trudged to the east, feeling his way between the tree trunks, mindful of any obstacles on the ground. He heard voices in the distance organizing a search.

Chase counted one hundred steps, which placed him roughly due north of the barn. Turning ninety degrees to the right, he continued his careful meander through the trees. Slowly, the light improved until he saw an open field ahead and bumped into a barbed-wire fence.

The north field. The barn was a vague outline in the increasingly foggy landscape.

The helo was nearly overhead and deafening, the pilot flying back and forth, working a grid as he drifted southwest. Chase stopped and crouched down to rest, hanging back under the cover of the trees until the helo moved on. In five or ten minutes, as he continued forward, they would deem this area clear.

Perfect.

Cops were walking in each direction along the tracks. Another stood on the rail crossing, watching the helo.

Chase wondered why they had focused on the tracks. Had they found the psychic? Had she survived? Was she working with them? Did they know about the barn?

Of course not. Those were stupid, paranoid thoughts. Why was he thinking that way again?

In reality, they were showing no interest in the woods or the farmstead.

He just had to relax and hold fast until the search moved on.

As the pilot pulled away, he heard an announcement from the police radio. He couldn't catch the details—the loud rotors above scrambled the message—but it soon became clear it was an order to move.

The cops walking the tracks ran for their cars and took off.

Probably a false sighting somewhere. It happened all the time and wasted valuable resources. A perfect break for him, though.

The cop on the crossing lingered for a moment. Something about the way he stood looked familiar.

Ah, Martin, the idiot detective.

Then Martin walked to his car, hopped in, and turned the headlights on.

Chase flipped him off, leapt up and ran, his eyes focused on the dim outline of the barn three hundred yards away.

He could walk, but opted for a steady lope. The sooner he slipped into the barn, the better. Out of sight. Changing. Becoming Karen Lathrop.

Chase Riddell was about to disappear forever.

The mists settling over the field were a curtain concealing him. He felt ecstatic, alive, as he ran toward a new life.

The grass was tall and whipped at his face. He didn't care.

Freedom beckoned.

Sixty-Four

Martin squinted.

What the hell was that?

As his headlights swept across the adjoining field, Martin thought he glimpsed something in motion, traversing a break in the fog. Probably an animal, a deer or something, but that notion didn't quite match what he'd seen.

He replayed the memory but it was too vague. A grey image, almost subliminal, nothing really.

Except he felt certain it was critical.

A gut feeling the shadow might have been a man running.

Martin stomped on the brake and jumped out of the car, plowing through the ditch and into a thick bank of fog. He ran cautiously, vigilant for obstacles, but missed spotting the fence anyway. Barbed wire snagged him below the left knee. He went down hard, losing his gun in the fall.

"Fuck!"

He lay stunned for a moment, then felt around for his weapon.

Luckily, he found it. He was essentially blind in the dark. Bloody fingers and throbbing pain confirmed the extent of the injury to his shin. He was going to need a tetanus shot.

Martin listened for the sound of movement but could only hear the helicopter returning, moving fast, chasing down the new lead to the east.

Rolling to his feet, he tested the leg. Sore but sound. He continued forward at a modest trot. Dangerous, yes, but the figure he saw—or imagined seeing—was running. There was no time for finesse now, even though he might be chasing a ghost. Or a figment of his imagination.

He seemed to be traversing a field, a wild place with long grass and saplings atop a hard, uneven surface. To the right, he caught glimpses of a dark looming structure, a farmhouse or a barn maybe. No lights, though.

A perfect hideout for a fugitive.

Was that where Riddell was running to? Was he there already?

If he was running...

Perhaps he *had* gone east. This felt like a fool's errand, but he couldn't get past the feeling he had seen someone. It had to be Riddell.

The night was an eerie tapestry of clear air and dense fog. Of whipping grass and random bushes. He tried to listen for footfalls or the sounds of someone thrashing through the prairie grass, but the approaching helicopter drowned out all other sound. Mostly, he was running blind, his chances of finding anyone almost nil. But if Riddell was running south, he had to be heading toward the farm off to the right.

Getting there first and lying in wait, or at the very least, arriving about the same time was the smarter option. Riddell wouldn't be expecting him. Martin was fairly certain the smug bastard thought he was home free. The arrogance of narcissists was often their downfall. He hoped this asshole was no exception.

He pivoted to the right, running southeast toward the buildings, keeping his eyes pasted a few feet ahead, wary of hidden obstacles and other dangers.

The helicopter flew over, ruining his night vision and revealing nothing in the surrounding field. It was a surreal sight, ground-level clouds diffusing the light, revealing narrow clear passages, all being churned by the rotors above. The wild vegetation further obscured his vision. His hair felt damp, his skin clammy, his leg hurt, and he knew the pursuit might be for naught.

He couldn't stop running. An inexplicable feeling in his gut said he was on the right track and any hesitation would cost him the collar. His gut had better be right. By now, Tisak expected him back at the station. He'd be in trouble soon.

Christ. The lieutenant would probably write him up.

What if Riddell had outsmarted them and escaped?

The possibility of failure gnawed at him.

And pushed him to run harder.

Sixty-Five

Chase heard the helo roaring back.

He dropped out of view and huddled as it screamed overhead, the blinding light dimming his night vision.

But the pilot was in a hurry to some other place, flying too fast to monitor the terrain below.

After it passed, he jumped to his feet and charged forward, elated. He would make it. They were heading away, in the opposite direction. The gods still smiled upon him.

His view of the field and barn disappeared as he ran into dense fog. No matter. He knew the way.

And he was so close.

He caught a flash of motion. Something closing fast—?

Wham.

He collided with a rock-hard moving object and took a stunning blow to the head like a smack from a baseball bat. He bounced to the left, falling hard, trying to parse the sudden change in circumstances. An animal? A deer maybe?

For a moment, his vision was a kaleidoscope of stars, his head a throbbing knot of pain.

When his sight returned, he looked back and saw the obstacle in the dim grey light. A body.

Jesus fucking Christ!

It was Martin Kettridge!

How?

Had that bastard spotted him somehow and chased him down?

No time to ponder. He recovered more quickly than Martin. Just microseconds faster, but enough to grab the advantage.

Chase rolled to his feet as Martin tried to push himself up. He stepped and kicked Martin in the ribs, a powerful punt that knocked the man sideways with an audible groan, his body crumpling into itself as he hit the ground. A couple more blows like that and the old fuck would be finished.

Chase stepped again, aiming a fierce kick to the head, but Martin anticipated the move and rolled aside.

With his leg already in motion and traveling through an arc, Chase teetered for balance. Martin grabbed his foot and yanked him down.

Dumb move, Martin.

Chase crashed down and lashed out with his fist, landing a solid blow to the face. He unleashed a series of fast jabs, but they were ineffective. Somehow, Martin's leg had gotten wedged between them as Chase fell on him. Martin kneed him away with a grunt and delivered a rib-bruising kick of his own.

Oof! Fuck!

With surprising speed, Martin leapt forward and slugged him with a plunging fist under the eye.

Chase gritted his teeth, trying to ignore the pain radiating through his face, throwing his arms out in a forearm-cross and blocking the next punch. As Martin recoiled to strike again, Chase kicked out viciously, his heel slamming into Martin's face.

The kick should have been enough to drop the bastard, but he bounced back, his nose bloodied, and fixed an angry eye on Chase as he shifted to strike again.

This wasn't going well. While he knew he could kick Martin's ass, he didn't have time to play games. He needed his gun to end this quickly before Martin had a chance to pull his weapon.

They eyed each other, breathing raggedly. As if reading his mind, Martin went for his weapon but came up empty, then stood there, as if confused by his empty hand.

As Chase leapt up and charged for a take-down, Martin faced him with a look of resignation. Didn't react or move until he snapped a swift, well-aimed knee to the nuts at the last second. Chase retched and went down, stunned. Fighting intense pain and nausea, he scrambled backward for a little breathing room, struggling to stay focused.

Fuck fuck fuck!

Feeling unnerved that the old bastard had suckered him, Chase grappled for his weapon, but the swim bag with the gun had slipped behind his back. As he tried to maneuver around to get a hand on it, Martin leapt at him, leading with his knee, throwing all his weight into a kill shot.

Chase rolled aside, evading the plunging knee, and lashed out with his foot, a hard kick to the ribs that sent Martin crashing to the ground. With a quick half-roll, he slammed a vicious rabbit punch to the base of Martin's skull.

The blow should have stunned him but Martin scrabbled away and reached for something in the grass.

His weapon?

Chase felt around for his gun. With that last twisting maneuver, the swim bag had rotated just enough to bring it within reach.

Martin reared up and charged at him with a primal yell, brandishing a rock. Chase yanked the Glock free and fired three quick rounds center mass with a firm double-handed grip.

Martin's face registered a microsecond of surprise as he continued forward and fell to the ground in a shapeless heap.

He remained still.

Dead.

Jesus, that was close!

Still, he had prevailed. The better man, as always.

Worried the gunfire would draw unwanted attention, Chase scuttled forward and ran for the barn.

Six steps out, his foot slapped down on something flat and solid. It sounded like wood planking. Whatever it was, it broke and gave way beneath his weight.

His body plunged downward into the void and he felt a dawning recognition of grave danger as the next seconds unfolded in slow, awful clarity.

The dark earth flew at him and he put his hands out to break the fall, but he was moving too fast. His hands slapped against a rough surface, snapping back with bone-jarring pain. The reaction threw his upper body back, his head smashing against something solid, like rock. Or concrete.

Chase plummeted into darkness, his left foot leading.

His mind tried to comprehend the sudden, unexpected change in circumstances when his leg slammed into a hard surface and snapped with a horrifying *crack.*

Excruciating pain shot up his leg and through every inch of his being as his head bounced off the wall.

For a long while, consumed by intense pain, he screamed in mindless agony. Then he attempted to collect his wits, his entire body shaking in shock as endorphins took some of the edge off the pain.

The space was midnight dark. He was blind. But it felt round. He had landed on a rocky surface.

He looked up. A faint grey circle lay far above, perhaps thirty feet up.

An old well. How ironic. At least it was dry.

Chase shifted, trying to imagine a way out, but grinding pain overwhelmed any attempt to move.

With a shattered leg, he wasn't going anywhere.

He checked for his swim pack, but the bag and the Glock were probably lying on the ground up above.

No way to signal for help.

A dark outcome teased his fearful mind. Only Martin knew where he was and Martin was dead. How would anyone find him here on an abandoned farm? Buried in long field grass, the well was invisible. He might die here.

His so-called friend had been right.

He was fucked.

But not if someone found him. The leg would heal. Escape was always a possibility.

In desperation, he cried out.

"Help!"

Sixty-Six

Lili stopped and watched Martin drive away.

She didn't know how long she stood there before turning and shuffling down the sidewalk toward her shop.

It could have been an hour. Or five minutes.

The last of the adrenaline leaving her system had left her washed out and dazed. Shell-shocked. Not a vaporous thought in her head. She only knew no one would be allowed to return to the mill until the police had fully searched and cleared the building. She felt even more adrift because her apartment was her sanctuary, a place to regroup and recharge. After today, would she ever feel safe there again?

She should be angry, but she wasn't anything. Just numb.

While she stood there, two stretchers rolled out and the injured were whisked off in waiting ambulances. Lili couldn't see who they were, though they appeared to be alive still. She prayed Olivia was one of them. Riddell was gone. Raleigh was probably dead. Nothing good had happened here.

She needed a place to sleep tonight. The sofa in her shop would have to do.

Would she sleep? She doubted it.

Lay awake all night?

Probably.

It was just after ten o'clock now. A long anxiety-filled night beckoned while she awaited word on Raleigh and Olivia.

Then she saw the glowing neon sign for On the Rocks, a cute, trendy bar that had opened the previous year. They had a decent wine selection and good food. Lili suddenly realized she hadn't eaten all day. She was starving.

Wine sounded like a brilliant idea.

Inside, it was dim and quiet with just a few couples out on a Tuesday night. The backbar was modern, all dark wood and mirrors with nooks for liquor bottles. It was well designed. Sleek.

A tall, hipster bartender moseyed down.

"Evening, miss. What can I get you?"

"Shot of Herradura and a glass of red, the Barolo."

"Excellent choice. Menu?"

"I know what I want." Throwing all caution to the wind, Lili ordered the loaded potato skins—about ten thousand calories' worth of comfort food.

The barkeep brought her drinks and watched as she slammed the tequila. She avoided eye contact.

He got the message.

Her phone pinged as the food arrived.

Martin.

Olivia K found unconscious. Should be okay.

Thank God! Finally, some good news. She typed: *Where is she?*

Ash Gen. Family on the way.

He must have read her mind. If the family was coming, they probably wouldn't want her there. Unlikely they would allow a night visitor, anyway.

She typed: *Raleigh?*

Alive but critical.

Riddell?

Nothing yet.

Thanks for the update.

She liked him and she didn't know why. He was an ass at first. Somehow, he started to take her seriously. Found some value in her insights. He wasn't some dinosaur set in his ways who was unwilling to change. No matter. He almost certainly considered her flaky and weird.

Thinking about him was silly.

End of subject.

Emma remained just below the surface, the past few days churning in an obsessive loop.

First, Emma seemed friendly. She wanted to help Danielle; wanted to nab Chase Riddell.

Until she aided in his escape. There was no other way to interpret her lies at that critical moment. Plus the lie about Olivia.

Lili felt angry and disappointed. Emma wasn't her friend, wasn't trying to help. She might be evil. If Chase escaped, it would be her fault. She must have known which way he was running. Lili was now certain it wasn't downriver. Thank God Martin seemed to believe her.

As she ate, Emma, Frank, Eamon, and Tommy played in a muddled loop in her head.

Four ghosts. So much conflict.

She didn't know what any of it meant.

The potato skins were delicious. The wine was better.

Time for bed.

Buzzing from the shot and the Barolo, she walked the two blocks to her shop, let herself in, and walked to the office without lights. She didn't need them. Stretching out on the sofa, she stared at the ceiling.

Lili tried to concentrate and untangle the mystery of the ghosts in the mill.

Her last cogent thought was the feeling that Emma, Frank and Tommy were alike in some undefinable way.

Then she slept.

Sixty-Seven

Martin stirred.

Where in the hell was he?

He was damp, his hair wet. He smelled dirt. A loamy scent. Mostly, he hurt. His chest felt crushed. The kind of damage one might receive in a car accident.

Except, as best he could tell, he was lying in the middle of a field.

The sky was growing lighter to the east, a hazy glow, shrouded by fog. The memory of a struggle came back in broken bits and pieces. A fight to the death with Chase Riddell. The bastard had pulled a gun and nailed him. Even with the vest, the impact of those three rounds had been stunning. It was still hard to breathe. He looked around.

No sign of Chase. Asshole must have gotten away. Great. Martin had lost the battle and the war. He had disobeyed an order and had nothing to show for it.

Voices mumbled in the distance.

He tried to call out, but only a squeak escaped. It hurt too much to even attempt speech, much less a shout.

Martin pushed himself up slowly. His forehead felt tight and sticky.

Blood.

He looked down and spotted a bloodied rock. Evidently, he'd fallen on it and hit his head.

It wasn't enough to get shot?

Gathering his wits, he rolled to the side and staggered to his feet.

He couldn't see a thing. Not the road. Not the barn. Nothing. The world was shrouded in fog, and he was deep in tall grass.

Voices continued mumbling off to his right. He turned and walked in that direction, limping. Something was wrong with his leg.

Oh yeah.

A barbed-wire fence took him down.

He was in no hurry. Wouldn't matter if he was. Between his ribs, the leg, and a blinding headache, he barely managed a limping hobble.

Suddenly, his right foot gave out beneath him—

Fuck!

He was falling.

He threw his arms out, grabbing a hold of a sapling. Held on tight as his chest slammed against the hard ground, sending an excruciating rush of pain through him.

Looking around, he realized he had nearly fallen into a hole in the ground. Probably an old well.

Jesus! That was close!

Martin held firmly to the tree until the pain receded and his breathing returned to near normal. He dragged his aching body out of the hole and crawled into a fetal ball next to the well, taking shallow breaths as the pain ebbed further.

He heard the voices again. It sounded like they were searching for something.

For Chase? Too late. Chase was gone.

More likely for him. They must have found the car he abandoned on the roadway.

Then he heard a whimper. He frowned and pursed his lips. Had he made that sound?

He didn't think so.

"Huh."

There it was again.

It was coming from the well.

"Hello?"

A feeble voice called out, "Help!"

Faint but unmistakable, it was the voice of Chase Riddell.

"Riddell? Are you down there?"

In a pained whisper, he said, "Yeah. Hurt bad."

Martin registered the comment and lay back, thinking about the last twenty-four hours. About Megan. Danielle. Olivia Kaplan. The siege at the mill. The stunning black eye Riddell had given the Ash Grove Police Department. About the fear that Chase would escape, that justice might never be done. The pain in his chest and his leg. About the absurdity of the moment and the downfall of an evil man in a cosmically fitting way.

Martin erupted in a belly-laugh.

Oh fuck, that hurt!

He couldn't stop. The unraveling of days of stress and tension gushed out in uproarious laughter.

Chase hadn't escaped.

Nope. The dumb motherfucker lay trapped and broken at the bottom of a well.

In that moment, it was the funniest damned thing Martin could possibly imagine.

Sixty-Eight

Lili stirred.

Someone was banging on her door.

Her phone was ringing too. What the hell?

Lying on her sofa at the store, she felt stiff, twisted, and cold. She'd been dreaming about a girl with flaxen hair who morphed into a monster.

Emma.

Slowly, reality dawned. She looked at her phone.

Martin.

She mumbled, "What do you want?"

"Open the door."

"Huh?"

"Open the door. Hurry! It's important."

The banging on her front door increased in intensity.

What the hell?

She stood unsteadily, ran her fingers through her hair and checked her look in the mirror. It would have to do. She walked through the shop and opened the door. Bright sunlight assailed her eyes. She took a moment to adjust. Martin stood there, disheveled and dirty, with a nasty bruise across the bridge of his nose and a gash on his forehead.

"You look like shit."

"And you look stunning. But right now, I need your help."

Lili felt too tired for flattery. "My help? Why?"

"Grab your stuff, whatever psychic stuff you normally use and get in the car. I'll explain on the way."

"It's in my apartment."

"Even better."

As Martin drove toward the mill, he described the situation. Travis Farber, a SWAT officer and his godson, had disappeared in the basement during clearing operations. Despite an all-night search, he was still missing. He wanted Lili to walk through the basement to see if she could find him.

"What about Riddell?"

"In custody."

"Good. How'd you catch him?"

"A long story for another day. A good story."

As they walked into the mill, Lili said, "Shouldn't you see a doctor?"

"I did. She said I was fine."

"Liar."

"No fooling you, is there?" Martin said flatly.

Lili grabbed her bag with the crystal and the candles and followed Martin to 139, down the iron rungs, and into the basement. There were cops everywhere. Everyone looked exhausted. Martin said they had been searching every square foot of the mill all night. No one had gone home. It all looked and felt surreal.

She set up in the room with the deck chairs and table, the TV, and the fridge. Adequate for her needs. She sent everyone away, including Martin, killed the lights and set to work.

Lili spent fifteen minutes relaxing and warming the crystal for the task. Waited for the mists, then peered into the crystal. She stood in a dark hallway, then walked down a long passage dimly lit by the candle behind her. She passed a dark patch on the floor. Smelled the metallic tang of old blood. Farther down the passage, she noticed alcoves along the inside wall, the type of space where someone might place a small table and hang a painting. A strange feature in a basement.

She stopped. The third alcove opened slowly, like a door. It was black within—nothing visible—other than a small cross carved into the brickwork above the opening.

Right there. Their missing man was behind the wall. She just knew it.

"Martin!"

He popped his head into the room.

She pointed to the left. "He's down that passage. Follow me."

Lili walked slowly, trying to maintain her bearings, following the path she had taken through the crystal. Halfway down the passage, she saw the bloodstain. She walked past two alcoves before reaching the one marked by the cross.

"He's in there."

Someone located two sledgehammers and a procession of cops took turns pounding their way through the brick wall.

Lili watched from a distance and listened as the cops talked about the night before. About the bizarre holograms and the barrage of bricks one group had dealt with. Incredible stories. She wished she had been there. But the events also shook her world view of ghosts and spirits.

While she believed ghosts could be malicious, she never believed they could inflict physical harm. The attack with bricks could have been deadly. The intense visions? Beyond her experience in the supernatural realm.

It wasn't over. Eamon was still around somewhere. This building would never be safe until he was forcibly evicted. Exorcised.

She also learned they credited Martin with catching Chase Riddell. Martin had tracked and attacked Riddell in a field, altering his route to his waiting getaway vehicle. From there, the evil bastard had fallen into an abandoned well, ending his well-planned escape.

Sounded like karma.

When the wall came down, they found Travis buried in loose dirt, unconscious but breathing.

After a round of congratulatory back-slapping and handshaking, relief at finding Travis Farber set in. Lili tugged on Martin's sleeve and pulled him aside.

Quietly, she said, "You still have a problem here."

He looked exhausted and cranky. "What?"

Lili understood the situation and explained it to him. The cross was the key. It was the place where Eamon had died.

"This is going to sound crazy, but someone needs to perform an exorcism to make this place safe again. I know just the guy."

He blinked. "Are you serious?"

Lili stared back. "Yes. And after everything that's happened, you need to trust me. Besides, how could it hurt?"

He stared for a long moment, shrugged, and walked over to confer with his lieutenant. Their expressions were almost comical. Skeptical, with a hint of resignation, before Sam Farber nodded.

Martin returned and muttered, "Okay—as long as your guy doesn't interfere with any evidence."

As Lili reached for her phone, Martin said, "And thank you. For finding Travis."

* * *

Mateo arrived sixty minutes later. Dressed in street clothes and carrying a small black bag, he looked more like a doctor making a house call than a priest.

Between Sam and Martin, they shuttled him into the basement with little fanfare, keeping him out of sight. Martin made some comment about his report listing the visit as clergy requested by tenant.

It was true, at least in theory.

Lili directed him to the spot where they pulled Travis out of the wall. Mateo requested a small table. Someone grabbed the one from Riddell's lounge area.

Mateo sent everyone away. Martin. Sam. Anyone within a hundred feet. He wanted the entire basement cleared but settled for everyone congregating in the entry room beneath the bathroom of 139.

Lili lingered. "Can I stay?"

"No."

Lili had never seen Mateo so focused and serious. She cupped her hands in supplication.

"Please?"

"You can't be here." He gave her a stern look. "Respect the process."

Lili walked back and joined the others as EMTs lifted Travis out. For twenty minutes, they heard nothing. Not a whisper. It was dull, frankly odd, and no one else really knew what was happening. A few cops drifted away.

A bright flash of light—like a flashbulb—lit up the passage. Then she heard a phrase shouted in Latin. Beyond *carpe diem* and such, Lili knew no Latin and had no clue what he was saying. The tone was angry, though.

Another flash.

The floor rumbled a little.

More yelling in Latin.

The rumble grew steadily until it seemed the entire building was trembling. Dust fell from cracks in the ceiling.

Lili looked up, wondering about the ceiling and building. Nervous chatter ramped up behind her. The vibrations continued for another minute or two, rising to a crescendo.

Suddenly, a tremendous *crash*, like a wrecking ball demolishing a wall, echoed through the basement.

The ensuing silence was eerie and preternatural. Lili could hear her own heartbeat. Several people muttered, "Holy shit."

She then heard a faint shuffling of feet, growing louder. She half-expected some strange beast to appear.

Mateo ambled through a moment later.

He looked bruised and beaten, his clothes disheveled, hair windblown, his face covered in soot like a chimney sweep.

No one spoke. Just stared, stunned.

"Is he gone?" Lili asked.

"I sure hope so." Without breaking step, Mateo walked through and climbed the metal rungs. Lili followed as conversation broke out behind her.

"Mateo? What happened?"

He stopped and turned. "Someday, I'll tell you. Not today."

"Really? Is he gone? At least tell me that."

"Probably." He shrugged.

"Mateo!"

"You know how this works. No guarantees. We'll know in good time."

Sixty-Nine

The angels never came.

Late at night, Emma wandered through the mill, musing about the angels, coming to rest on the crane in 114.

She had no idea how long she waited for them. In her resting state, she had little concept of time. It might have been hours, days, or weeks. But while she rested, she meditated and tried to make sense of the craziness in the preceding weeks.

In a series of revelations, she untangled the various facets of her confused existence.

Emma had spent a lot of time reading books on psychology and psychiatry. She did so to better understand the cop. Had read about anxiety, depression, paranoia, and psychosis plus mood, personality and substance abuse disorders. She concluded that Chase Riddell was a muddled combination of power rapist and sexual gratification rapist, though his motives for killing were less clear. He could be classified as a mission-oriented serial killer, but he was also a malignant narcissist and undoubtedly had other defects.

In other words, a monster.

She wasn't a doctor but felt pretty good about her diagnosis.

Through her studies, Emma realized she had issues, too.

She fought the idea at first. To acknowledge it was to accept she might be mentally ill, but she then wondered: was that even possible in a ghost? But she couldn't deny the cascade of odd events in the last few weeks: the random coming and going, the missing hours in her day, the inability to visit parts of the mill, her troubles using the iPad. Eamon and his magic had caused some of it but couldn't explain all of it—certainly not the clear connection to Tommy and Frank who seemed to exist somewhere in her head.

The first hint came while reading about DID, or dissociative identity disorder, once known as multiple personality disorder. Ruminating while she rested, the connections and awareness grew as she thought about DID and considered her circumstances and history. The disorder was often associated with overwhelming trauma.

Her abusive childhood and violent dismemberment had been harrowing experiences. She recalled the newspaper article about her death: *The face presented an appearance of peaceful repose, as though she had fallen asleep.*

What a bunch of hooey. She had been ripped apart by a paper machine!

Her brief life had been extremely traumatic—

Only she couldn't have DID.

People with DID created alternate personalities. She hadn't created unique alters. She had adopted known identities from people who had died in her presence. The lengthy time lapse between her death and adoption of alters? That didn't sound like DID at all.

Emma had felt unsettled from the start, naturally. She had gone from planning a wedding to haunting a paper mill. But if she had the disorder, the symptoms would have presented right away.

What then? Why had she connected with Frank and Tommy when plenty of other people had died here? Had she identified more closely with them? The violent nature of Frank's murder had affected her deeply and Tommy died young, just as she had.

Plausible, but how?

Emulated their personalities? Pretended to be them, like playacting?

Wouldn't she have known she was doing that?

A darker possibility unfolded in her head. An action both frightening and dreadful in the same breath.

What if she had stolen or appropriated their spirits?

She had been reading about psychology, but also reading about the spiritual elements of her existence. Such things were possible in the supernatural world. Was she some kind of freak with demons trapped inside her? That sounded ridiculous. Frank and Tommy were no such thing.

Being a ghost, stealing their spirits seemed a reasonable explanation, but she had no memory of doing so. And why would she?

Maybe she nabbed Frank because he was better at expressing her anger. She got so tired of being nice. And when existence became overwhelming, did she assume quiet Tommy's persona and hide out in 106? Did she do it out of desperation? Loneliness? A way to cope with circumstances? She didn't know, but it hadn't been born out of malice.

Emma could prove none of it, but little else made sense.

It explained many of the problems she'd been having. She concluded the shifting rules were a consequence of the other spirits struggling to get free, hindering her awareness and muddling her thinking.

She just wished she'd seen it sooner. Maybe she could have saved that girl in the cellar.

But Eamon was also to blame. He meant to destroy her and had engaged in considerable trickery.

Now he was gone. Someone had sent him away. An exorcism maybe.

The cop was gone too.

Quiet had returned to the mill and she felt safer. Saner.

She concluded the whole going-to-heaven-with-the-angels moment had been a psychotic break. The chaos of the final few weeks a consequence of the internal battle with Frank and Tommy and the strain of dealing with Chase and Eamon. She had unraveled under the stress. Who could blame her?

Besides, heaven was such a whimsical idea. Did it even exist?

She decided karma was nonsense, too. In reality, people were rarely punished for their misdeeds. History was full of awful people who had behaved horribly and faced few, if any, consequences for their evil acts.

So many answers eluded her. Why had only she and Eamon been marooned here? Why none of the others who died in the mill? Would Tommy and Frank have passed on if she hadn't waylaid them? Unsolvable mysteries of the universe...

No matter. She was dead. The mill was her only concern.

She needed to release Frank and Tommy, though. Maybe if she had a proper friend, like Lili, she wouldn't need them anymore.

Things were already changing. She was no longer limited by geography. This was the first time she had ever set foot in 114. Strangely, when she spoke in this room, she sounded like Frank.

Weird.

Maybe she had taken the first step by acknowledging the truth. She would figure out how to let them go so they could move on. Become sweet little Emma again, the ghostly girl of the night shift. Take evening walks to restore her reputation.

First, she had to find a way to make up with Lili.

Seventy

Lili lay in bed, dozing.

It was 7 a.m. Too early to be awake.

Three days had passed since Olivia's kidnapping and everything that followed.

Poor Olivia still hadn't woken after her ordeal. She remained in an induced coma while they allowed a subdural hematoma to heal. They expected her to recover completely. Lili had gone to the hospital once, but Olivia's family seemed cool and unwelcoming.

Raleigh clung to life in the ICU. One bullet had penetrated his vest and another nicked his femoral artery. While he wasn't her favorite person, he had shown great courage trying to save Olivia. He evidently loved her far more than she realized. Still, his brazenness had almost gotten him killed.

A spoon flew off the counter.

Lili rolled over and mumbled, "Go away."

She ignored the fork that fell as well. She had no desire to talk to that lying bitch.

As she drifted back to sleep, a female voice spoke in her head.

I'm sorry.

Lili flipped onto her back. "Emma?"

Yes. And I am sorry.

"You lied to me."

I was deceived too. By Eamon.

"Why should I believe you?"

He wanted me to look bad. He set me up. But I have other issues, too.

"Besides being a liar?"

Yes.

Emma explained and Lili listened, drawing an increasingly conflicted image of the girl, feeling one part incredulous and one part awed. Was her outlandish story even possible? A ghost with a mental disorder? Confused and messed up by circumstances? Stealing souls? All that could exist beyond the grave? Not an auspicious sign for people who committed suicide and thought their problems were over. Jesus! It was mind-boggling. And fascinating as hell.

Emma finished with: *Any chance you believe me now?*

"I don't know. Sounds like a pretty tall tale to me."

Frank spoke. *I understand. I'd be skeptical too.*

Lili sat bolt upright. "Holy shit!"

⋆ ⋆ ⋆

Olivia came home five days later.

Subdued and somber, she had said few words. Who could blame her? Kidnapped and left for dead, nearly losing her husband, she had lived through an ordeal most people couldn't even imagine.

Lili helped her put together an overnight bag. She was staying with Lili until Raleigh came home in two days.

Once Olivia settled in, Lili called from the kitchen, "Coffee?"

"Please."

They snuggled into chairs in the sitting area.

"Raleigh looked better today."

"He's an idiot," Olivia said dismissively.

"You don't mean that."

Olivia sipped her coffee. "No. That big galoot risked his life to save me. That's more romantic than a Hallmark movie and twice as dumb. He's no use to me dead."

Lili chuckled silently. Olivia's sense of humor was returning.

"I'm sure he felt the same way."

* * *

Two weeks passed.

During that time, the store had become a madhouse. Lili had blogged about her experiences in Rock River Mills and it had gone viral in the paranormal community. She opted to capitalize on her fifteen minutes of fame and had started writing a book about it.

But this afternoon, she was off and had a date. Martin had called yesterday and asked her out. Something casual, he said. No big deal. She accepted and found herself excited at the prospect, even though she still couldn't fully explain the attraction. It probably wouldn't work out, but why not try? She wanted to restore some sense of normalcy to her life.

Lili checked herself in the mirror. She had chosen a lovely blue sundress with matching clogs. A silver pendant and earrings. Light make up. Stylish, subtle.

Perfect.

Emma whispered in her head. *You look great. Have fun.*

"Thanks!"

Lili grabbed her purse and ran out the door.

They met at Cafe Adora, an eclectic cafe serving lunches, coffees and teas, and wines.

Quiet, cool, and dark, a half-dozen booths ran along one wall. They had permanently decorated the interior for Christmas and Lili loved it.

It was the perfect place for a first date. Not quite the commitment of dinner, but more than a casual cup of coffee.

Martin sat in a booth at the far end. He waved, and she thought he looked quite scrumptious, even if he did look like a cop. He stood as she approached. Something of a gentleman when he was off duty, but dressed casually, wearing a stylish graphic tee, shorts, sandals.

They sat and exchanged the usual pleasantries.

Lili said, "I've never dated a cop before."

"This is a date?"

"Sort of."

"I should've dressed better."

"Nonsense, you look fine."

"You look stunning."

Lili felt her face warm with a blush. "Thank you."

The waitress came and took their order. Lili ordered a rosé, Martin a bottle of ale from the local microbrewery.

"How's the case going?"

"Looks like they're trying to set up an insanity defense. It's not going to fly. He's going to jail forever."

"Good."

"Indeed. Enough about him. How's Olivia?"

"Better. She has nightmares about the well. She also has a good therapist. It's going to take time, but Raleigh's doing well and staying home with her while she mends."

Martin nodded. "So, tell me more about your psychic powers."

"I thought you were a skeptic."

"Recently, I've had a change of heart."

Thank you!

Thank you for reading *The Mill.* I hope you enjoyed it. As an independently published author, I rely on all of you wonderful readers to spread the word. If you enjoyed *The Mill*, please tell your friends and family. I would also sincerely appreciate a brief review on Amazon.

Again, thank you!

Cailyn Lloyd

`http://www.cailynlloyd.net`

Acknowledgments

Many people advised and assisted in bringing this book to publication. They are:

Amanda Manns and Jennie Lloyd who read and critiqued the first drafts of The Mill.

Sara Kelly who copyedited the final draft and the revisions to the final draft.

Katie Lloyd who proofread the final draft.

Patrick O'Donnell, a retired Milwaukee police officer, who provided advice and tutelage on police policies and procedures. Plus the many fine people on the Facebook group, Cops and Writers. I modified a few situations to suit the story. If I got anything wrong, it's on me.

Thank you all for your time, advice, wisdom, and patience.

Content guidance: Sexual assault (non-graphic). Profanity. Violence. Abduction.

Books by Cailyn Lloyd

Shepherd's Warning (2019)
The Elders Book 1

Quinlan's Secret (2020)
The Elders Book 2

Hayward's Revenge (2021)
The Elders Book 3

The Mill (2022)

Printed in Great Britain
by Amazon